Praise for the Otter Lake mystery series

"Delightful . . . with laugh-out-loud moments, a touch of romance, and a fun, sassy style. Readers will enjoy every moment spent in Otter Lake."

—Diane Kelly, award-winning author
of *Death, Taxes, and a Shotgun Wedding*

"A frolicking good time . . . with a heroine who challenges Stephanie Plum for the title of funniest sleuth."

—*New York Times* bestselling author Denise Swanson

"Time spent with the folks in Otter Lake is well worthwhile, with writing that is witty, contemporary, and winning." —*Kirkus Reviews*

"Wonderfully entertaining!" —*RT Book Reviews*

"This story has everything a reader could want—murder, mystery, a love interest, a small town, and a flamboyant best friend on the side."

—*Night Owl Reviews* (Top Pick) on
Skinny Dipping with Murder

Also by Auralee Wallace

Skinny Dipping with Murder
Pumpkin Picking with Murder
Snowed In with Murder
Ring in the Year with Murder
Down the Aisle with Murder

HAUNTED HAYRIDE

With

MURDER

Auralee Wallace

St. Martin's Paperbacks

HAUNTED HAYRIDE WITH MURDER

Copyright © 2018 by Auralee Wallace.

All rights reserved.

For information address St. Martin's Press, 175 Fifth Avenue, New York, NY 10010.

ISBN: 978-1-250-15149-0

Our books may be purchased in bulk for promotional, educational, or business use. Please contact your local bookseller or the Macmillan Corporate and Premium Sales Department at 1-800-221-7945, ext. 5442, or by e-mail at MacmillanSpecialMarkets@macmillan.com.

Printed in the United States of America

St. Martin's Paperbacks edition / October 2018

St. Martin's Paperbacks are published by St. Martin's Press, 175 Fifth Avenue, New York, NY 10010.

10 9 8 7 6 5 4 3 2

HAUNTED HAYRIDE

With

MURDER

A Ghost Story

"Okay, all of you shut up. I'm going to tell you a story."

"Oh my God. A story? Like a bedtime story? That is so lame."

"No, not like a bedtime story. What is the matter with you?"

"Then what kind of story?"

"Seriously? What are they teaching you in Girl Scouts these days? We're camping. We're sitting around a crackling fire. We don't have any marshmallows left—not mentioning any names, Brittany. Obviously, I'm going to tell you a ghost story."

"OMG. That's even lamer."

"That's one, Carly."

"What's one?"

"Let's just say you don't want to know what happens if you get two. Now, for real, shut up. You're all going to like this story. It's about the Apple Witch."

"The Apple Witch? None of us believe in the Apple Witch."

"Well, Brittany, by the time I'm through, you just might change your minds."

"When Mrs. Landry led our camping trip, she let us watch movies on our phones."

"Well, I'm not Mrs. Landry."

"Why are you leading this Girl Scout trip anyway? You don't even have kids. At least Mrs. Landry—"

"Oh my God, enough about Mrs. Landry! You want the truth? Mrs. Landry doesn't want to lead any more Girl Scout trips. Mrs. Landry said she would light her hair on fire before she'd take you people camping again. So you're stuck with me. And I'm stuck with you . . . and hopefully when all this is through, I will get a nice contract to install a security system in Leanne's father's sporting goods shop."

"Just let him tell the story already."

"Thank you . . . girl . . . with the dead emoji patch stitched onto the front of her hat. I'm sorry. I don't know your name."

"It's Morticia."

"I'm going to take that at face value. Now, before I start, this story is very scary, so I just want to make sure that you're old enough to hear it. What are you guys, eight? Nine?"

"We're fifteen."

"Excellent. So you've seen far worse on the Internet by now."

"Did you ask our parents if you could tell us this story?"

"Did I ask your—What is this, the special snowflake troop? Julie, your parents have probably already fallen asleep on the couch after two wine coolers and half a Will Ferrell movie. They really aren't going to care if I tell you guys a ghost story. Besides, scouting is about survival. You need to know fear. How else are you going to live through the zombie apocalypse?"

"Holy crap, just get on with it."

"*Thank you, Morticia. I will. Okay, so, prepare your-selves, ladies. You are about to hear a tale that will send shivers racing down your spine. It will make the hairs on the nape of your neck stand on end. It will—*"

"*What's a nape?*"

"*Yeah. That's a weird word. Nape.*"

"*For the love of— It means the back of your neck.*"

"*Why not just say neck?*"

"*Well, because your throat is part of your neck too. And you don't want that part to be hairy.*"

"*But men shave their necks. Don't you shave your n—*"

"*That's it. I obviously can't help you. You're all going to die in the undead wars. A zombie will be coming toward you, and you will be asking some poor adult ridiculous questions, and before you know it, it will have ripped open your stomach and be munching on your entrails.*"

"*Dude. Too far.*"

"*Okay. Stop talking. For real now. And pay atten-tion. My partner and I barely escaped our encounter with the Apple Witch. The lessons we learned could one day save your lives.*"

Chapter One

"I can't believe you got us into this."

"Here we go."

"Seriously, it's freezing out here."

"It's not the cold that's bothering you. And we both know it." I put my flashlight under my chin. "We're in Apple Witch territory."

The man in front of me stopped walking.

Freddie Ng. Best friend. Business partner. Devoted boyfriend to his boyfriend. Total scaredy-cat.

"What are you supposed to be right now?" he asked, his frosty breath rising between us. "The flashlight monster? Put that thing down. And, for the record, I am not afraid of the *Apple Witch*."

I smiled. "Then why does your voice drop to a whisper every time you say her name?"

"My voice does not drop to a whisper every time I say *her* name."

He totally just said *her* in a whisper.

"Let's just find the kids, so we can get out of here," he said, spinning away. I trotted after him on the winding trail that led deeper into the forest.

We were on our latest job for Otter Lake Security, hashtag OLS. The one and only security company in . . . well, Otter Lake, New Hampshire. Our business had been picking up lately thanks to our third business partner and only fully licensed private investigator, Rhonda Cooke. She had managed to impress an insurance company with her skills, so we had been gathering evidence on a number of people committing insurance fraud. We were also taking on the odd adultery case. She wasn't working with us tonight because she was on another case, but all that being said, we weren't doing well enough that we could turn down any business that came our way. So we were currently employed by the Honeycutt Apple Orchard to help oversee their Halloween festivities. Every year the orchard had a number of themed attractions—a haunted barn, a maze, a scary hayride. It was lots of fun. I had been the one to bring this job in. I used to babysit the Honeycutt kids a couple of times a week for a few months a really long time ago. It had been . . . an experience. But, all that was history. Tonight, we had been called upon to search the woods for a campfire party and to send the young derelicts at said party home. Even though it was a long-held tradition for teenagers in Otter Lake to seek out the Apple Witch this time of year, the Honeycutts had been trying to put a stop to the practice. They were worried the kids might end up getting hurt on their property.

"It is pretty cold out here," I said, stepping over a fallen log. "I'll give you that."

Freddie huffed a laugh. "I would have thought that the woolen monstrosity on your head would be keeping you warm."

"It is. And it's not a monstrosity," I said, tugging down the hat I was wearing while still clutching my flashlight. And, okay, fine, maybe it wasn't so much the hat *itself* that was keeping me warm as the *thought* of the hat. My *friend* Sheriff Grady Forrester had made it for me. He'd recently gotten into knitting. He found the yarn arts to be relaxing. And he needed a lot of relaxation. Being sheriff in Otter Lake, Live Free or Die, New Hampshire, was not always easy. Sure, our small town had a lot to offer if you were into things like docks stretching out into lakes, nights with a billion stars, and fall foliage that could make you believe in higher powers. But small towns always seem to come with their eccentricities, and Otter Lake was no exception. In fact, just last week Grady had investigated a reported Peeping Tom at a local's cabin. He set up a security camera to catch the perpetrator in the act, and it turned out there was indeed a Peeping Tom—a moose—peering into the bedroom window. Three nights in a row. Grady recommended to the owner that he call Fish and Game for advice, but in the end, the local man decided he could live with a peeping moose. He was even thinking of starting an Instagram page. I didn't think that was wise. Moose could be really mean. But to each his own.

"Admit it. You're scared. We're in Apple Witch territory, and it's getting close to Halloween. And you hate Halloween," I said, stumbling over a rock sticking out from the hard-packed trail. "Actually, you're like the Ebenezer Scrooge of Halloween. Soon you'll be visited by—"

Freddie let out a garbled yell. I think he was trying to say *What are you doing?* while also trying to shout *Stop!* Once he got himself together, he pointed his flashlight directly at my face and said, "Were you about to wish ghosts on me?"

I smiled . . . and squinted. The flashlight was very bright. "I thought you didn't believe in ghosts."

"I said I wasn't *afraid* of ghosts." He darted a look

around the shadowy forest closing in on us. "I'm not sure what I *believe*."

"Seriously?"

"Well, we don't know everything that happens under the moon and stars."

"I don't know if we are technically under the moon—"

Freddie swatted my arm. "What are you, a scientist now? Nobody likes scientists anymore, Erica. Read the papers. And the point is," he said, voice rising from its whisper, "seeing as nobody really knows for sure whether or not ghosts exist, whispering a ghost's name in ghost territory is just smart. Precautionary. Like wearing a seat belt."

"A seat belt?" I asked with a smile. "Really?"

"You know what?" Freddie said, whirling back around. "You are being awful tonight. I hate it when you're in a good mood."

I chuckled. I was in a good mood even though my face was a little numb and my nose was running from the cold. I loved fall. Cozy sweaters. Stunning vistas. Pumpkin spice. Couldn't forget the pumpkin spice. Oh! And hot sheriff friends who liked to snuggle around warm fires. Those were pretty nice too.

We walked on a few moments, the only sound being the crunch of our footsteps on the frosty trail.

"Besides, if anyone should be worried about ghosts," Freddie suddenly whispered, "it's you. *She* only—"

"By *she* you mean the Apple Witch that you're not afraid of?"

"*She* only goes after young, nubile women," Freddie continued, ignoring me. "And you fit those categories, if we're talking broad strokes."

"What?" I shone my flashlight directly at the back of his head—which really had no effect. "That's not true."

"Which part? The young? Or the nubile?"

"Har, har, har," I said, turning my flashlight back to the path. I really didn't want to trip over any more rocks. "But no, the other part. The Apple Witch only goes after men for her revenge."

"That's ridiculous," he said, stopping short. "What story have you been listening to? She doesn't go after men. Everybody knows the *Apple Witch,* with her rotten-apple face, uses her knobbly tree-branch fingers to pierce the flesh of supple young women to drain them of their beauty like maple syrup from a tr—"

Suddenly a strange sound cut him off.

"Did you hear that?" I don't know why I bothered asking. Freddie had instantly stiffened. He looked like a dog with his ears perked up, but, you know, without the ears.

"That was weird," I said, dropping my voice to a whisper. "It almost sounded like—"

Freeeeedie . . .

I whipped my head toward the sound.

Freeeeedie . . .

I scanned the trees with my flashlight. "I think we've found our— Freddie? Where did you go?" I spun my flashlight around only to have it land on him perched atop a boulder at the side of the trail. "What are you doing? Get down from there."

He just looked at me.

"It's the kids," I said. "And why would you climb up a rock? I'm pretty sure both teenagers and ghosts could get you up there." I rolled my hand. "Come on down."

"How was I supposed to know it was them with all your talking about the . . . *you know who.*" He slid down from the rock. "And don't you judge me. It's not like they were calling *Eeeeeerrrrica. Eeeeerrrric—*"

"Okay, knock it off." It was kind of spooky.

But, of course, none of the local kids would be calling my name. Freddie and the teens—hey, that sounded kind of like a band—had a long and convoluted history. It had all started a few years ago when he had been running security for the fall fair. Freddie had taken it on himself to give the kids a pretty hard time over stuff like littering and loitering, and they had responded by taking his boat for a joyride . . . and accidentally crashing it into some trees. They were fine, but the boat was not. That had landed them in some pretty hot water. Freddie opted not to press charges—at the pleading of their parents— and in return the parents offered the kids up to the town for indentured servitude under Freddie's supervision. If you had a gutter that needed cleaning, you knew just who to call. In some weird Otter Lake way, this had bonded them, and Freddie had ended up becoming a kind of mascot slash drill sergeant for the adolescents. It really was a sign of affection that they were picking on him.

"Besides," Freddie whispered, "that didn't sound like any of the kids I know."

Just then the wail started up again, *"Freeee—"*

This time the ghost's voice cracked.

"Okay, I take it back. I know that voice. That was Austin."

I grimaced. "He still hasn't made it through puberty?" Poor kid. He had to be almost sixteen.

"No," Freddie said, shaking his head, confused squint on his face. "It's almost like he's going backward."

"Come on," I said. "I think I see their fire over there. They're right by the house."

We cut through the trees toward the dilapidated structure—the dilapidated structure that once housed the Apple Witch. The stone foundation was still in pretty good shape, but the rest of it looked like it would have trouble withstanding a sneeze. Unfortunately, by the time we got to the clearing, there were no kids, just a small fire and junk-food wrappers.

I sighed. "They are not going to make this easy, are they?"

A tree branch snapped in the distance.

"Come on," Freddie said. "Let's go after them."

"Nah, forget that. Let's just wait until they get bored and come back. We can't leave the fire unattended." Besides it was nice and warm. "Only you can prevent forest—"

A marshmallow pinged off my brow. "Hey!"

"We have a job to do. And I want to do it and go home."

"I know, but they'll be back, and I don't think the Honeycutts would appreciate it if we burned down the fores—"

Freddie picked up a two-liter bottle of soda from the ground and dumped it on the small flames. "There. Let's just get this done. Stanley's going to need to pee."

Stanley was Freddie's ancient French bulldog. He was a real sweetheart. Freddie didn't like to leave him alone for too long because he was his baby . . . and he did have a weak bladder.

"Fine, but we're not chasing after them." There had to be an easier way. I swung my flashlight over the trees again. "Okay, guys, you've had your fun," I shouted. "Come on out now."

No answer. But there was lots of rustling and hushed laughter.

"Seriously?" I muttered. "How is this a good time for them?" Just then I heard quick footsteps. They were running around us now. I tried to catch them with my flashlight, but they were quick. "You're going to run into a tree," I called out again.

More laughter.

"They're teenagers, Erica," Freddie said. "They don't care about physical safety. Let me handle this." He cleared his throat then shouted, "Last one out here has to clean the goose poop from Mrs. Moore's lawn." That's right, Mrs. Moore had a pet goose named Buttercup, and boy, could that bird poop.

Freddie's band of three merry teens came tearing through the trees.

"Hey man, why did you put out our fire?" Austin whined in his cracked voice. "We were just messing around."

"Yeah, well, it's time to go home."

"Aw, come on," another boy said. "What's the hurry? We're waiting for the Apple Witch."

"She's not coming," Freddie said, adjusting his gloves. "Your excessive use of body spray has scared her away."

"Seriously, man. Be cool." A fourteen-maybe fifteen-year-old girl said that. She had braids coming down from either side of her hat.

"Krystal," Freddie said, pinching his temples. "There is nothing *cool* about *freezing* to death in the woods waiting for a ghost witch that is not coming." She looked like she was about to say something when Freddie pointed at her. "And so help me if you pick apart any bit of that sentence, I will . . . do something you are not going to like." He looked at me and added, "God, I hate teenagers."

"You love us," Austin said happily.

"I can't even . . ." Freddie just blinked and shook his head. "Let's go."

"We can't," the other kid said. "Josie and Tyler aren't back yet."

"Josie and Tyler are here?"

All three teens nodded.

"Well, where are they?"

"They wanted to be alone," Austin said with a double pop of his eyebrows.

Freddie groaned and threw his head back. "So they want to die. That's what you're telling me. Because that's what happens to teens who make out in the woods." He whirled away from the kids and muttered to me, "God help them if Josie takes her top off."

I wagged my finger in the air. "I don't think you're giving ghosts enough credit."

"I'm sorry, what are you talking about now?"

"Well, they are not as slut-shamey as they used to b—"

"Please, Apple Witch, take me now," Freddie said, throwing his arms wide. "I wish to die in your tart embrace."

I chuckled. "Careful. She might hear you."

"I don't care anymore. It's better than hearing your feminist ghost theories." His eyes were darting side to side though. Looking for the Apple Witch. You know, in case she had heard him.

Just then a girl came running out into the clearing wearing jeans and a heavy flannel jacket. Josie. She did a quick double take at the sight of Freddie and me, but quickly dismissed whatever she had made of our arrival. "Tyler found something. I think you guys need to come see." She rolled her hand for us to follow and whipped back around.

We all hurried after her, our many flashlights bouncing over the trees. It didn't take long before we spotted Tyler standing at the bottom of a slope. We eased our way toward him on what I was guessing was a dried-up water runoff. It had been a particularly stormy spring and summer. The water had carved a few new paths in the trees.

Unfortunately, it made for pretty slippery terrain. We were all leaning back at steep angles toward the ground so that we didn't end up sliding all the way down.

Tyler had glanced up at us a few times as we made our way toward him, but he never kept his eyes long from the spot on the ground lit up by his flashlight.

"What's going on?" Freddie asked. "Are you okay?"

"I . . . I don't know."

I trotted over to get a closer look at the spot. "Is that a boot?"

Tyler nodded his head. "I picked it up. For just a second. It was stuck at first, like half-buried, so I yanked it and—" He shook his head again. He suddenly looked like he might be sick.

"And?" I asked carefully.

"When I yanked it . . ." His wide eyes met mine. "There was a crack."

"A crack? Like a branch?"

"I don't know."

We stared at each other a moment. Suddenly I was too afraid to look back down.

Everyone fell silent.

"Tyler," I finally said in an unnaturally calm voice, "I need you to swear on everything you have ever loved that this is not some stupid Halloween prank."

He nodded.

"Do it, Erica," Freddie hissed in my ear. "Look in the boot."

I whipped around so that my face was about an inch away from Freddie's. "Why don't you look in the boot?"

He planted his hands on my shoulders and turned me back around. "You're the feminist scientist. It's only right that it be you."

"I don't even know what that means," I mumbled.

But no one answered. They were all waiting.

I looked down at the boot. It was standing straight up—Tyler must have dropped it that way—but it was too dark to see anything beyond its black mouth. I swallowed one more time then pointed my flashlight toward it and—

"Bones! Run!"

Chapter Two

"Run?"

"Yeah," I said, slipping my fingers underneath my hat to scratch my brow. "I wasn't really thinking. I might have been in shock." I looked up at the fantastically hot man in the sheriff's uniform before me, holding out a steaming mug.

"Did anyone do it?"

I accepted the drink. "Do what?"

"Run?"

I nodded. "Austin did. Ran right into a tree. We all slowed down after that."

"So that *is* why the paramedics are looking at his nose. The kids said he ran into a tree, but I wasn't sure I believed them."

I looked over at the ambulance pulled up on the lawn of the orchard. "Is he all right?"

"I think he's just bruised."

I nodded some more.

"Nice hat, by the way," he said with a smile.

"It likes you too. I mean, I like you too . . . or . . . I don't know what I mean." Finding a dead man's foot will do that to you. I raised the mug to my lips, sugary steam wafting up to greet me. Mmm, apple cider. Nice. I loved apple cider. Hopefully I didn't start associating dead feet with apple cider from here on out. That would suck. On second thought . . . I put the mug down on the floor of the hay wagon I was sitting on. Best not take any chances.

"You okay?"

I smiled. "Are you asking as sheriff? Or as my friend?"

He smiled back at me. "Both."

Ah . . . Grady Forrester.

Sheriff, most handsome man in the universe, on again, off again love of my life . . . now *friend*. We shared quite the history. We had liked each other back in high school, but that was all cut short in a strange series of events that had ended with me accidentally flashing the entire town at the annual Raspberry Social holding Otter Lake's mascot—a beaver named Betsy—in my arms. Yup, that had kind of put a stop to our budding romance for a while. Then when I had moved back to town a couple of years ago, we had tried to rekindle things, but, *well,* we both had some commitment issues, and some conflicting professional issues—given that he was sheriff and I was working on my PI license. We also had some family issues . . . and some Freddie issues, couldn't forget those . . . and probably some other issues I was forgetting. Basically every time we had tried to make a relationship work, it had ended very badly. As a result, we had decided that maybe we should just try being friends for a while. Friends who don't date other people. It was working out really well. We weren't fighting. We were getting to know each other in ways we never had before. And we were spending all sorts of time together. The only problem was that the whole not-sleeping-together thing was kind of . . . hot. I wasn't sure either one of us could take it much longer. But then again we were also pretty worried that sex would ruin everything. Like instantly. In an epic fashion. So we were hanging on.

"I'm fine," I said. "I mean, it's not like I saw an entire body this time. It was just a foot, so all in all . . ." I finished the sentence with a shrug.

"You know," Grady said with a smile, "you find one more body, and the FBI is going to have to open a file on you."

"Shut up," I said with a small laugh. A laugh Grady did not return. "Wait . . . that's not true, is it?"

He chuckled.

I flicked him on the arm with the back of my hand then looked over at the twinkly lights outlining the porch of the red farmhouse that served as the apple orchard's gift shop and café. This whole place was so cute. There were scarecrows and sunflowers. Hay bales set up for kids to climb on. There was a corn maze—which Freddie would avoid at all costs. He had a nanny leave him in one once as a child. It had left him with some issues. And, of course, there were rows and rows of mini apple trees blanketing the surrounding gentle hills.

Yup, it was all so cute.

I was finding it hard to reconcile all that cuteness with the . . . boot in the woods.

"So," I said, drawing out the word, "was there a body that went with that foot?"

He pinched his lips together and nodded. "It's looking that way."

"I don't suppose you know who it belonged to?"

He shook his head. "It's early, but judging by the state of decomposition . . ." He looked up at me. I shook my head like I was totally cool with decomposition talk. "I'm guessing the body was buried at least a couple of years ago. We'll start going through the missing persons files when we get back to the station."

I nodded.

"I still have to ask you a few more questions though," he said, looking over to the group of people standing by the ambulance. "Are you okay with that? Or do you want to talk to Amos?"

I squinted at him. Amos was Grady's deputy. He was also apple-cheeked and generally nervous. It would take a lot of reassurance to get him through an entire questioning, and I was pretty tired after the night's events. "Why would I want Amos to do the questioning?"

"You know," he said, rocking on his feet, "because we're friends now, and we're doing really well as friends. And part of that is due to the fact that we're keeping work separate from our personal *friendship*."

I nodded. "We have been doing well."

"So well, in fact," he said, looking down at the ground before peeking up at me, "I was thinking that maybe we could start talking about becoming even *closer* friends. If you were interested in maybe becoming closer friends."

I gave my head a shake. What? Holy crap . . . had Grady seriously just suggested we become closer friends? Huh, maybe this wasn't such a bad night after all. And just like that the boot flashed through my mind. Nope, still bad. Any time you find a dead body it's bad. Especially for the dead person. But you know, this time *I* didn't actually turn it up. A teenage boy did, so—nope, still bad. But still . . . maybe not all bad?

See, I had been waiting for Grady to make the first move on this particular topic. He had been the one to suggest we be friends in the first place, so I didn't want to rush him or anything. But if he thought we were ready . . .

I cleared my throat. Suddenly it was very tight. "I . . . would be open to becoming closer friends."

"Good," he said. "We should talk about it."

"Yeah," I said, trying to hold back the smile that was

threatening to take over my entire face. I mean, this was no time to appear joyfully happy. A foot had died. I mean person! A person had died.

"You seem a little surprised?" he said with a shy smile. Oh boy, Grady with a shy smile was one of my favorite Gradys of all.

"I guess I am. I mean, we've both been so busy lately," I said with a little shrug. "We haven't had a whole lot of *friend* time." Most of our apple orchard security work took place at night, so it was kind of hard to mesh our schedules as Grady mainly worked days, you know, when people weren't finding feet. And when I did have free time—the apple orchard wasn't open seven nights a week—my friends, well, one friend in particular, Rhonda, was, well, let's just say Rhonda was demanding this time of year.

"I know," he said. "We need to make time to . . . talk. Maybe not tonight though."

"No, no, no," I said with extra side-to-side head-shaking. "I touched bone tonight." I cringed. That didn't sound right.

"Why do you have to make everything sound so dirty?" a new voice suddenly said.

I hadn't seen Freddie coming—what with all the stars in my eyes—but there he was, hopping up on the wagon beside me.

"Hey, watch my cider," I said, scooping up my mug.

"Cider. Nice. Did you get me one?" he asked, pulling his hat from his head and rubbing his hair.

I shook my head. "Grady got this for me."

Freddie rolled his eyes over to Grady.

"I didn't get you cider."

"Why not? We're *friends*," Freddie said, putting his hand to his chest. "Isn't that why you got Erica a drink? Because you're *friends*? Or is—oof!"

I had backhanded him in the belly.

"There's lots more inside," Grady said. "Grandma Honeycutt made some for everyone."

"Oh ho ho, no way am I going in there," Freddie said, waving his hands. "Not if Grandma Honeycutt is in there."

I frowned at him. "What's wrong with Grandma Honeycutt? She is like the sweetest old lady in Otter Lake. And she looks like Mrs. Claus."

"Exactly," Freddie said, nodding. "It freaks me out. And she's not my grandma." He shuddered. "Oh, and by the way, I got Betty to go to my place and let Stanley out for a pee break in case you were wondering."

I had not been wondering. Nor could I wonder about how his neighbor, Betty Johnson, hadn't killed him yet, because I was still stuck on the other thing he had said. "So let me get this straight. You're afraid of Grandma Honeycutt too? I thought you were just afraid of witches, ghosts, and—"

"Ghost witches, actually," he said with a sniff. "Get it right."

"And corn mazes," I said with a point.

"Those are all good choices," Freddie said. "But as my poppo—my real grandmother—always says, someone who uses that much sugar to get their medicine to go down has to be pretty rotten."

I frowned. "I think Mary Poppins said that."

Freddie shot me a look. "No, it was my grandmother, but she said it in Cantonese, and it was rice syrup instead of sugar, and—You're missing the point. Grandma Honeycutt is creepy. And isn't she a descendant of the *you know who*?"

"No, I don't know who," Grady said, looking to me.

"The Apple Witch."

Freddie scoffed. "God, you just really want to die, don't you?"

"Well, I don't know if the Honeycutts are related to the—"

Freddie cut him off with a look.

"But I do know that Grandma Honeycutt makes the best baked goods."

"The best," I added.

Grady nodded. "And I think she also makes teddy bears for children in the hospital. With little outfits. And hats."

"Yeah," Freddie said with a disturbed chuckle. "Little teddy bears that probably come alive at night and stab you with their little knives."

Both Grady and I blinked at Freddie as he grabbed the apple cider from my hands and took a sip.

"This is good," he said, lifting the mug. "Not too hot."

I shook my head. "That's it. You're not allowed to watch any more horror movies."

We had been watching way too many as of late. Remember how I mentioned Rhonda, our other OLS partner, was demanding this time of year? Well, Halloween was her favorite holiday, and in exchange for her giving up all of her choices for movie night during the year, we had agreed to participate in thirty-one horror movies in thirty-one days for the month of October. It had seemed like a good idea last November, but now that we were in the thick of it, I wasn't so sure. I didn't think it was having a good effect on Freddie. I looked back at Grady. "What were we talking about?"

Grady looked as confused as I felt. "Questions. I need to ask you some more."

"Shoot," Freddie said.

"Right." Grady took out his pen and notepad. "Um,

okay, as you know, I've already talked to some of the kids, and they said . . ." He looked up at me. "Did you really kick the boot when you saw what was inside?"

"Yeah, that was just after I shouted for everyone to run." Hmm, maybe the horror movies weren't having a great effect on me either.

"She toe-punted it into next week," Freddie said over *my* mug in his hands.

I sighed. "I just . . . reacted."

Grady nodded, but the furrow between his brow was deepening. That was a sure sign of stress. I should maybe buy him some new wool. "Did you then pick up the bones and put them back in the boot?"

"I told her not to touch the evidence," Freddie said. "But she never listens."

I cut him a look. "It was just like one bone. A toe, I think. And I was wearing gloves."

"I'm just saying, people are going to start calling you 'cadaver dog' again." Freddie took another sip of my cider.

"I didn't find the body this time. Tyler did. I just confirmed it."

"Yeah, but how many dead bodies do you think the average person, who isn't in a dead-body profession, touches?" Freddie asked. "I'm starting to think your number is not normal."

"Hey, I don't think you are in any position to judge anybody on what is norm—"

"Guys," Grady said. "Guys?"

We both looked back at Grady. Oh boy, he was clutching his forehead under his sheriff's hat. He was going to need a lot more wool. I wanted him in the right frame of mind for the next level of our friendship.

"Do you think we could just stick to the questioning?" he near-pleaded.

"Shoot," Freddie said again.

"Don't tempt me," Grady replied.

I snickered.

"Okay, where were we?" Grady looked back at his notebook. "Actually . . . I think that's all I need for now. I just wanted to confirm the kids' accounts with yours."

"Cool," Freddie said, hopping off the wagon.

"But, uh . . ." Grady wagged a finger in the air. "There's just one more thing."

Freddie groaned. "I knew this was coming."

I looked back and forth between the two men. "Huh? What's coming?"

Freddie rolled his eyes over to me. "He wants to know if Otter Lake Security is planning to get *all up in his* murder *grill*."

"Oh," I said. "But are we sure it's a murder?"

"Well, I doubt the body buried itself," Freddie said.

"True, but the ground is pretty muddy there in the spring. Maybe—"

Grady cleared his throat. It had a desperate-sounding quality to it.

Freddie looked back at Grady. "While I'm sure you won't believe me, I'm going to tell you the God's honest truth." He put his hand on his chest. "I have no desire to go back into *you know who*'s territory. Not ever again."

I smiled at Freddie. "You're totally regretting asking her to take you away in *her tart embrace,* aren't you?"

"Little bit," he said. "You finding the foot didn't help."

"Okay," Grady said, once again looking confused. "That's good. I mean, I respect your business, but I think it might be better for all of our friendships," he said, making sure to swirl a hand around all three of us, "if this was left to the sheriff's department."

"Fine by me," I said. "I don't want to stick my nose

into this—" I cut myself off with a frown. "I suddenly feel like I have dirt up my nostrils."

"Bone dust," Freddie offered.

"You want a tissue?" Grady asked.

"No. I'm fine."

Grady snapped his book shut. "Good. And Amos may get in touch with you tomorrow if we have any more questions."

Freddie nodded. "Let's go, E."

I hopped off the wagon too, and wouldn't you know, I was standing quite close to Grady. Like "I could totally smell his aftershave" close. "And we'll pick up the conversation we were having earlier . . . um, later?" I asked. And hopefully that later would be sooner than later. If that made any sense.

He smiled. "I think that's a good idea."

"Get a *friend*-room," Freddie drawled as he walked away.

I shot Grady a wave then hurried after him.

We had made it almost all the way back to the parking lot when Freddie stopped suddenly. "Oh crap, I left my flashlight back at the café."

"What's the big deal?" I asked, still walking. "You can get it when we come back for work tomorrow."

"I can't. It's my lucky flashlight," he said, setting off in a jog back toward the orchard. "I'll be right back."

"Wait, what?" I called after him. "You want me to wait here? Alone? After we found a foot tonight?"

"Relax. I'll just be a second," he called back to me.

"But . . ." I resisted the urge to run after him. "Is this payback for me making fun of you and the Apple Witch?"

"Oh my God, stop saying her name. And yes," he shouted before disappearing from view.

And suddenly I was alone on a gravel path that led to a near-deserted parking lot of a very dark apple orchard.

I crossed my arms over my chest.

So yeah . . . this was fine.

I wasn't afraid of ghosts. Or witches. Or sweet old ladies.

I was just afraid of being left alone in parking lots.

But it was fine. Those bones we had found were pretty old, so the murderer would be long gone.

Probably.

Unless he or she lived nearby.

I rocked a little on my feet as I waited.

This was ridiculous. I just needed to distract myself. Think of other things than my current predicament, like . . . bones!

God, no! Not the bones! What was wrong with me?

Just then I heard a rustle in a nearby bush. Not a big rustle. Good chance it was like a squirrel-sized rustle. Were squirrels nocturnal? I didn't think so. But it definitely could have been a raccoon-sized rustle . . . or a "human trying to be quiet" type rustle. That wasn't good. No matter what though, I did not believe it was an Apple Witch rustle. Ghosts did not rustle.

I looked back toward the farmhouse.

How long did it take to get a flashlight?

I could go after him . . . but then he'd just make fun of me. Kind of like I had made fun of him. And that wouldn't be fun.

I whipped my head back toward the bushes when I heard a branch snap. At least I thought it was a branch snap. I mean, it could just have been my imagination, but—

Grady! I could think about Grady, and becoming closer friends with Grady. That . . . that was a thought that could warm you from the inside. I mean, I wasn't entirely sure we were ready for the closer-friendship step, but it was certainly worth thinking about. Much better than thinking about . . . *bones*!

Okay, screw this. I didn't have anything to prove to Freddie.

I sped-crunched my way over the gravel back toward the farmhouse.

It was very noisy gravel.

Not loud enough to cover up the growing rustling sound in the bush though.

Oh God, that was definitely a human-sized rustle, and that human wasn't even trying to be quiet anymore.

"Is somebody out there?" I called out. I don't know why. I already knew the answer. "What do you want?"

There was no answer, but I could now see the silhouette of a person emerging from the bushes.

"Stay back!" I shouted. "Or I will—"

"—wah!"

Chapter Three

"Please don't scream."

Easier said than done when someone jumps out in front of you in a dark parking lot.

"You don't have to scream." The woman put her hands up. "It's me. Mandy."

Mandy. Of course it was Mandy. I mean it definitely wasn't the Apple Witch. Because I didn't believe in ghosts. So if it had been the Apple Witch, well, that might have been really embarrassing. I dropped the hand I had covering my heart. Mandy was the youngest of the four Honeycutts, and the only girl. She worked at the orchard with her brothers. That, of course, didn't explain why she had just tried to scare me to death, but it was a start. Once I got a good look at her though, my fear changed to concern. She had her wispy blond hair pulled up in a hurried bun, and she was wearing an oversized corduroy jacket that made her look like a kid wearing an adult's coat. And that all would have been fine if her eyes hadn't been huge and teary.

"Hey," I said with a chuckle. "I didn't recognize you in the dark."

She hurried toward me. "I'm sorry," she whispered. "I didn't mean to scare you."

"No problem, but why are we whispering? 'Cause that's kind of freaking me out too."

"I need to talk to you," she said, clutching my elbow, "but not here."

Yup, I was definitely becoming alarmed once again.

"I don't want my brothers to see us," she said, looking around. "And I don't have anyone else to turn to."

Very alarmed.

"Cam's probably already looking for me."

Cam was the youngest of the three brothers. All four of the siblings kept the apple orchard going for their grandmother. Their parents had died when they were young. Everybody in town liked them. Kind of in the way you might like a well-intentioned pack of golden retrievers. They were super fun and cute, but you might not want to invite them over to your house all at once. They'd probably break something. But maybe that's just how they had been when they were kids. They were pretty wild back then. Like playing tag football wouldn't have been enough for them. They'd have to play it on the roof . . . while their poor, poor babysitter shouted for them to get down.

"Mandy, what's going on?" I grabbed her arm gently, trying to get her to focus. Her eyes were still darting all over the place. "Is this about what happened in the woods tonight?"

She nodded quickly. "I'm really freaking out. I think I might know who was—"

"Mandy?" a voice called out.

She jerked away from me as we spotted both her brother and Freddie walking toward us. Cam was as large as his sister was tiny.

"Take this," she said, pressing a piece of paper into

my palm. "And promise me you won't tell anyone what we talked about."

"But I don't even know what we talked about," I whispered. "Should I go get Grady?"

"No. No." She shook her head violently. "Please don't tell Grady."

"I . . ." I didn't want to make a promise to her when I didn't understand what it was that I was promising, but when I met her eyes . . . well, they were all round and desperate like that cat clutching its hat in that Disney movie I couldn't remember the name of and—

"Please." She blinked at me. "I know you of all people can keep a secret."

Oh sure, and now she had to go and bring *that* up.

"Okay, fine," I mumbled. "I promise. I won't say anything to Grady until we—"

"Mandy, where have you been? You know I freaking hate writing posts for the Web site," Cam said, coming up to us, "And Adam's going to be all over me if I don't get it done tonight. We have to *reassure* the public."

"I found my flashlight," Freddie said, holding it up in the air. "What are you guys chatting about all huddled up? You look like you're conspiring."

Mandy folded her arms over her chest and smiled nervously.

"We were just . . . cold," I said in a tone that would let Freddie know that this was definitely not something he should pursue.

"Really?" he said. "You look kind of freaked out."

Well, that hadn't worked.

I shot Freddie a look. It was of the "please stop talking before I kill you" variety.

"What were you talking about?"

Nope, he was not picking up on my signals at all.

"Oh . . . uh," Mandy said, rubbing her hands together

and placing them on her belly. "I was just telling Erica about the paintball tournament we're having in a few days. She said you guys might be interested in coming."

Wow. Okay. I was kind of impressed with the way that had just flown out of her mouth. No hesitation whatsoever. She didn't even look that nervous anymore. Her eyes were still teary, but that could have been easily explained away by the cold.

Unfortunately, I could also tell by the look on Freddie's face that he knew those were words that would never ever come out of my mouth. Now, if he could just pick up on the fact that this was a lie I was in on—so it was therefore obviously not a lie I would want him to pick apart—we would be fine.

"Erica never would have said that."

Son of a—

"No, no, actually I did. Don't you remember, Freddie?" I said tightly. "I was talking about paintballing just last week. I was saying that I'd like to give it a try?"

He pinched his lips together and shook his head. "You did not say that."

For the love of . . .

"No, no," I said with a nod. "I'm pretty sure I did."

His eyes narrowed.

"Well, hey," Cam said, sidling up to me. "If you want to give it a try, Erica, I'd be happy to show you a few things."

Good Lord. Was he hitting on me? I was his babysitter!

Freddie looked back and forth between my horrified face and Cam's face, full of . . . seduction? Then he smiled. "You should do it. The paintballing, I mean. I remember that conversation now. You were really excited about trying it out." I could always count on Freddie to make things more awkward.

I tried to stretch the corners of my mouth into a smile,

but it was pretty shaky. I turned to Mandy. "But won't we be working? I mean, you guys are keeping us pretty busy."

"The tournament's in the morning," Cam said. "First thing. We always start at dawn."

Dammit.

Dawn. Of course they started at dawn. The Honeycutts probably didn't need sleep. They just fueled themselves with applesauce, Mountain Dew, and adrenaline. But . . . while I may not have known it until just this very moment, it turned out the absolute last thing I wanted to do first thing in the morning was go paintballing. Like ever. So help me, whatever this secret was I was hiding for Mandy, it had better be important, and not something like . . . like . . . I didn't know what lame secrets siblings kept from one another because I didn't have a sibling, but I was willing to bet there were lots of different ones. And what was up with all this cloak-and-dagger stuff anyway? Why couldn't Mandy just tell me what—

"Hey Mandy," I said, reaching for my phone. My internal rants sometimes gave me good ideas. "I just realized I don't have your number—"

"I never use my phone," she said.

Her brother looked a little confused at that.

Wow, she really was fast with the lies. I guess she didn't want to talk on the phone. I couldn't help but wonder what reason she'd give her brother for not wanting to give me her number. At least he was smart enough not to probe it, unlike some Freddies I knew.

"Right. Well, why don't we just play it by ear?"

"Come on," Cam said. "You have to come. After what happened tonight, I bet you could use something to keep your mind off of things."

"Yeah, Erica," Freddie said with another smile.

"And you should come too," Cam said, slapping him

on the shoulder hard enough that he had to take a step
forward to regain his balance.

"Oh," Freddie said with a chuckle, "I'd love to, but,
uh, my gun's in the shop."

Cam clapped him on the shoulder again. "You have
your own gun? I didn't know you were into paintball."

"Yup, Freddie loves paintball," I said. I felt a tiny bit
guilty. But then again, he had started all this.

"Then, for sure," Cam said. "You guys should totally
come. And don't worry, I have plenty of extra guns."

"You know, I believe you when you say that," Freddie
said. "Okay, well, we'll check our schedule and get back
to you. Right, Erica?"

"Sure."

"Awesome. There's a link with all the information on
the orchard's Web site. Oh, and it's a costume thing," Cam
said, leading Mandy away. "I don't think that's there."

"Great."

Once they were out of earshot, Freddie looked at me
and said, "What the hell just happened?"

"I . . ." I took a quick look at the piece of paper in my
hand.

Meet me at the outbuilding off the 8th side road. 10 a.m.

". . . seriously have no clue."

Chapter Four

"Hello?" I cracked open the door to the brand spanking new cottage. "Anybody home?"

It was a gloriously sunny fall day. Thank God. I needed a gloriously sunny fall day. Last night had been *a lot*. Foot bones . . . nonexistent ghosts . . . secret notes . . . paintball? When I first woke up, it took me a second to believe all that had happened, but there was Mandy's note just sitting on my dresser. I couldn't have dreamed that into existence.

Meet me at the outbuilding off the 8th side road. 10 a.m.

That was it.

I couldn't help but wonder if this was some sort of elaborate prank. The Honeycutts did owe me one. Those boys had played a lot of practical jokes on me back in the day. At least they had . . . until I got them back. Well, the whole "getting them back" thing was really more of Mandy's idea, but . . . let's just say, everything got out of control pretty quickly, and I was the babysitter, so the whole thing was on me. The whole, weird, messed-up thing. So yeah, this could be payback, but Mandy had seemed genuinely freaked out last night. I just couldn't believe this was some kind of joke.

I had of course told Freddie about it. One, because he saw the note in my hand, and he was not the type to stomach curiosity well, and two, I didn't want to die in an outbuilding alone without anyone knowing I was there. Actually . . . I'd just rather not die. Not that I thought Mandy would kill me, but who knew what could happen in an outbuilding on an apple orchard the day after finding a foot in the woods right around Halloween?

I had definitely been watching too many horror movies.

So while I had no idea what was going on with Mandy, I was going to find out. After one quick errand.

"Hello?"

That one quick errand had brought me to the door of the only other inhabitants on my mother's island in the middle of Otter Lake, Kit Kat and Tweety. They were identical twins in their seventies and had matching white perms and dentures. They liked to eat meat, drink whiskey, and tell dirty jokes. On occasion they would stick their fingers into cupcakes they weren't ready to eat yet, but had dibs on for the future. They were also like family. Their place had burned to the ground a while back, but the rebuild was finally complete, which was good for everyone. They had been staying with my mother and me while construction was going on, and that . . . that was just too much.

I took another step into the cottage.

"Erica, what are you doing here so early?" Kit Kat said, coming out from the kitchen. "Shouldn't you be tired from digging up another body?"

I scratched the side of my head. "Heard that already, huh?"

"Betty Johnson told us," she said matter-of-factly. "She

still listens to her husband's old police scanner when she
has trouble sleeping."

Nothing like keeping tabs on your neighbors to bring
on the sweet dreams. But in fairness, Betty Johnson was
the same Betty Johnson Freddie had woken up to let his
dog out. I stepped all the way into the cottage and shut
the door behind me. I had to resist the urge to leave it
open in case I needed to make a quick getaway. See, before the fire the twins had had a bit of a problem with
hoarding. Actually, I don't know if you could call them
full-on hoarders, but they were definitely borderline. I
had been thinking the whole situation had taken care of
itself when the place burned down, but then their cousin
shut down his souvenir shop in Florida. They were temporarily holding some of his stock until he could find a
buyer. So now their new little log cabin was filled with
gator heads. It was not . . . welcoming.

"Oh, stop staring at Billy," Tweety said, coming out
from the kitchen to join her sister. "He never did anything
to you."

"I doubt *Billy* ever did anything to anyone," I said
under my breath, "and yet here we are staring at his
head."

"You're sounding more and more like your mother
every day," she said with a point.

My jaw dropped. What a terrible thing to say. Not that
my mother, Summer Bloom, was terrible. She was
just . . . extreme in her beliefs. The lodge that we lived
in was actually her business. Earth, Moon, and Stars. A
women's retreat for spiritual healing. She was also a
vegan, a yoga addict, and a naturopath . . . which many
around Otter Lake equated with being a witch. Not like
the Apple Witch, but . . . whatever.

"Besides," Tweety said, stroking the gator head, "think
about it. If you were killed before your time, wouldn't you

want to be stuffed, so that people could appreciate your beauty for years to come?"

I frowned. "I . . . don't think so."

Kit Kat lifted her mug to me, but her eyes were on Billy. "And you know he would have eaten you given half a chance."

I frowned some more. "He's the size of one of those little weiner dogs. It would have taken a really long time."

"Well, thanks for the visit," she said. "See you soon, Erica."

"No, no, I'm sorry," I said, waving. "I was just teasing. Don't kick me out. I came for a visit . . . and a favor."

The twins scrunched their faces up with identical suspicion.

"I was hoping that you guys could feed Caesar for me tonight?"

"Oh," Kit Kat said with a shrug. "Sure."

Her sister nodded. "No problem."

"You going out with your *friend*?" Kit Kat asked, waggling her eyebrows.

"I wish. No, I'm working." My mother was away doing a retreat with her boyfriend—best-selling author and guru Zaki. She wasn't getting back until late tonight, and Caesar had a very specific schedule. If it wasn't adhered to, he barfed on my bed. Our relationship was like that.

"Don't tell me you're going back to the apple orchard," Kit Kat said, heaving herself down into an armchair.

"Yeah. Of course. I told you we'd be there until Halloween."

"I just mean, they're not shutting down the festivities given the . . ." She grimaced. "Foot?"

"Not until they know more," I said, shooting a look at Billy. It was like he was always watching me. "I mean, yes, that part of the woods is technically on their property, but it's not exactly on the orchard grounds, and this is their busy time of year."

The twins exchanged glances.

"What?"

Tweety sniffed. "You people are nuts, that's what."

I sighed. "Don't tell me you guys are scared of the Apple Witch too?"

She whacked me on the arm. "Don't say her name out loud. She'll hear you."

"Um, ow," I said, rubbing the spot where she'd got me. "And I will take that as a yes."

Kit Kat leaned forward in her chair. She squinted and pointed at me, "Let me tell you something, missy. You are talking about things you don't understand. If you know what's good for you, you won't mess around with the . . ."

"Apple Witch?"

The twins threw all four of their hands up in the air.

"What?" I asked with a chuckle. "You can say her name. She's not *Voldemort*."

The sisters exchanged looks and said, "Who?"

I suddenly had the feeling that this was going to be a very long day. "It doesn't matter." I shook my head. "This is ridiculous. You two are like the least superstitious people I know. Why—"

"Strange things have happened in those woods," Kit Kat said, once again pointing at me.

Her sister nodded. "You need to show some respect."

"You want me to show some respect to the ghost that doesn't exist? Maybe I should construct her a little apple shrine," I said, making a building motion with my hands, "and bring her apple presents and—"

Tweety swatted my hands this time, destroying my imaginary apple shrine. "That attitude is going to get you apple-killed if you're not careful." Suddenly she was standing awfully close to me. "You can't throw a rock in town without hitting someone who has heard that witch's strange, ghostly cries."

I stepped away from her . . . but, unfortunately, that brought me closer to Kit Kat.

"And people have gone missing," she said, leaning even closer to me in her chair.

I took a step away from both of them. "What people? I've never heard of anyone going missing in Otter Lake. You made that up."

Kit Kat leaned back into her chair. "I most certainly did not."

I planted my hands on my hips. "Okay, well, what people?"

"Just . . . people," she said.

"Like over the years," her sister added.

"Oh. Of course. Just people." I nodded. "Hey, has anyone checked out the dates? Like maybe a person goes missing every seven years—for the seven men she killed—on the anniversary of her death." Rhonda had made us watch a horror movie just like that the other day.

"That's just ridiculous," Kit Kat said with a fair amount of disgust. "Be serious."

"I'm not the one who's being ridicul—"

"We've lived in these parts a lot longer than you have," Tweety said.

"And men do go missing," her sister threw in.

"Cheating men."

"People say they run out on their wives, but really . . ." Kit Kat shook her head and made a very strange face.

I stared at her. "I don't know what that face means."

"It means they go into the woods and never come back out." Kit Kat clapped her hands together. "Bam! The Apple Witch gets them! Oh shoot, I said her name. Now Tweety's going to die."

"Me?" Tweety shouted at her sister. "Why would I die?"

"Well, there's no way I'm letting that ghost witch near me, so I figured she'd just take you instead. I mean, we are identical and—"

"Okay," I said, cutting her off with a wave. "As informative as this has been, I have to get going. Thank you for feeding Caesar."

"No problem," Tweety said. "But Erica?"

"What?"

"You need to listen to us."

"Stop going into those woods," her sister warned.

"Or you'll regret it."

Well, I wasn't going into the woods, *exactly*.

I was going to an outbuilding *in the woods* for a super-secret meeting with a woman whom I barely had had any contact with for years who was acting super-sketchy after a body was found on her family's property. So really . . . who had time to be afraid of a witch? I had other problems.

"Why did I let you talk me into this?"

But at least I wasn't alone.

"Because I'm your best friend?"

Freddie shook his head. "That's not it."

"Because I promised we could go for pizza afterward?"

"That sounds more like me."

I was glad he had agreed. Not just because I didn't want to die alone . . . or at all . . . but I was tired of biking everywhere. It wasn't hard to figure out why Mandy had chosen the apple orchard's outbuilding for this *private* meeting. It was far away from the main hub of action. I think it was used for storage way back in the day when the pickers were working on the outer boundaries of the property. You could also get to it from the road without having to park at the main lot. Which would have really helped out if, you know, I had a car. I couldn't afford one. Nope, every cent I made went toward saving up for a down payment for a place of my own. Not all of us had rich parents like Freddie, and real estate was hard to come by in Otter Lake. A development company had been trying to turn our quaint little community into a cottage playground for the rich and famous. So far they had managed to attract some rich folks, so maybe one day the famous would follow. In the meantime, Freddie and Rhonda drove me most of the places I needed to go. The rest of the time, I took my bike. I had bought it off Big Don's nephew who worked at his uncle's restaurant slash bar, the Dawg. Yup, he had upgraded. Apparently even busboys had more money than I did these days.

"Are you sure Mandy didn't tell you anything about why she wanted to have this creepy meeting?"

"I'm sure," I said, rolling my eyes . . . before tripping on a raised tree root. "She didn't have time. You and Cam interrupted."

We walked a little farther in silence. The trees were crowded over us and the old wagon drive that led to the outbuilding. Not that it was much of a drive, just two hard-packed dirt tire tracks barely visible in the grass. The tang of overripe apple hung in the air.

"This is a bad idea," Freddie said. "You know, it's not just Grandma Honeycutt that's creepy. The entire family is creepy. We never should have gotten involved with them."

"They're not creepy," I said. "Have you been into the Halloween candy again? You know it makes you grumpy."

"My candy consumption is none of your business,"

Freddie said. "And if they're not creepy then why do they all still live together?"

"It's a family business. And a big property," I said, throwing my arms out to the trees blazing with fall color. "Why wouldn't they all live together? And I think you're forgetting that I still live with my mother."

"No, didn't forget that," he said matter-of-factly.

"Relax. You're going to get yourself all worked up," I said. "You really don't do well with this time of year."

"It's like the *Texas Chainsaw Massacre* family," Freddie went on. "Leatherface with apples. That's why I didn't bring Stanley by the way. No reason why he should get murdered too."

"Okay, you're seriously cut off from the candy and the horror mov—"

"And who names their kids after the alphabet?"

I stopped walking and looked at him. "Names their kids after the alphabet? What are you talking about?"

Freddie stopped walking too. "Adam, Brandon, and Cameron?"

"Oh my God, I never realized that before," I said, rubbing my arms. Even with my heavy wool sweater, it was pretty cool in the forest. "But what about Mandy?"

Freddie blinked at me. "You mean Amanda? The first girl in the family?"

"Huh." I started walking again. "That seriously never occurred to me."

"Wow," Freddie said, falling into step. "You know, you'd be the first to die in a horror movie. Like right away. You wouldn't even have to be running in heels. And while we're on the subject, why did they all take their mother's last name?"

"I don't know. Maybe their dad wasn't close to his family. Maybe they just liked the way it sounded. And naming the kids after the alphabet isn't creepy. It's . . . cute."

"Maybe if you're a rabbit," Freddie grumbled, kicking a pile of yellow leaves. "I mean, how many kids were they planning on having?"

"Okay, too far," I said, pointing at him. "You know that's a sad story."

He held his hands up in defeat. "I know. I know."

We walked on a little more in silence. I mean, it wasn't too silent. It had been a warm fall, so the odd cricket was still chirping, but otherwise it was silent.

I felt bad every time I thought about the Honeycutts and their mom. She had died giving birth to Mandy. I think she had that condition . . . preeclampsia? She was warned about having more children, but I guess she felt it was worth the risk. Her husband died not long after. Heart attack. Most people thought it was brought on by grief.

"You know what else is creepy?"

But I guess not everyone was feeling sad. "What else is creepy, Freddie?" I asked before startling at a chipmunk zipping by.

"They're all blond haired and blue eyed."

"Okay," I said. "Now you're just getting crazy. They're family."

"But that's a lot of recessive genes," he went on. "It's like that other horror movie with all the little blond-haired, blue-eyed children who—"

I frowned. "Weren't they aliens?"

"You're missing the point."

I sighed. "That is because there is no point to all this craziness."

Freddie stopped walking again. To an outside observer it might look like we were delaying going too far into the woods. "Why are you always so protective of the Honeycutts anyway?"

I looked at him. "You know I used to babysit them."

"Yeah, no," he said, shaking his head and squinting suspiciously. "There's something more you're not telling me."

I planted my hands on my hips and sighed. I did not like talking about this . . . which was probably why I never had. There was no way to tell the story—the story of the revenge prank Mandy and I had pulled on her brothers—that didn't make us all look bad. "No . . . well, maybe. It's just . . . like, have you ever experienced something really unpleasant or awkward with someone? And even though you don't like the memory . . . it kind of like *bonds* you to that person?"

"You mean like you and me and every day of our high school experience?"

I frowned and started walking again. "No, that's not what I mean."

Freddie trotted after me. "Hey, did you and the Honeycutt children accidentally kill a drifter? Is it *his* foot in the woods? You can tell me."

"I don't know why I even bother. Hey, look, there it is," I said, pointing up ahead.

The outbuilding had definitely seen better days. I was kind of surprised it was in such a state of disrepair. The rest of the orchard was so well maintained. But I guess only family made it out here these days. It was basically a minibarn painted green with red trim, but that paint was pretty worn and faded now. It was probably cute at one time . . . actually, who was I kidding? Whatever it may have looked like in the past, it looked like a murder barn now. Not that I had ever seen a murder barn. But it probably didn't take an expert.

"It looks like a murder barn," Freddie suddenly said.

There was a reason why we were friends.

I took a hard swallow and walked up to the wooden door with the rusted iron handle. "Well, here goes nothing."

I stepped inside the dusty barn and—

"Whoa . . ."

Chapter Five

"Mandy. Hi," I said quickly, to cover up for my earlier *whoa*. I mean, the earlier *whoa* was totally justified, but I didn't want to be rude. It was indeed pretty *creepy*—to use Freddie's word—in here. And it had an abandoned smell. Like old turpentine, grease, and hay, all mixed together. The rust-covered harvesting tools hanging on the wall didn't help the atmosphere either.

"Sorry," she said. "I know it's kind of creepy in here."

"You said it," Freddie muttered, looking around. He swatted at the air, sending dust motes spinning.

I shot him a look before saying, "I . . . uh, brought Freddie. I hope that's okay."

"I know," she said, crossing her arms over her chest. It almost looked like she was trying to give herself a hug. "I heard you guys coming. It's fine."

Freddie hissed some air through his teeth. "When you say you heard us coming . . . ?"

"Yeah, I heard the murder barn part."

"Really?" Freddie asked, before whispering to me, "She must have ears like a bat." He then turned back to Mandy. "I'm sorry. I was just being—"

Suddenly Mandy dropped her face into her hands and started to cry.

I shot Freddie another look.

He shrugged and mouthed, *What did I do?*

"Mandy? What's going on?" I asked, going up to her.

She looked at me, eyes full of tears. "I'm so sorry. It's just . . ." She closed her eyes and put her hands on her stomach. That was the second time she had done that. If I didn't know better . . .

I squeezed her shoulder. She was wearing a cream knit sweater and jeans. She looked so cozy . . . and little . . . and sad.

"I'm sorry. I'm sorry. I know it probably seems crazy, and that's why I didn't want you to tell anyone. I just didn't know what else to do. I know you're dating Grady and—"

"We're just frien—" I shook my head. "Sorry. Doesn't matter. Go on."

"I wanted to know if Grady told you anything. You know something more than he would have told us?"

"I don't think so," I said, trying to remember the very little Grady had said last night. "Why?"

"He didn't tell you who he thought it was? Or how they died?"

"No," I said, straightening. "He just said that it was still early. That's all."

She threw her hands weakly in the air. "I don't know why I even asked. It's stupid. I haven't been sleeping." She shook her head and put her hand to her mouth like she might be sick. "I . . . need to sit down." I helped her over to a workbench, exchanging looks with Freddie.

"I feel like I'm going crazy," she said a moment later. "I don't even know what I'm saying."

"It's okay," I said. "Take your time."

"I know this isn't good for me. It isn't good for . . ." She looked down at her stomach.

"Are you . . . ?"

She nodded.

"Is she what?" Freddie asked. "What are you two talking about?"

I stared at him, then directed his gaze to Mandy's stomach with my eyes. She even patted her belly.

"What? Do you need an antacid?" Freddie asked. "'Cause I don't have one. But I might have a piece of gum."

"Freddie," I hissed, "gum is not going to help her situation."

"Why not? I find that gum helps most situa— Wait. You're pregnant?!" Freddie shouted.

I closed my eyes and took a breath.

"Well, why didn't you say so?" he said, rushing over. "We'll do whatever you need. Pregnancy rules apply."

"Pregnancy rules?" I asked, not at all sure that inviting him to elaborate was a good idea.

"Yeah," he said, frowning at me. "You have to do whatever a pregnant woman wants at any given time."

"That's just one rule."

"But it applies in many different scenarios. I mean, we can't let you go skydiving or anything," he said to Mandy. "But any reasonable request must be granted. Just rub the lamp—or your belly—and the baby genies will make your wish come true."

I looked at him.

"What? Everybody knows this."

I blinked a couple of times before turning back to Mandy. "Do you . . . know something more about what happened in those woods? Something that you don't want the police to know?"

She shook her head. "No, I swear. I don't know what happened. It's just . . . again, if I tell you, you're going to think I'm crazy."

"Mandy, I've known you most of your life and—"

"It was the Apple Witch. I think the Apple Witch killed whoever it was out there."

Chapter Six

"The Apple Witch?"

Freddie and I had said it at the same time, but in very different tones of voice. Mine was of the "are you kidding me right now?" variety and Freddie's was just filled with horror.

"See?" She shrugged a little. "I told you."

"No, no," I said, patting her shoulder. "I don't think you're crazy." It was probably a good thing that she couldn't see the look on my face.

"I know how it sounds, but . . . things have happened in those woods."

"I tried to tell her that," Freddie said with a crazy point at me. "Didn't I? I tried to tell you not to mess around with the . . . *you know who.*"

I ignored him. "What kind of *things* are you talking about, Mandy?"

"Things I can't explain," she said. "Look, I grew up hearing about the Apple Witch. Obviously. She's a big draw for business. I never really believed in her though. Then I dated this guy for a little while, Danny, and—"

"Oh yeah," Freddie said. "I remember Danny." He

looked over at me. "It was while you were in Chicago. Wasn't he some sort of ghost hunter?"

"That's how we started dating," Mandy said with a nod. "He wanted permission to ghost-hunt on the property at night. My grandparents thought it might be good for business. And . . . he showed me the tapes." A shudder ran over her. "He had video of *something*. Lots of videos."

I crossed my arms over my chest before quickly uncrossing them. It looked very judgmental. "Again, what do you mean by *something*?"

"It looked like a woman in a cloak," she said. "And the time stamp was always the same. Ten minutes after midnight. Every night in October. He said she always came out at that time to roam the forest around her house. Danny thought that must have been when she died."

"Or maybe she had to stop off and kill Cinderella first. Like every night. On a ghost loop," Freddie said with a chuckle before catching the look on Mandy's face. "I'm sorry. I make jokes when I get scared."

"Do you have any of these tapes?" I asked.

"No, Danny has them all. He was going to do a Web series."

I swatted at a cobweb floating in front of my face. "And where is Danny now?"

"He's in Vegas," she said. "Probably hunting more ghosts."

"Mandy . . ." I didn't know what to say. I just wanted to make this better for her, but I didn't want to make her feel like I felt. Like the whole thing was ridiculous.

"Look, I know what you're thinking. And sitting here now, in the light of day, I agree with you. Ghosts aren't real. My baby is fine."

Whoa, my baby is fine? What did that mean?

"But then I wake up in the middle of the night, and . . ." She bit her lip and looked down at her hands.

"And what?"

"I feel like I'm being haunted." She swiped a tear from her cheek. "I just can't stop thinking about the Apple Witch, and that . . . this pregnancy might be cursed."

"Cursed?"

"You know how my mother died, right?"

I nodded.

"Did you also know that some people believe the Apple Witch can't rest in peace because she's looking for the baby she lost?" Her eyes darted over my face. "All the women in my family have had a tough time with pregnancies."

Well . . . crap. It didn't matter if I thought this was ridiculous or not. The whole thing was real enough in Mandy's head. "You need to talk to your family about this. You need their support. And what about the baby's father? Can he help?"

"It's Shane's," she said, picking at the skin around her thumbnail. "And he doesn't know yet."

I didn't really know Shane, but I thought he helped out at the garage in town.

"I don't know how he'll feel. He's always joking about commitment, and this wasn't planned. But now that it's happened . . . I just want this baby so badly." She let out a shaky breath. "My brothers are going to freak out when they find out it's Shane's. Especially Adam."

"I take it they don't like him?"

"No, they're like best friends. But Adam thinks Shane is a total dog."

Freddie nodded. "And does Shane know the child's name has to follow with the alphabet?"

I swatted at him. "What is the matter with you?"

He cringed. "I'm sorry. I'm freaked out, and pregnancy makes me awkward."

"I thought it made you a genie?"

He frowned at me. "I can be both. Don't put me in a box."

Mandy laughed. It was a very sad sound though. "No. He's not that far off, Erica. I mean, the name doesn't matter. But . . . my family, we're close. It seems stupid, but that kind of thing is important. And my brothers have always been so protective. You know that. They had to be both mother and father to me." She laughed again. It sounded even sadder. Man, if this hilarity kept up, she was going to make me cry. "Then there's my grandma. I don't know what she'll think of . . . a child out of wedlock. And her health's not great."

"I've known your grandmother a long time. I'm sure she'll love any child of yours. You need to tell her."

"I will. I will. I just need to get my head together first. I mean, I started thinking about the Apple Witch the second I found out I was pregnant. Then when you found the . . . body . . . I guess I was just looking for reassurance."

"We'll do it," Freddie said.

I whipped my gaze over to him. "Do what?"

"Get her some reassurance. We'll talk to Grady. Or Erica will. What's the big deal?" He shrugged. "Say, *Hey Grady, 'sup? What's the 411 on the foot in the woods?*"

"Because that's how I talk?" I asked, before adding a finger-point at his chest. "Don't answer that." I looked back at Mandy. "I mean, yes, we can do that. But I don't know if this really solves the problem. Mandy, if there's no wallet, it might take a long time to get an ID on the body. And with . . . how old the body is, it might take some time to get a cause of death too."

She took another shaky breath and nodded. "I'm sorry. I never should have asked you guys to do this. I'm just hormonal. It's ridiculous. I know it's all ridiculous. And please don't tell my brothers I'm freaked out about the witch. You know how they are." This time she looked to Freddie instead of me.

I looked at him too and raised an eyebrow in question.

He scratched his arm. "They may have been razzing me a bit about my . . . *you know who* beliefs."

"Right," I said, giving my head a little shake. "But, Mandy, I don't like leaving you like this."

"I'll be fine. Really. I'm just so tired, you know?" She ran a hand over her face. "If I could just get a good night's sleep, I know I could think straight . . . and face everyone."

I sighed. "I wish there was some way I could convince you that all this Apple Witch stuff is just . . . not true." I blinked a few times. "Wait, you said that in the tapes Danny took, the time stamp was always 12:10? And it was every night in October?"

She nodded.

"Erica," Freddie said with lots of warning.

I threw my hands in the air. "Well, then there's the solution."

"I can't go into the woods," Mandy said. "I can't do it. Not like—"

"Of course you can't," I said, patting her shoulder. "I didn't mean you."

"Erica," Freddie said again.

"Freddie and I will do it. We're working tonight anyway, so we'll already be here. We can just stop by the Apple Witch's house after the gates close. Record the whole thing—or the whole *no* thing as will likely be the case."

She shook her head. "I couldn't ask you to do that."

"You're not asking. We're offering. We're the baby genies, remember?"

"I just . . . I feel so ridiculous for—"

"Stop. It will be fun. And you can finally get a good night's sleep once you know for sure there's nothing out there."

She looked torn. "Are you sure it's not—"

"It's no problem at all," I said with a big smile. "Right, Freddie?"

I waited for him to answer and got nothing.

"Right, Freddie?"

"Of course not," he said brightly. He then shot me a look that had so much restrained anger in it, it probably could have brought the Apple Witch back from the dead.

I smiled. "Great."

Chapter Seven

"Trick or treat."

"Hey, you. Come in," Grady said, leaning back in his chair behind the desk. "This is a nice surprise."

At least someone was happy to see me. Freddie definitely was not. He actually said something about never wanting to see me again, and then he stopped talking to me altogether. That being said, after he dropped me off in town, I watched him go into the corner store and pick up a bag of marshmallows. He was obviously campfire-snack shopping, so I was thinking we were good to go. Well, good to go if I could get past this next little hurdle.

See, if we were going Apple Witch hunting that obviously meant we needed to set up near the Apple Witch's house. And if we were hanging out near the Apple Witch's house, that would mean we were also hanging out somewhat near a crime scene. I wasn't exactly sure how Grady was going to take that particular piece of news. In the past, Grady and I had had a lot of trouble navigating the waters of our conflicting careers. As sheriff, Grady got really protective of his crime scenes, and, admittedly, Freddie and I had not always followed all the rules when investigating. But the good news was we weren't investigating this time. At least we weren't investigating the cause of death of the foot in the woods—and yes, I know it was a person I found, but for my sanity, I felt temporarily better referring to it as a foot. And Grady and I had been working really hard on our relationship, and I was really hoping that this wouldn't throw a wrench into all that.

"I brought you a coffee." I lifted a paper cup in the air. "And a muffin."

"Thank you. I'm starving," he said. "And you know—"

"Amos makes lousy coffee," I finished with a smile.

Grady smiled back. "He really does. I keep offering to do it myself, but then his feelings get hurt."

I suddenly felt all warm and tingly inside. I mean, look at us with our own private jokes about our day-to-day lives.

I sat in the chair across from Grady as he unfolded the wrapping of his muffin. "So what's the occasion?"

"I just felt like doing something nice for you."

He looked up at me and froze, hand midway to mouth with a hunk of muffin.

"What?" I asked, straightening in my seat. "I do nice things."

He just looked at me. That sheriff's glare of his always made me feel so guilty.

"Fine," I said with an eye roll. "I wanted to talk to you about something."

He leaned back in his chair and templed his fingers. "Okay."

"And I'm hoping we can use all of our new communication skills to make sure that this doesn't become a thing."

He pushed his muffin away. "I knew it was a dirty muffin."

"Grady, that is not a very mature start. And it is not a dirty muffin. You can eat the muffin regardless of how this conversation goes."

He took a deep breath. "Fine. You're right. My bad. Let's try this again." He smiled. "Please, Erica, tell me what it is that brings you to my office today."

"Well, don't say it like that," I said, wrinkling my nose. "That was just weird."

He pinned his lips together a moment then said, "Erica. 'Sup?"

"Now you sound like Freddie."

He threw a hand in the air. "Just tell me what's going on."

"Okay. Okay," I said. "Keep your pants on." It took everything in me not to add *or don't* with a lascivious eyebrow pop. I didn't think he'd appreciate any more tangents. So I just launched right into Mandy's fears about the Apple Witch, and that she was in a really vulnerable place right now what with the discovery of the body, without telling him about her pregnancy. I know I had promised Mandy I wouldn't tell Grady any of this, but . . . well, I didn't know what the *but* was to that particular point, *but* . . . it wasn't like I was telling him the full story, and . . . and I could only do so much! I ended my explanation to Grady with, "So Freddie and I thought we might go and check out the ruins tonight to prove that there is no Apple Witch killing people in the woods."

"I see."

"I realize you might have some concerns about us going out so close to the crime scene, but I promise you, we have no intention of going anywhere near there."

He looked at me a moment then said, "Okay."

"Okay?"

"Okay."

"That's it?"

"That's it," he said with a shrug. "I mean it's weird that a grown woman is so freaked out about a witch living in her woods, but I know you used to babysit the Honeycutts . . . and it's nice of you to do that. I assume you got her permission to go exploring out there."

"Yeah, totally," I said, straightening in my seat. "But . . . you're not worried about the crime scene?"

"No," he said carefully. "You said you're not investigating the murder, right?"

"Right."

He nodded and leaned back again in his chair. "Then I'm not worried about the crime scene."

I cocked my head. I mean this was great. Wonderful. Exactly what I wanted to hear from him. I just couldn't quite believe it. "So none of this bothers you? You have no concerns?"

"I am a little concerned that you and Freddie are going to get so freaked out that you turn feral . . . like *Lord of the Flies* or something, and I'm going to have to clean up what remains of you two tomorrow, but no, other than that, no worries." He shot me a smile.

"Well . . . good."

He smiled again. "I'm also really glad that you gave me the heads-up and told me about this in advance. That way if somebody reports seeing you out there, Amos won't shoot you thinking you're the Apple Witch."

I smiled back at him. "I am also glad that we are avoiding that scenario. And you're not worried about us running into the murderer on the loose?"

"Whatever happened in those woods . . . it happened years ago. And contrary to what you might read in books, most murderers aren't stupid enough to go back to the scene of the crime." He tapped his desk with a pen. "But if you do get murdered, I'm assuming only the Honeycutts know you're going out there, so I'll start by questioning them first."

"Cool," I said. "Thanks."

"And take your phone obviously," he said. "I mean, I doubt I'll get to you in time if anything happens, but again, your death screams could provide me with useful evidence."

I smiled some more. "Look at you making all the jokes."

"I am a new man, Erica." Suddenly he frowned. "But maybe don't go into the house."

"Sure," I said quickly, then added, "Not that I was planning to—" I mean, I may not believe in ghosts but even I had my limits. "But why not?"

"I don't think it's safe," he said. "That house could have had a cold cellar or subfloor. With its age and all the damage it has sustained over the years, I doubt it's safe."

"Got it."

He smiled again.

I smiled back again.

"I feel like we need to high-five here," I said, leaning across the desk with my hand in the air. "Don't leave me hanging."

"Yeah," he said, smacking my palm. "We totally handled that like pros."

"No fighting."

"None."

"Just honest, respectful communication."

He nodded. "It feels good."

I raised an eyebrow. "Like next-step good?"

He nodded some more. "Like I don't see why we need to wait any longer. I think this conversation right here proved it."

"So, what are you doing tonight?" I asked quickly.

His eyes darted side to side. "Aren't you ghost-hunting?"

Dammit! "Right. Right. Forgot all about that for a second there."

"But soon," he said, smiling again.

"As possible."

"Agreed."

"And we're still meeting up for the pumpkin races?" I asked. Every year Otter Lake had a tradition of throwing jack-o'-lanterns into the river to, well, race. The name was pretty self-explanatory. It was a fun fall activity. Just the kind of cozy thing I wanted to do with Grady.

"For sure," Grady said. "We're meeting at the bridge, right?"

"Absolutely." I smiled again like an idiot. We were meeting at a covered bridge just on the outskirts of town. That way we could see the pumpkins, but we would still have a bit of privacy. "Well . . . I should probably go," I said, getting to my feet.

He nodded. "Probably a good idea. Because *soon* suddenly isn't seeming *soon* enough."

"Right."

"Right."

"Could *soon* maybe be . . . right now?" I asked, shrugging a little.

His eyes widened. "That probably wouldn't be appropriate . . . at work. I'm sheriff." I couldn't tell if he was trying to remind me of that or himself.

I nodded. "And we might traumatize Amos."

Grady nodded too. "That is true." He was breathing kind of heavily though.

"Okay, well . . ." I said, trying to back-step toward the door, but not getting very far. "If you really want me to go."

"Not nice, Erica," Grady said.

"What? You think I'm teasing?" I asked. "Because I could seriously lock that door and—"

"Please go."

"Are you sure?"

"Like right now."

"Okay," I said with a smile. "I'm really going . . ."

He crumpled up a sheet of paper and threw it at me. "Get out."

I popped outside before it hit me.

Chapter Eight

"Freddie?"

Nothing.

"Freddie?"

Still nothing.

"Are you seriously not going to talk to me all night?"

He just stared at me—angrily—from across the camp-fire and popped a marshmallow into his mouth. We had set up the fire about an hour after the gates closed at the apple orchard. Mandy didn't want us to tell her brothers that we were going into the woods for her sake, but ever since Grady put the thought of being shot in the woods into my head, I really wanted to avoid that possibility too, so we ended up telling the guys that Grady thought it would be a good idea if we kept an eye on the crime scene, just in case more kids showed up. We threw in that we'd do it for free as it counted toward the security hours we needed to apply for our private investigator licenses. You could tell the brothers found the whole thing a little strange—given Freddie's fear of the Apple Witch—but in the end they just said thank you and lent us some pretty awesome lanterns.

"This next half hour is going to be the longest half hour of our lives if you don't start talking to me." Actually, it was probably a little less than half an hour until the Apple Witch was to appear, but the point still stood.

"Fine," Freddie said in that controlled voice people use when they are really angry but still want to sound rational. "I am very upset with you."

"I can see that."

"You knew I had . . . concerns about the . . . *she who shall not be named,* but you volunteered us to do this anyway."

"What was I supposed to do?" I asked, poking a stick in the fire. Unfortunately, it didn't have a marshmallow on it. Freddie wasn't in the mood to share yet. "Mandy was all pregnant and upset . . . and she's got those big eyes." I pointed the stick at him. "And you're the one who said we have to follow the pregnancy rules."

"You should have asked me first," he said before eating another marshmallow.

"You're right," I said. "I should have asked you first."

He held his angry face for a second longer, before he broke out into a smile. "Okay, now that that's all over, so while I was all angry at you, I had a great idea."

I had really thought that would have been harder. "You did?" I held out my hand for the marshmallows, and he tossed the bag to me.

"Seeing as we have to take video anyway, I was thinking we could do a *Blair Witch* type thing for the OLS Web site."

I tried to say *What?* but my mouth was too full, so I just looked at him quizzically.

"You know. People love ghost-hunting stuff. It will totally up our Google ranking."

I swallowed the sugary lump. "But given your *concerns* about—"

He pointed at me.

"We both know who," I said. "Won't taking scary video make this experience that much worse?"

"I don't know yet," he said matter-of-factly. "But I think it might distract me."

I guess I could see that. "Okay, well, what exactly did you have in mind?"

"Well, we can do a little history on the place," he said, looking over at the house. "We may have to edit that in later because I don't actually have any history on that, but then we can take some scary footage of you—over by the house—crying with your nose running saying good-bye to your mom."

I wiped my nose with my glove. "I'm not sure I can do the crying part."

"Sure you can," Freddie said, suddenly pulling a pretty expensive-looking video camera out of his bag. "You just need to believe in yourself. And think scary things."

"I don't know," I said with a sigh. "I'm not really feeling scared. I'm feeling cold. And I just want to get this footage for Mandy and go home."

"I know what'll get you in the mood," Freddie said, pointing the camera at me. He pressed a button and a light hit me in the face. "Tell me what scares you."

"What? What are you talking about?" I asked, trying to look at Freddie but only seeing the light at the front of the camera.

"We're always talking about what scares me," he said. "But what about you? What freaks you out?"

I frowned. "I . . . don't know."

"Don't give me that *nothing scares me* crap."

"Well, confronting my mother about the identity of my father scares me." I had come to the conclusion this past spring that an important part of my journey to becoming a fully functioning adult was finding out the identity of my father. It was not an easy subject to broach with my mother. When I was little, she never talked about him. For the longest time, I thought I might have been brought into this world with some sort of Wiccan cere-mony. Probably involving herbs. Maybe some yoga. It was a confusing concept. But as I got older, I realized that wasn't likely the case, so I had confronted my mother. On a few occasions. But the topic had really upset her, so I always ended up letting it go. Now that I was older, though, I kind of felt like I deserved an answer. I was just too afraid to ask the question.

"You still haven't done that?" Freddie asked. "No, of course you haven't. You would have told me. But that's not what I meant. I don't mean scared like 'my father came from a sperm bank and I have two hundred sib-lings' scared."

I clenched the marshmallow in my hand. "Holy crap. Do you think that's possible?" I mean, I had thought of the sperm bank thing, but not the two hundred siblings.

"Don't worry. I think they put a limit on it. But what I meant was, what gives you the heebie-jeebies?"

I frowned. I was having a hard time transitioning away from the siblings thing. "Well . . . I don't know. When I was a kid, I watched *Friday the 13th* at Janis's tenth birth-day party. That kind of freaked me out."

"Ten?" Freddie asked. "That seems young. Where were her parents?"

"Who knows?" I said with a shrug. "But for a long time after that, every time I walked up the steps to the retreat, I was sure Jason was going to jump out of the woods and get me with his machete."

"I hear ya," Freddie said.

"Oh!" I pointed at him with my free hand. "I also don't like windows without curtains at night. That totally creeps me out."

"Nobody likes that." He shuddered a little. "You know what I'm scared of? I mean, aside from all the other things I'm scared of?"

"What?"

"Little-kid ghosts." Freddie looked at me from around the camera and shook his head. "Like in movies they always have those high-pitched voices, and they're always singing nursery rhymes."

I nodded. "Yeah, that's just wrong."

"Oh! Or when they bounce those bouncy balls down the stairs?" Freddie said. "I'm sorry, kid ghost or not, I'm taking you out."

"But you can't take them out. That's the whole thing. They're already dead."

"There has to be some way to banish a ghost," Freddie said, looking at me from around the camera again. "I mean, vampires you got stakes and garlic and holy water. Werewolves have silver bullets."

"Salt."

"Salt?"

"I think salt banishes ghosts," I said, eyeing the marshmallow I was currently roasting.

"Why salt? What would you even do with it? Sprinkle it on their food?"

"No . . . I don't know what you're supposed to do with it actually." I frowned. "But I think you are also supposed to burn their bones."

"Really?" Freddie asked. "But do bones burn?"

"I think. Wait . . . of course they do. People are cremated all the time!"

"Oh yeah, but I don't like that," Freddie said. "It sounds like a lot of work. I mean, we both know how hard grave-digging can be, and it also just seems rude . . . and illegal."

"Well, I doubt anybody is going to make you burn a

ghost's bones," I said. "It's not something you *have* to do."

"But what if a ghost is haunting me?" he asked.

"Then go with the salt."

"I just can't see how salt would work."

"Oh my God," I said, throwing my head back. "Then I guess you would just have to live with the ghost."

"Who wants to live with a ghost?" Freddie squealed. "They'd always be moving your stuff around and—"

"That's it!" I pushed myself to my feet. "Let's go take your stupid footage."

"Are you scared?"

"No, but I'm ready to cry." Not to mention my marshmallow had melted off my stick and fallen into the coals because I hadn't been paying attention. I made my way around the fire toward Freddie while pulling on my woolen mittens.

"Okay." He got up too. "You go first."

I stopped walking. "What? Why can't we just go together?"

"Because I need you in the shot."

"That's awfully convenient," I grumbled.

"What's the big deal? I thought you didn't believe in ghosts. Isn't that the whole reason we're out here, so we can prove to Mandy and her baby that there is no Apple Witch?"

We warred with our eyes a moment.

I cracked first. "Right you are."

"Then please," Freddie said, swinging out his free hand. "After you."

I nodded. This was fine. Sure, Freddie had been goading me, but I *didn't* believe in ghosts. There was nothing to be afraid of. I was only sorry that I wasn't that good of an actress. Freddie was going to be super-disappointed with the calm, cool, brave face I had on. I started off toward the dilapidated house at a crisp pace, while watching my footing on the uneven ground.

"You getting all this?" I called out without looking to see if Freddie was following me. I didn't need that kind of reassurance.

"I am getting it all," he said. "Anything you want to say to your loved ones before we get to the house?"

"Nope."

"What?" he called after me. "Not even to your mother?"

"Nope. Don't have to," I said. "I'll be seeing her tomorrow."

"Anything you want me to know?" he shouted.

"Nope," I said, slowing my pace. The light from Freddie's camera lit up the old wooden plank door in front of me. "Well, here it is."

"Right," Freddie said, keeping the camera steady.

Neither one of us said anything for a moment.

"Well, aren't you going to open it?" Freddie asked.

My chin dropped to my chest. "You want me to open it? I thought you just wanted me to act all scared."

"Yeah," Freddie said, giving me another look around the camera. "But people are going to want to see what's inside."

"It's an abandoned house. That's like a hundred and fifty years old."

"Exactly."

"I can't even see if there's . . ." I looked back at the door. Yup, there was a doorknob. I took a deep breath. "Okay, but I'm just going to open the door. I'm not going in."

"Got it."

"Hold on to yourself, Freddie," I said, reaching out for the doorknob. "Because I'm really going to do it."

"So do it."

"Okay. I'm really going to."

"Any time."

"I'm really—"

"Open the door!"

"All right. All right. Sheesh." I gripped the doorknob. It was rough and flecks of rust caught in the wool of my mittens. I gave it a test turn and suddenly the door gave way and swung in. I jumped back. And next thing I knew there was a blinding light in my face.

"You all right?" Freddie asked.

"Yes," I said, swatting at him. "Just get that camera out of my face."

Freddie swung the camera toward the house.

"Oh my God," I whispered. Not sure why I was whispering, but it seemed like a good idea. "It's a mess in there." The floor on the far side of the room was covered in soot? I guess there had been a fire at some point. Maybe just outside the house? The back wall had collapsed so it was only about half the height of the other three. The glass was gone from the windows. But it still had a creepy lived-in feel. There was still an old potbellied woodstove in the corner. And a table with two broken legs.

"Okay," Freddie said. "That's good. Now get in there."

"What?" I screeched, but, you know, in a whisper. "I'm not going in there. I told you I wasn't going in there."

"Just one shot," Freddie pleaded. "It will only take a second. You owe me this."

"I owe you nothing, sir."

"But it won't be any good unless the viewers can sense a real live person's fear."

"I don't care."

"You made me come out here."

"Don't care about that either."

"Please, Erica," Freddie said. He then pushed me pretty hard on the back. "And try to cry." I stumbled inside a few steps before turning around to look at Freddie.

"Is this—" Suddenly the floor creaked. Actually it kind of sounded like it was cracking. "Oh crap! I just remembered. Grady said not to go into the—"

Too late.

Chapter Nine

I screamed as the floor gave way from under my feet.

"Erica!"

"Fre—" I couldn't even get his entire name out before my fall was abruptly cut short. "Whoa. Okay. Ow. It's fine. Just a subfloor."

"Oh my God," Freddie said. "For a second there, I thought you were dead."

"Me too."

He started laughing. I tried to resist joining him because me dying really shouldn't be that funny, but I couldn't help myself.

"And in that split second," Freddie said a moment later, still laughing, "all I could think was her mother is going to ask what her last words were, and I was going to have to say *nope*."

I laughed harder at that while pulling my foot out of the hole. I tapped around for a solid plank, adjusted my weight, then moved to bring my other foot up when—

"Hey," I said, gulping down a breath and looking at my feet. "There's something down there."

"What kind of something?" Freddie asked, voice instantly changing into something much more serious.

I felt around a little with the tip of my boot. "I don't know."

"So help me," Freddie said, "if you have found another body I am never going anywhere with you again."

"No, it didn't feel like a body part." I waved a hand at him. "Shine the light on the floor."

I could tell Freddie was freaked out by the shaking of his camera beam, but I wasn't that scared because whatever I had kicked . . . well, it felt kind of like plastic.

I lowered myself to the floor and looked down into the crawl space. There was something there. I reached toward it.

"What are you doing?" Freddie hissed.

I looked up at him. "I'm just going to see if I can get it."

"Have you not been paying attention to all the horror movies we've been watching? If you put your hand in there, you're going to be pulled right down into—"

"Got it," I said.

"Well, that was anticlimactic," Freddie said. "Hey, is that a—"

"Videotape," I said, holding it up.

"No way," Freddie said in a whisper. "I bet you it's one of Danny's tapes of the Apple Witch!"

"Maybe," I said, slowly getting back up onto my feet. I tiptoed my way toward the door, testing each step. Wouldn't want to fall those twelve inches again.

Freddie held his hand out to me when I was still a couple of feet away. I took it and he pulled me out of the house like the floor was lava or something.

We both stared at the tape in my hand.

"Okay," Freddie said. "I've completely changed my mind. I wasn't sure that ghost-hunting was going to be fun. Even with my *Blair Witch* idea. But it is totally fun."

"I know. We discovered lost footage," I said, still looking at the tape. "But why would Danny put this in the floor?"

Freddie chuckled. "Maybe Danny didn't. Maybe the Apple Witch—"

Suddenly a chill ran over me. "Freddie? What time is it?"

His face dropped. "We totally lost track of time, didn't we? Oh God! And I said her name!"

I pulled my phone from my pocket. "It's just after midnight." I swatted him on the arm. "Get the camera ready."

Suddenly all the good happy fun ghost-hunting feelings were gone. Again, I totally didn't believe in ghosts or witches, or ghost witches, but that didn't mean I wasn't just a little bit freaked waiting for one to show up.

"Where do you think she's going to appear?" Freddie whispered.

"I'd say most likely at her house," I whispered, suddenly too afraid to look over my shoulder at the house directly behind me. Freddie and I scurried back toward the campfire we'd built earlier then turned around.

He lifted the camera up again. "Okay, I don't see anything yet."

"And you're not going to," I whispered. "Because ghosts aren't real."

"Then why are you whispering?"

I shot him a look.

We both fell silent and focused on the house.

"What time is it now?" Freddie asked a moment later.

"Six minutes after."

"Right," Freddie whispered.

Another moment of silence passed.

"Hey, Erica," Freddie whispered.

"What?" I whispered back.

"Do you think she really wears a long black cloak?"

"No." I looked at my watch. Eight minutes after.

"Do you think she really has a rotten apple for a face?"

"No." Nine. Nine minutes after.

"Do you think she really has gnarled twigs for fingers?"

"No."

"I can almost feel her dragging one of the tips of those twigs down my cheek."

"Oh my God, stop it." I looked down at my phone. "It's almost time."

"If we die," Freddie whined. "I want you to know that you are my best friend, and I love you, and this is all your fault."

"Got it."

Freddie and I waited. No sound but the crackling of the fire.

I was staring so hard at the house in the darkness, I was worried my eyes would start playing tricks on me. I was sure nothing was moving, and yet the shadows seemed to be fading in and out . . . almost like something might be swirling together . . .

I looked down at my phone again. Relief washed over me. "Twelve eleven. It's twelve eleven. It's over."

"Oh thank God," Freddie said, releasing a whoosh of air. "I mean, it would have made for great video, but—"

Just then a loud crack sounded behind us.

We whipped around.

"What is that?!"

Chapter Ten

"So you saw the Apple Witch?"

"I don't know what we saw."

"Oh my God, would you stop saying that? It was the Apple Witch. You know it was the Apple Witch."

I ignored Freddie and focused all my attention on Rhonda. "I don't know what we saw."

Rhonda grabbed the camera hanging from her neck to steady it as she stepped over a pumpkin. "Well, what did the video show?"

"You mean, Freddie's video?" I asked. "A couple of crazy shots of the ground, that's it. But you could hear us screaming." Yes, we had done a lot of that. "I don't think we'll show it to Mandy. I doubt she'd find it reassuring."

Okay, yes. Freddie and I had seen *something* in the woods last night, but I was not at all convinced it was the Apple Witch. It had been a largeish shape, and it had moved, much like a human would, and that was all I knew for sure. I mean, the campfire had been between us and the shape, so with the glare, I was kind of surprised that we had seen anything at all. It was all shades of black. And now that we were in a pumpkin patch on yet another beautiful fall day, I was finding the entire thing to be even harder to believe.

Rhonda had asked us to come out to help with her cheating-spouse case. She needed to get pictures of the guy with his girlfriend, but given that we were in a pumpkin patch, there wasn't a lot of cover. Rhonda wanted it to look like she was taking pictures of Freddie and me, but really she'd have the camera focused on our target. Hopefully, she'd be able to wrap this up today and join us at the apple orchard. Things seemed to get out of control when Freddie and I spent too much time alone.

"As I tried to explain to Erica," Freddie went on, "I've done some research and ghosts do not show up on digital recordings. You have to use videotapes. Which explains why Danny used VHS. So even if we hadn't freaked out, we wouldn't have gotten anything anyway."

"Hmm, right. That makes perfect sense," I said.

"It's science," Freddie said before turning to Rhonda. "I totally think I saw her face."

Rhonda's eyes widened.

"No he didn't."

"Well, I did see her long dark cloak."

"No you didn't," I said, finally turning to address him head-on. "You saw no such thing. For all either one of us knows it was a deer . . . or a bear." Normally I'd find that idea terrifying, but I'm pretty sure if it was a bear, Freddie and I, with all our screaming, had put it off humans for life.

"It was totally the Apple Witch," Freddie said.

"I can't even . . ."

"Well, I guess we'll know more when we look at Danny's tape," Freddie said. "Oh! Maple syrup lollys. I'll be right back."

"Freddie," Rhonda shouted. "We don't have time for—"

"I'll be right back!"

He was already gone, headed off to the little shack that was selling pies and other treats.

I shook my head and stepped over another pumpkin. Why did people like coming to pumpkin patches? This field was very tough going. One of us was going to break an ankle. Well, it might be nice on a date with . . .

Grady.

That was another issue. Grady was going to want to see the tape, and we were totally going to give him the tape. I mean, Freddie wanted to see what was on it first, and, truth be told, I kind of wanted to too. Mandy had been so upset. I wanted to put this whole Apple Witch thing to rest as soon as possible, and if we saw the tape, and it was one of Danny's, and it did have the Apple Witch on it, there would be a way to debunk it. And I couldn't really explain all this to Grady because that would mean telling him Mandy was pregnant. And that was definitely not my place, regardless of how close Grady and I were getting. There was girl code about that kind of thing. Actually, maybe not girl code, just human decency. So yeah, we were definitely going to take a look at the tape, before we gave it to Grady. And, besides, it probably didn't have anything to do with the murder anyway. Probably. I mean, it had occurred to me that maybe that body in the woods belonged to Danny. But Mandy was convinced he had moved to Vegas, so I looked him up on Facebook—not because I was investigating, but just, well, because—and there were pictures from Vegas. Not a lot of pictures, but pictures, so it probably wasn't Danny. So really, looking at the tape should be fine. Besides, I was working for the Honeycutts. And any good security person would look at footage found on the property before turning it over to the police. So yeah . . . it was fine. Grady wouldn't be mad. At least that's what I was telling myself.

Freddie and I were going to go to the library after the pumpkin patch. Neither one of us owned a VCR. Then we'd hand it straight over to Grady.

"Are you going to go back out into the woods tonight?" Rhonda asked. "Try to get more footage of the witch?"

"No." It was the one thing Freddie and I actually agreed on.

"But you haven't finished the job," she said.

"It was not a job. It was a favor. And I'll just try to find some other way to reassure Mandy that there is no Apple Witch."

Yes, I was hoping the tape we had found would be the key to debunking the Apple Witch, but even if it didn't, I had been giving it some more thought, and really, the best thing for Mandy to do was to talk to her family. She needed their support right now. The secret of the pregnancy was her biggest problem. And really, it was kind of crazy that it was a problem at all. After all, what century were we living in? Granted, Mandy was young, but she had employment, and I bet Grandma Honeycutt would love to be a great-grandmother. She was just that type. And maybe Shane would be on board with the whole thing, but even if he wasn't, it wasn't like Mandy would be the first single mother ever. If she needed someone to be with her when she told her family, I would for sure do that.

"You know people in town are starting to talk about the Apple Witch too," Rhonda said. "Mr. Coulter said he spotted her walking down Main Street after midnight last week."

"What was she doing? Window-shopping?"

"I don't know, but people are getting antsy."

I sighed. "Rhonda, we are not going back into the woods." The ghost may not be real, but Freddie-induced hysteria was, and I was pretty sure that could be even more dangerous. "I cannot control what this town th—"

"Hey," Rhonda said in a low but commanding voice. "That's the guy."

I glanced in the direction she had indicated with a small nod. He looked like a really sweet, handsome dad, taking his toddler to explore a pumpkin patch. He just put his daughter down so she could toddle among the pumpkins. He had been giving her a shoulder ride. They actually looked like they belonged on the cover of a catalogue or something. "He doesn't look like a cheater."

"Oh, he's a cheater," Rhonda said. She had her head tilted down to make it look like she was focused on her camera, but she only had eyes for the target.

"How do you know?" I asked. "I don't see any girl-friend."

"Men don't take their kids to the pumpkin patch alone."

"Sure they do." At least I thought they did. Maybe. It seemed possible.

"No they don't," Rhonda said with a sigh.

"I think all these cheating cases are making you cynical." We only had two cheating cases so far. But the targets had in fact been cheating in both cases, so I think my point stood. Rhonda also wasn't dating anyone at the moment. The last guy she had been seeing had been transferred to another state for work, so I didn't think she was exactly in a loving frame of mind. "You should wrap this thing up and come to the apple orchard with us."

"So I can find a foot?" Rhonda started walking in the direction of our target, being careful to keep a good distance. I fell into step behind her.

"Okay," she said a moment later, "so we're not ghost-hunting, but when do we start investigating this murder at the apple orchard?"

"We don't."

"What? You're kidding me, right?"

"Nope," Freddie said, walking up to us with a maple syrup lollipop in his mouth. "Erica's right. We aren't touching this one."

"But . . . but this is right up our alley," Rhonda spluttered. "We always look into murders that happen in town."

"Those have all been very unique circumstances," I said. "We always had a personal stake involved."

"And they didn't involve ghost witches," Freddie said.

"But you have a personal connection to the Honeycutts, and you found the body on their property."

"For which I have already said, *Hey guys, sorry about that foot I found on your property,* but, you know, in better words, and I think that's all proper etiquette requires. Besides, Grady and I are on the verge of becoming even closer friends—"

"Barf," Freddie said.

"I do not want to jeopardize that in any way, and you know Otter Lake Security getting involved in any investigation is a really big trigger for him."

"That's right," Freddie added, lollipop hanging from the corner of his mouth. "And as Erica just said, she wants to become even closer friends with Grady's other big trigg—"

"Whoa!" I shouted. "There will be none of that."

"I can't believe I'm hearing this," Rhonda said. "Freddie, you can't honestly tell me you don't want to investigate this. I mean, fine, I get it, you don't like the Apple Witch, but—"

"Don't like her?" Freddie pulled the lollipop from his

mouth. "You make it sound like I don't want to go to the movies with her Friday night—which, for the record, I don't—but this is a little more about mortal danger. I saw her once already . . ."

"No you didn't," I threw in.

". . . and lived to tell the tale," Freddie said, shooting me a look. "I don't want to push my luck."

"But," Rhonda reasserted, "what about the excitement? The glory? The media attention of OLS solving yet another murder?"

He shoved the lollipop back into the corner of his mouth and shook his head. "The only time we get media attention is when Erica falls off a Ferris wheel, and I really don't know how much that helps us overall."

"But how can you just let this go? Freddie, you're . . . you're like the love child of Agatha Christie and the Pink Panther!"

"The Pink Panther," Freddie said in a pretty scary voice. "The Pink Panther? You did not just say the Pink Panther."

"What's the Pink Panther?" I asked.

Freddie shot Rhonda a withering look, but said to me, "I'll show you clips later."

"And Erica," Rhonda went on. She was pretty upset now. "I know *you* can't let this go. "You're like . . ." She shook her head, struggling to find the right words. "You're like a cat in a room with five hundred doors. Only one of them is closed, so that's the one you want to go in. Not to mention the fact that you have white-knight syndrome."

I propped my sunglasses up on my head. "What?"

"You feel like it's your job to save everyone. There you are . . . a cat in knight's armor scratching on the door with your little cat lance."

I frowned.

"And the person on the other side is all like, *There's nothing in here for you, cat!*"

"Okay, I think I get your point." Actually, I wasn't sure if I did at all. I was stuck wondering if my little cat-self had a little cat-horse.

"And there's catnip in those other rooms with the open doors. And mice. Wrapped in bacon! And everything a cat could ever want. But you don't care—"

"Rhonda," I said. "Why are you so upset about this?"

She took a deep breath and her shoulders slumped. "I became a cop to help people. To put bad guys in jail." She threw a dejected hand in the air. "Now all I do is take pictures of people cheating on their spouses and trying to scam their insurance companies."

Rhonda had lost her job as a police officer trying to save my life. I knew it had been really hard for her, despite the fact that she didn't like to talk about it much. "I'm so sorry. I didn't realize you were having such a rough time."

"I'm sorry too, Rhonda," Freddie said.

She scowled at us. "Oh, stop looking so sad. I really like this job most of the time, but when an opportunity like this comes up to do more, I kind of feel like we should seize it. Make that sheriff's department regret ever firing me."

"Rhonda, I don't kn—"

"Let me handle this," Freddie said. "Rhonda, as much as we feel for your situation—and your happiness *is* very important to us—OLS is a democracy. And unfortunately in this circumstance, it is two partners against one, so—"

Suddenly Rhonda's camera was up. "Quick. You two. Stand together. Freddie, put your arm around Erica. Make it look like you're a couple, and I'm taking your engagement photos or something."

"Ew," Freddie said.

"Just do it."

Freddie obliged and Rhonda started clicking away.

I took a quick peek over my shoulder. Cheating couple twelve o'clock. And . . . oh my God, they were kissing! Right in front of the toddler!

"Now, do you see what I'm dealing with?" Rhonda asked, still clicking away.

"Yeah," I said sadly as I turned my head back around. "I hear you."

Freddie elbowed me in the ribs. "Would you please smile?"

I looked at him. "What, why?"

"I don't know," he said with a shrug. "We don't have any nice pictures of us."

"You are so weird," I said, but I put on a smile.

"Oh, I didn't mean like that," Freddie said.

I tried another smile.

"Really?"

I growled and smiled again.

"Just . . . you know what? Never mind."

"Freddie!"

"Hi, Mrs. Robinson."

We had just walked into the red brick Victorian building that housed Otter Lake's library. Mrs. Robinson was the librarian, and she loved Freddie. Freddie had spent a lot of time in the library as a child. His various nannies were always leaving him for storytime. His parents, real estate speculators, were often off traveling the world. Mrs. Robinson got used to having Freddie as her library companion. Plus she never had children . . . which I think she really, really wanted. They were a natural fit. She always had cookies and milk on hand to offer him as snacks.

"Where have you been?" she asked with a warm smile. "I've missed you."

Freddie smiled back. It was a shy smile that he only used with Mrs. Robinson. "I was here two days ago."

"Exactly," she exclaimed. "Two days is too long. Now, what would you like for your snack? I have those little cookies with the jam centers."

"That'll do," Freddie said with a smile, then turned to me and added, "She didn't have them two days ago. I gave her hell."

I just shook my head.

"What? It makes her feel important. And she knows they're my favorite. That's how our relationship works."

"Oh, but Freddie," Mrs. Robinson said, coming back to the desk and waving him over. I followed, so she tagged on, "Hello, Erica."

It was a totally normal adult hello. "Hello."

She leaned over the counter and whispered, "While I get the cookies, would you two be dears and keep your eye on those three boys over there?"

I looked over to where she was pointing. Three pre-teen boys were sitting at the library computers looking sketchy.

"You never know what the kids will be getting up to on the Internet."

"No problem," Freddie said.

"Thank you, dear." She patted his hand and turned to walk to the back.

"You're going to bring the milk too, right?" Freddie called after her.

"Of course," she trilled.

"In the cup I like?"

"I won't forget."

Freddie caught me looking at him. "What? Stop trying to make it weird. It's not weird."

I shook my head. "So weird."

Both Freddie and I leaned our backs on the counter, so we could keep an eye on the boys. As soon as we did, they looked over.

"'Sup," Freddie called out.

They didn't answer.

"Keep it PG," I added.

Still no answer.

Freddie and I exchanged glances.

"I think they get it," he muttered.

I looked around the library. I hadn't been in for a while. Mrs. Robinson had a display set up on the front table for the season. Lots of scary-looking Halloween books . . . and a history-looking one. I squinted to read the title. *Ghosts of New Hampshire*. Hmm, probably had the Apple Witch in there. I might actually be interested in checking that one out. Find out the origin story of our resident witch. It all probably started with some poor widowed woman trying to hold on to her orchard while the townsfolk started rumors to steal her land. And yes, I guess I did have feminist ghost theories, but that was because they usually applied.

"I'm back," Mrs. Robinson said, carrying a plate and a cup. "I'm so sorry, Erica. I forgot to ask you if you wanted anything."

"That's okay," I said. "I'm good." I wanted no part of whatever this was. One mother was more than enough for me.

"So did you two just come by for a visit, or is there something I can help you with?"

"We wanted . . ." Freddie had to stop for a moment. He already had a cookie in his mouth. "We want to use one of the VCRs downstairs."

"Freddie, dear, eat over your plate," Mrs. Robinson said. "And of course, you're welcome to use the machines.

We're down to just one VCR. The other two broke, and we don't have the budget to replace them. Hardly seems necessary anyway."

I nodded. Nope, nobody used videotapes anymore, except for ghost hunters, apparently.

"Well, we only need the one," Freddie said with a chuckle.

She smiled. "You're so clever."

Freddie beamed.

"Okay then, you know the way," she said. "I'd better stay up here and keep an eye on the boys."

We turned to leave when she added, "Freddie?"

He turned back around.

She shot a stern look at the plate he was still holding.

"Can't I take the cookies downstairs just this once?"

She peered at him over her glasses that were resting far down her nose. "You know the cleaner only vacuums down there once a week."

"I won't make a mess."

"Freddie."

"Fine." He shoved two cookies in his mouth and put the plate back on the counter. "Can I at least take the milk?" he mumbled.

"Yes, just this once," she said. "And don't talk with your mouth full."

He shot her a thumbs-up with his free hand.

"Oh, and try to keep it down this time," Mrs. Robinson said. "You two got quite noisy the last time you viewed a tape down there."

Okay, so we had used the library VCR once in the past to view some surveillance tapes of the fall fair. And yes, we may have gotten a bit loud when a stupid bird popped its head right in the middle of the screen—not in the library, on the tape—so we couldn't see the little bit of video that was particularly important to that particular investigation. It was really frustrating. Anyone would have reacted . . . noisily.

"That was one time," Freddie said. "And it was mainly Erica doing all the shouting."

"We'll be quiet," I said, leading him away. "Promise."

We took the very narrow steps down into the basement. A lot of work had been done to make the basement a usable space, but it was still kind of creepy. The ceilings were really low and it had that damp feel that basements in old houses do.

"That must be the one that's still working," Freddie said, pointing at a desk with a TV and VCR. It had a back and side walls for privacy. Not that there was anyone else around . . . except for maybe the serial killer who lived down here. It totally had that feel.

"Okay," Freddie said, settling himself into a sturdy plastic chair with metal legs. "Let's see what Danny was able to get."

"If it is Danny's," I reminded him. "Do you think the tape will even work? He's been gone for years, right?"

"Only one way to find out," Freddie said, popping the tape in the machine. Luckily whoever had recorded this tape had used one of the video cameras that took full-sized tapes, instead of those mini ones that had to be fitted into other cassettes. A moment later he hit play.

Black-and-white dots filled the screen. I could barely hear the sound of static. "Turn it up," I said. "The volume's too low."

Freddie turned it up just as the screen came to life. I couldn't quite figure out what we were seeing at first. I squinted. I mean, I guess that was to be expected. Danny was filming in the woods at night . . . but there were greenish shapes and . . .

Suddenly a loud moan filled the air.

What the . . . ?

"Oh my God," Freddie said, fumbling for the volume again. "That is not the Apple Witch."

"It's . . . it's a . . ."

Sex tape.

Chapter Eleven

"Holy crap," Freddie said. "What do we do?"

"I don't know," I hissed.

Freddie hit the pause button.

"Oh God, not there." The picture frozen on the screen was something I didn't feel I'd ever be old enough to see.

He fumbled with some more buttons, then paused it again.

"Not there either! That's even worse!"

"Sorry. Sorry," Freddie mumbled.

"Keep it down please, Erica," a voice shouted from the top of the stairs.

"Sorry, Mrs. Robinson," I called back.

Freddie snickered, but managed to stop the tape at an indecipherable moment. "Well," he said with a long pause. "That was unexpected."

"What do we do?" I said with a head shake. "I've never found somebody's sex tape before."

Freddie's eyes narrowed. "You say that like you assume I have."

"Sorry."

We didn't say anything for a very awkward moment.

"Should we wait to see if we recognize who is, you know, in the tape?" Freddie asked.

"What for?"

"Stop making that face. A murder happened in those woods, Erica. This could be evidence."

"Oh right." I was still having trouble processing what we had found. "Well, let's just go take it over to Grady. Actually, I'm meeting him in like half an hour." Our date for the pumpkin races. "We probably should have just given it to him in the first place."

Freddie rolled his eyes. "Always so worried about Grady. If Grady wanted to watch the tape first, then Grady should have found the tape first."

I nodded. "You're absolutely right. He should have had Amos push him through the door of a dilapidated house, pretty far from the crime scene, on private property, so he could fall through the floor and find the tape."

Freddie shrugged. "It's not my place to tell him how to do his job, but if you say so."

I swatted him before folding my arms over my chest.

"But what if it's Danny and Mandy?" Freddie went on. "She said he was all into the Apple Witch. We know he was filming out there. What if they decided to . . . you know, make a tape of their love."

"Never say that again," I said. He had a point though. Mandy would be so embarrassed. And she was already going through so much. "But we still have to give it to Grady."

"I know."

We stared at each other a moment.

I cracked first. "But if it is Mandy, I would want to give her a heads-up." Stuff like this had a way of spreading through town like wildfire. I mean, I wouldn't tell anyone about the tape, and I'd make sure Freddie didn't either, and I completely trusted Grady and his people, but even so . . . it's like there would be a disturbance in the force, a ripple across Otter Lake, and everybody would just know.

"So we're watching it?" Freddie asked.

"I guess."

Freddie reached to press play then snatched his hand back. "Even if this particular film doesn't cater to my orientation, I can't watch it with you. It's like watching an X-rated movie with your mom."

I tilted my head side to side. "Or Mrs. Robinson."

He swatted me this time.

"Well then, what do you suggest?"

"I don't know," he said with a shrug. "You close your eyes or something and I'll watch. Or I'll close my eyes—"

"No, you better watch," I said, fluttering my hand at the screen. "I might not recognize Danny." I mean, I had seen his Facebook photos, but those were not like this.

"Okay."

I put my fingers over my eyes. "Go."

I waited a moment then said, "Did you turn it back on?"

"Yes."

"I can't hear anything."

"I don't need to hear it to recognize Danny."

"Good point."

"Ugh," Freddie said a moment later.

"What?"

"I hate watching amateurs have sex," he said with a sigh. "It's like watching animals do it on National Geographic. Like would it kill you to have some nice lighting? Makeup?"

I snickered under my hands. "You watch animals do it on National Geographic?"

Freddie scoffed. "No, I was just making an analogy— oh God."

"What?" I asked, fingers still pressed against my

eyelids. "Did you see Danny? Mandy? Hey, Danny and Mandy. That's kind of cute."

"No," Freddie said with more tired-sounding disgust. "I just don't understand people sometimes. Why would anyone like that?"

I almost dropped my hands from my eyes.

"Keep 'em shut. You don't want to see this."

I sighed, but kept my fingertips in place. "You know, I am starting to feel ridiculous about all this." Given the scenario, that probably wasn't surprising. "I can't imagine why—"

"Whoa. Yup. That's Danny."

"It is?"

"I'm pretty sure."

"Whoa!"

"What whoa?"

"But that's not Mandy."

I opened my eyes for real that time. Freddie had paused the tape again. And he was right. That was definitely not Mandy. You couldn't really see who it was exactly because of the angle. But the . . . build in the . . . chest area was definitely wrong.

"Okay, well, I think we're good. That's definitely not Mandy," I said. "Let's just get this over to Grady."

"Right," Freddie said, but instead of pressing the eject button, he pressed play again, which would have been fine if . . .

"Freddie Benjamin Ng, what on earth are you watching?"

. . . Mrs. Robinson hadn't walked down the stairs at that very moment carrying another plate of cookies. I guess she'd had second thoughts about letting us snack down here. And for the record, Benjamin was not Freddie's middle name.

"Erica made me do it."

Chapter Twelve

This. This was the New Hampshire fall I wanted. I leaned my forearms on the railing of the bridge, so that I could soak in some of the gorgeous autumn sun. The bridge had a roof but the sides were open, allowing the deliciously cool wind to rush through. New Hampshire was famous for its covered bridges, but this one was a little off the beaten track. Foot traffic only. Best part of all? I was meeting Grady.

Too bad I was about to ruin it with a . . . tape.

But it was fine. I'd just give it to him right off the top and then we could get back to our date.

It was a bit of a walk to get here—away from the center of town—but it seemed like a romantic spot to meet up. We could walk together back into town and take in some of the fall colors. Yup, all this situation needed was a Grady. Hmm, maybe in a cozy fisherman's sweater. I could give him a friendly hug. That would be very cozy. Maybe without the tape. I could put it on the railing of the bridge and—bad idea. It would end up in the river for sure.

I took my phone out.

I was still a few minutes early.

Maybe I could just check my messages though to see if I missed anything. Nope. No messages. Well, that was fine. I could just take in the splendor of this day . . . or I could . . .

And just like that I was browsing social media. Not for anything in particular really. But . . . well, maybe I could check Danny's Facebook page one more time. Not at all because I was investigating. But I was worried about all of Mandy's worrying . . . and I had only looked at it quickly before, and there had been something a little off about his photos.

I scrolled through his page. Yup, the last post was a couple of years old. It was a picture of the Las Vegas sign. I mean, not everybody posted a lot, but . . . nope, and there were no selfies . . . not even a group shot with him in it. The pictures before that were all in New Hampshire. And he posted a lot back then. Not a lot of selfies, but a lot of links to ghost stuff. Maybe he had given up on that particular dream. Well, there was one way to find out.

Suddenly my thumbs were flying over the screen of my phone. I'd just send Danny a quick message saying I was from Otter Lake and had a couple of questions about the Apple Witch then—

"Hey."

I quickly hit send then looked up to see—

Oh yes. This . . . that . . . he! *He* was exactly what I wanted.

Fall Grady standing in the mouth of the covered bridge. Turned out, I liked Fall Grady, just as much as I liked shy-smile Grady. He wasn't wearing a fisherman sweater, but the olive-colored men's utility jacket also looked very huggable. And was it just me, or was everything better in autumn? "Hey."

"You weren't waiting long?"

"Nope," I said, sliding my phone into my back pocket as we walked toward one another. This greeting part was always a little awkward. We were never quite sure how to receive each other. I mean, a greeting hug had always seemed a little too friendly. A handshake definitely too formal. So we usually settled on the awkward raised hand of greeting before we both stuffed said hands into our pockets and rocked on our feet.

This time was different though.

He was coming right in. Stooping a little. Oh yeah, we were officially closer friends now because he was going right in for the hug.

Chills raced over my body as the warmth of Grady wrapped me up. Yup, hugs were definitely better in fall. Oh wow, and he smelled so good. I brought my nose in close to the skin of his neck. Grady mixed with after-shave was so my very favorite smell.

"Whatcha got there?" Grady asked.

And just like that. It was over.

I almost lost my balance as Grady pulled away. He reached a hand out to steady me. "What?" I followed his gaze to my hand. Oh, the tape. I knew the sex tape would ruin the mood. "It's for you actually."

He frowned as he took it from my hand. "What is it?"

"We found it at the apple orchard last night," I said. "Given all that's going on, we thought you'd want it."

"Did you watch it?"

"Did we . . ." I chuckled for a moment, but I couldn't keep it up. "Let's be real. You know that we did."

He nodded.

Huh, that was easy. He didn't even flinch. I mean, I doubted he was impressed because I just said that we had suspected it was evidence and all, but—

"What's on it?" he asked, looking up at me.

"Oh . . ."

He shot me a sideways look. "What? Why do you look so . . . are you blushing?"

"It's just that it's, uh . . ." Oh my God, talking about it with Grady was even more embarrassing than discovering it with Freddie. I mean, I guess because it put the topic of such things on the mind, and we were standing so close, and I could still smell his aftershave, and— "Sex."

"Sex?"

"It's a sex tape."

He blinked a few times. "Oh."

"Oh yes. We were like *oh!* too when we figured out what it was. At the library no less."

Grady shot me another look. "You watched a sex tape with Freddie in the library?"

"I didn't. I kept my eyes closed. Most of the time. And we didn't know it was a—and neither one of us owns a VCR, and we were in the basement."

He smiled. "Oh good."

"Mrs. Robinson still caught us though."

This time his chin dropped into his chest. "Mrs. Robinson knows about this?"

"She doesn't know where we found it or anything, just that we were watching . . . it." I put my hand over my face and shook my head.

Then miracle of all miracles, Grady started to laugh.

I dropped the hand. "Wait . . . you're not mad."

"I would be. I mean, I am. You should have brought it to me first, but I think the look on Mrs. Robinson's face was probably punishment enough." He shook his head. "So, who's on the tape?"

"Freddie thinks it's a guy named Danny. He used to date Mandy?"

And just like that, every part of him hardened. Fall Grady was no longer standing before me. He was all

Sheriff Forrester. "Okay, well, I'd better get this back to the station."

"What?" I asked, reaching for his arm. "We're not going to watch the pumpkins?"

"I've got a lot to—" Suddenly he frowned and pointed at me with the tape. "Where exactly did you find this?"

Uh-oh. Suddenly this was all going downhill pretty fast. "Funny story actually . . . kind of like the library situation."

Grady tilted his head . . . and I swear it was almost like I could see the sheriff's hat materializing on his head.

"See, Freddie wanted to take some *Blair Witch*-type video of me outside the Apple Witch's house. He thought it might distract him from all his ghost fears if he could, you know, focus on something else, and . . ."

"Erica," Grady said, tilting his head to an even more extreme angle.

"He pushed me inside."

Grady just blinked.

"And . . . I fell through the floorboards." I said the last part super-quick. Just like I was ripping off a Band-Aid.

Whoa. Okay . . . he was rapid-blinking now. He looked quite angry, or like he might be having a seizure.

"It was fine," I said, waving a hand. "It was just a sub-floor, but . . . yeah."

He stared at me a moment longer then said, "I've got to go."

"Grady . . ."

"I need to get a forensics team back out there." He took a couple of steps away before pointing at me with the tape again. "Did you touch anything else in the house? Were there any more tapes under the floor?"

"No, I didn't touch anything . . . and I didn't look to see if there were any other tapes."

And he was walking away again.

"You're mad," I called out after him.

"I'm not mad," he called back, still walking.

"Yes you are. We should really talk about—"

He swirled around. "I'm really not mad. Do I wish you had handled things differently? Yes. But you did come to me *eventually,* so—"

"You're really mad."

His face twitched for a moment before he said, "I'm not mad. I'm just . . ." He held up a hand. "What if it hadn't been a subfloor? What if it had been a cellar?"

"But it wasn't."

"Oh well," he said, throwing his hands in the air. "And, you know, I expect these things to happen when you and Freddie get together. I've accepted that. And I was really good about the whole thing when you told me about your plan back at my office, wasn't I?"

"You were awesome."

"All I asked was that you not go into the h—" He cut himself off suddenly. Something had caught his eye. I followed his gaze over to the walking trail by the river.

It was a couple walking along the path by the river.

Wait . . . that wasn't just any couple.

Come on, now . . .

Was that . . . ?

No . . .

Matthew?

Chapter Thirteen

It was Matthew . . . and his girlfriend, Jessica.

Well, this was awkward . . . and complicated.

All sorts of quick glances darted around the four of us. See, Matthew—handsome architect and all around nice guy—had come back to town a couple of years ago just around the same time I had. And for whatever reason, he had expressed a bit of interest in me, but, I, of course, made it clear in no uncertain terms that it was looking like I was a lifer when it came to Grady. Things got a little bit complicated, though, when Grady started dating Candace, another newbie to town, and told me—on New Year's Eve, no less—that we were never, ever, ever getting back together. I, being hurt, may have kissed Matthew Matterson that night. Which Grady didn't take all that well. New Year's also happened to be the night we all met Jessica—beautiful, perfect veterinarian, and Rhonda's cousin—for the first time. And now she and Matthew were together, so . . . yes, this was definitely awkward and complicated.

It wasn't a jealousy thing though. Because I certainly wasn't jealous. Well, at least I wasn't jealous beyond the totally normal tiny, tiny amount one would be jealous given this situation, and I didn't think Grady was jealous . . . because we had come a long way in that department. And frankly, Matthew and Jessica looked really happy walking hand in hand down the path . . . not fighting. So I was happy for them. Not at all jealous of the perfect picture they made with their good looks, well-made hiking clothes, and intimidating professions . . . while Grady and I argued about whether or not he was not mad. Not even a little bit.

Grady and I looked at each other.

"Quick," I said, "hold my hand."

"Forget hands." He draped his arm over my shoulders.

"But we're just friends."

"They don't need to know that."

We both leaned on the railing and smiled at the couple approaching us.

"I'm still not mad," Grady muttered in my ear.

"Oh no, of course not," I whispered in a sarcastic voice, before calling out, "Matthew! Jessica! Hi!"

"Hi guys," Matthew called back. Jessica just waved. Hmm, if I had any doubt about whether Jessica knew about the kiss Matthew and I shared, I didn't anymore. That was a very cold wave. I mean, seriously? I expected more maturity from a vet. "Beautiful day, huh?"

And I swear to God, Grady muttered, "Oh, you think so, Matthew?" before calling out, "Sure is!"

I shot him a quick look before turning back to Matthew. "I didn't realize you were back in town."

He had been spending lots of time in New York. He had kind of implied that I had a bit to do with that decision, but no one needed to be reminded of that fact.

"Well, you know, Otter Lake. It's like a black hole. No one escapes."

We all chuckled. Awkwardly.

"Well, you two enjoy your day," he said.

"You two . . . too," I called out with a chuckle.

Grady kept his arm around my shoulders as Matthew and Jessica, the vet, walked on. Once they were out of sight, we fist-bumped, and backed away from each other.

"So where were we?" Grady asked.

"You were saying you weren't mad when we both know that you're totally—"

"I'm not mad!" he shouted. He walked a few steps away then turned and walked right back over. "I just want to know one thing. Are you and Freddie investigating this case?"

I put my hands up. "No, I told you that already."

"Yeah, but I'm kind of having a difficult time believing you."

"And that right there," I said, pointing at him, "is a problem."

Suddenly Grady went still and muttered, "Pause fight."

"What? Why now?"

"And put your finger down."

I followed his gaze. Oh, for the love of . . .

Seriously?

Grady and I exchanged looks, and he came back over to put his arm around my shoulders.

"What is it, the freaking parade of exes today?" I muttered.

"I know," he mumbled back just as I called out, "Candace! Joey! Hi!"

That's right. Now it was Grady's ex walking by the river with her new husband. Now I really liked Candace. I counted her among my closest friends, but she did used to date Grady . . . for a longer period of time than I had ever dated Grady. And before we had become really close friends, she had once said that Grady and I were bad for each other, so did I really want her to see us fighting on this beautiful fall day? No, no I did not.

"Hey guys!" Candace called out sweetly. She did everything sweetly. "Beautiful day, huh?"

"Gorgeous," I called back. "The best."

"I guess you guys wanted to get away from the crowd at the pumpkin races too," she said, giving her handsome werewolf of a husband a squeeze. Seriously, he looked like a handsome werewolf.

"Yes, we did," I said, giving Grady a squeeze of my own.

"We should meet up for coffee soon," Candace said.

"You know it," I called back.

We all waved at each other before they followed the trail under the bridge and away.

Grady's arm dropped from my shoulder and he backed away again. "So is OLS investigating or not?"

"I just told you we're not!"

"I know what you said." He planted his fists on his hips. "But are you just saying that because it's what I want to hear?"

"No, there is no investigation."

He stared at me a moment. "Okay."

"Okay?"

He nodded.

"We still friends?"

"Still friends," he said, turning. "But I really do need to get going though."

"Are we still going to talk about becoming closer friends?" I called after him.

He didn't turn this time, just shot a thumbs-up in the air.

I sighed and leaned my elbows once again on the railing of the bridge and looked down at the water . . . only to see a pumpkin face smiling back up at me. I guess the race had started. This must be the front-runner. Too bad it had grounded itself between two rocks.

"He's mad," I said. "He says he's not. But he's mad."

The pumpkin just laughed silently at me.

"Yeah, right back at ya."

Chapter Fourteen

"Well, this has been a day."

"Uh-huh."

"And we haven't even started our shift at the apple orchard yet."

I nodded.

"I mean, Agatha Christie and . . . the Pink Panther?" Freddie said, taking his eyes briefly from the road to look at me. He had showed me some clips of the latter. I could see why he was upset. But in fairness I could also kind of see why Rhonda had made the comparison in the first place.

I nodded again.

"Oh, cheer up," Freddie said. "Grady always over-reacts to stuff like this."

I didn't answer.

"Like what does he want? An apology? Like, *I'm so sorry I pushed Erica into an abandoned house without her father's permission*?"

I shot him a warning look.

"I really am sorry about that by the way," he added

quickly. "I didn't think about a cellar. I probably could've killed you. I blame the Apple Witch."

I slid my eyes briefly over to him. "Are we saying her name now?"

"Only when we're driving. I don't think she can hear us when we're driving."

We were in Freddie's Jimmy headed over to the apple orchard for our shift. The days were so much shorter now. A harvest moon hung on top of the trees. The orchard would be busy tonight.

"It's just that things have been going so well between us," I said.

"I know, but there were bound to be bumps in the road, and it's not like he dumped you. Again."

I shot him another look.

"And he even tried to pretend like he wasn't mad. That's new. You might even call it progress."

I shook my head and looked out the window.

"So," Freddie drawled. "What are we going to tell Mandy about last night?"

"I have no idea."

"Do we tell her we found the tape?"

"Um, no. I don't think now is the time to tell her that her old boyfriend was cheating on her." Even though she was with someone new, nobody liked finding out that kind of news, and she had enough on her plate. "Besides, we don't know what we don't know. Maybe they were on a break or something." I looked out at the trees zipping by. "I'm just going to try to convince her to tell her family what's going on. I think that's what's really bothering her. But aside from that, from now on, we do security and that's it."

"I hear you," Freddie said, tapping the steering wheel. "We out."

"I am so completely fine with leaving this one alone."

"Absolutely," Freddie said. "And if Rhonda calls me Pink Panther again, she's fired."

"No she's not."

"Ugh, fine. We won't fire her, but you're HR. There has to be some sort of disciplinary action we could take? I've got it! She can—"

"She's not cleaning your toilets, Freddie."

"Um, I believe they are the office toilets."

"She's not cleaning the toilets," I said. "And what was all that stuff about me having white-knight syndrome? I don't have white-kn—"

"Be happy with your white-knight syndrome," Freddie said, shooting me a super-annoyed look. "It's way better than Inspector Clouseau."

He had a point.

I eyed a scarecrow out the window. "Well, at least we're on the same page for once."

"We are?" Freddie asked. "What page is that again? I forgot what we were talking about."

I sighed. "We're on the same page about not getting involved in this murder."

"Oh right. Yeah, no way," Freddie said, tapping the steering wheel again. "But do you really think it's Danny we found?"

"I don't know. But Grady had a pretty strong reaction when I said you thought it was him on the tape." And Danny never had responded to my Facebook message, not that that meant much. But speaking of Facebook, maybe I could go through his contacts and—"But it's not our business!"

"Why are you yelling? I'm right here."

"Sorry," I said with a sigh. "And maybe it's not even murder. Maybe . . . maybe the person with the boot just died of like a brain aneurysm or something, and leaves fell on him, and it could have been muddy and—"

"The Apple Witch buried him."

I threw my head back against the seat. "For the love of— The Apple Witch did not bury him. I'm just saying we don't know anything for sure. And we're not going to know it because we're not investigating."

"Oh no, totally not investigating."

"I promised Grady. OLS is getting nowhere near this—"

I screamed.

Person! In the headlights! Waving her hands out!

Mandy!

She had jumped right into the path of the SUV!

Freddie slammed on the brakes.

I fumbled with my seat belt then jumped out of the Jimmy. "Mandy! What are you d—"

She grabbed my arms. "They're fighting! You've got to help me!"

"Oh my God, what are you doing?" Freddie shouted, racing around the vehicle. "I think I just had your baby."

But Mandy had already taken off for the barn.

Freddie and I exchanged looks.

"Come on!" she shouted.

We took off after her.

Chapter Fifteen

"Hurry!"

Mandy didn't go in the main doors of the barn. She ran around the side to the steel stairs anchored to the outer wall that led up to the second-story loft.

"But who's fighting?" Freddie yelled after her.

"Adam and Shane."

Mandy's oldest brother and her boyfriend.

"He knows Shane and I are dating. He heard us talking. I was going to tell him—" She cut herself off. I guess she still wasn't at the "scream out your birth announcement for all of your family to hear" stage of pregnancy yet.

As we pounded up the stairs, I could hear Freddie mumbling, "It's probably nothing. We're not going to die. The family's not that creepy. This is not a terrible idea."

Mandy whipped the door open and ran inside. I caught it just before it closed.

"They're probably just coming to an agreement, back-woods style." Freddie stumbled into my back and we pitched forward through the door. "It's probably no big—whoa."

This was bad.

This was very, very bad.

Adam had Shane backed up to the edge of the loft—right where the floor ended and dropped to the level below. And while Adam wasn't as big as his baby brother, Cam, he was more intimidating. He had a high and tight military haircut and everything about him was just . . . hard. He also had a pitchfork pointed at Shane's chest.

"Adam, stop," Mandy cried. She was edging toward them. Freddie and I fell in behind her.

Adam didn't say anything. Shane didn't either. He was probably too focused on gripping the outer prongs of the pitchfork pinned to his body. Their eyes were locked.

I slowly reached my hand into my pocket for my phone. I didn't want to take it out just yet in case it set Adam off, but this really seemed like a 911 type of deal.

"Adam," Freddie called out. "'Sup?"

I guess Freddie felt this situation was a little more casual.

Adam kept his eye on Shane for a second longer before he tossed his pitchfork to the side. It clattered against the planks of the floor. He then looked up at Freddie and said, "Hey man."

Mandy ran to her boyfriend.

"Everything all right up here?" Freddie asked.

"It's all good," Adam said with a sniff. "We just needed to clear some things up." He then grabbed a rope hanging from the eaves of the barn. "I got stuff to do. See ya in a bit." He then swung off the loft over to a stack of hay bales and jumped to the ground. I mean, why take the stairs?

Freddie collapsed to his knees. I rushed over to him. "Oh my God, you were awesome. You totally defused the situation."

"Is Tarzan gone?" he asked with a quick swallow.

I peeked over to the floor below. "I think so."

He took a few shaky breaths. "I'm so glad I used the bathroom before we came." His eyes flicked up to mine. "But don't tell anyone that part when we retell this story."

"Of course not." I looked back at Mandy. "We have to call Grad—"

"No," Mandy near-shouted. "Don't."

"But he had a pitchfork and—"

"It was nothing," Shane said. "And that's what I'll tell Grady if you call him. We were just horsing around."

I blinked a couple of times. "He could have killed you."

"I had it coming," Shane said, exchanging looks with his girlfriend.

If dating Mandy meant Shane had it coming, I could only imagine how bad the pregnancy news would be.

Freddie shot me a super-knowing look and mumbled, "I told you this family was—"

"There you all are," a kindly voice called out.

Freddie yelped, jumped to his feet, and whirled around to face the door. "Grandma Honeycutt."

I hadn't heard her come in either, but there she was. She had her white hair pinned up in a bun, and she was wearing baggy jeans with a red fleece.

"Oh, those stairs are going to be the death of me," she said, trying to catch her breath. "I thought I saw you two headed up here. Would you and Erica like to join me for some tea in the house before we open the gates?"

Mandy quickly came up to our backs and whispered, "Please don't tell her about this. She's not well. It will just upset her."

I shot Mandy a quick look over my shoulder.

Again with the big eyes.

I cleared my throat. "Maybe now's not the—"

"It's been so long since we've had a chat, Erica," she

said, clutching her hands to her chest. "And I just took some apple crumble from the oven."

"I . . ." I didn't know what to say. We had just witnessed something pretty intense and I was having trouble switching gears from pitchfork impalement to apple crumble. I looked to Freddie. I could almost hear him screaming *No!* in my head. But there was another voice in my head, and it was reminding me of how much I enjoyed Grandma Honeycutt's baking, and really, what soothed frazzled nerves better than apple crumble? "We're in."

"Wonderful." She turned and headed back down the steps.

"Thanks a lot," Freddie hissed in my ear. "Now we're really going to die."

Maybe. But it was going to taste so good.

Chapter Sixteen

"Oh . . . oh my . . . Mrs. Honeycutt," I mumbled before swallowing. "This is so good."

"Erica, I've known you your entire life. Call me Grandma," she said with a sweet smile.

I looked over at Freddie. "You have got to try this," I said, pointing at the bowl with my fork.

He chuckled politely, but the translation was . . . not so polite.

"Oh!" Mrs. Honeycutt was suddenly on her feet. "I forgot the maple syrup. You have to try it with maple syrup drizzled on top." She looked at Freddie. "Are you sure I can't get you a bowl?"

"Oh, I'd love to," he said, tossing Grandma a pained smile as she headed back to the kitchen, "but my stomach is really . . ." He grimaced and patted his stomach.

"Can I make you some ginger tea?"

"No, no, thank you."

"Okay, well, let me know if you change your mind, dear."

Once she had left, I looked up at Freddie and said, "Seriously, you are missing out."

"She's fattening you up, Erica," he said with a quick shake of the head—so quick, it was more of a shudder. "I bet you anything she's got a cage in her basement, and she is going to feed you apple crumble until she's decided you're fat enough, and then she's going to roast you like a pig. Probably in that old-timey oven in the café."

"That sounds awesome," I said, taking another bite. "Seriously, there are way worse ways to go." All the sugar and carbs really were calming my nerves.

"And have you noticed that"—Freddie darted a look around—"this dining room is super-creepy."

I looked around. I didn't see creepy.

"This striped wallpaper is like bars on a jail cell—"

It really wasn't like that at all.

"And what's with all the shelves with the knickknacks and figurines?"

"They're cute," I mumbled as my eyes trailed over the walls covered with built-in shelves laden with . . . stuff. "People like to collect things. That's not weird."

"I bet each one of those figurines houses the soul of one of her victims. I saw a show just like that on Netflix."

I rolled my eyes. "Okay, you need to chill out. I realize that we just witnessed a man holding up another man with a pitchfork, but"—as I said it out loud I realized that perhaps I was the one underreacting, but the apple crumble was really that good—"you don't have to worry about Grandma Honeycutt. She is just a nice old lady who bears a striking resemblance to Mrs. Claus and shows her affection with—oh yes, maple syrup." I smiled as Grandma Honeycutt swirled back into the room with a small earthenware pot of what I was assuming was maple syrup. Freddie was probably thinking it more like the potion the Evil Queen had made for Snow White's apple, but that was neither here nor there.

"Here you go, dear," she said, passing it over the table

as she sat down across from me. "Now, tell me all about how you have been, Erica. It feels like ages since we've talked."

I nodded. I had said hello to Grandma Honeycutt once or twice since I'd been home, but that was about it.

"It's been so long. I have to admit I still sometimes think of you as the young lady we hired to babysit the kids."

I smiled.

"You'll never know how much you helped us out in those days. We never expected to be raising four children at that point in our lives. And after my darling Jeannine passed . . ." she said, looking at the picture on the wall of her deceased daughter. "Well, I'm not sure how Barney and I would have managed without you." We all looked over at the picture of Barney on the wall. "He loved his grandkids so much."

I had always liked Barney. He never said much but always shot me a wave when he was riding around on his big, red tractor. I was in Chicago when he passed. I suddenly felt kind of guilty for not going to the funeral. It was a community thing. "Oh, I don't think I did that much."

"Nonsense," she said, reaching over to pat my hand. "The kids loved you."

"Cam, in particular, still has an affection for Erica," Freddie said with a very still face. I tried to kick him under the table but I couldn't find his leg.

Grandma Honeycutt smiled. "Oh, they all did. And I know my grandchildren could be a handful. Erica was the only babysitter in town who would take them on."

I frowned then mumbled, "I was?" I grabbed my napkin and wiped at the crumbs sticking to my lips.

"Oh yes. We went through so many girls before we found you."

I smiled, but I was suddenly enjoying my dessert a lot

less because I guess that meant I had been the Honey-cutts' last choice. And I knew those kids were crazy! But I didn't have any siblings. How was I to know what kids were like at home all together?

"I don't know what you did, Erica, but whatever it was, you sure got those kids to fall in line."

"It was all Mandy's idea," I said before I could stop myself.

"What's that, dear?" Grandma Honeycutt asked.

"Nothing." She didn't need to know about all that. She wasn't well. And that memory would only upset her . . . and then she might lock me in the basement for real. "Uh, I'm so full. That was wonderful, but I think we should be getting to work. People must be showing up by now."

As we were getting to our feet, Freddie leaned over and whispered into my ear. "What did you do to those poor innocent kids, Erica Bloom?"

"Nothing," I hissed between my teeth. "Drop it."

"Of course," Grandma Honeycutt said, also getting to her feet. "I feel so much better knowing that you're here watching over everything. Especially after what was found in the woods." She shook her head, looking sad. "But before you go, I have to ask you something."

I raised an eyebrow.

Her rounded shoulders slumped. "Did I hear some sort of fight going on up in the barn earlier?"

"Oh . . ."

"I saw Adam come storming out of the barn." She straightened a napkin on the table. "But he never likes to talk about things that are upsetting him."

I pinched my lips together and nodded. "I think he and Shane needed to come to an understanding of sorts."

She studied my face, waiting for me to say more, but, again, even though she really did look like Mrs. Claus, I wasn't about to crack. It wasn't my place to say anything.

Finally she said, "I hate asking this, dear, but . . ."

I waited.

"You won't tell Sheriff Forrester about it, will you?" She came around the table to take my hand. "It's just that, well . . . you must know that Adam is on probation."

"I do?" I was pretty sure I did not know that.

"Oh, well, he was innocent, but that lawyer of his convinced him to take a deal, so we could get it over with quickly. Bad publicity, you know. And it wasn't for anything violent."

"What was it for then?" Freddie asked.

"I probably shouldn't talk about it," she said with another little headshake. "I just wouldn't want Sheriff Forrester making this little . . . understanding . . . wasn't that what you called it, dear?"

I frowned. Had I? Suddenly I wasn't so sure.

"I wouldn't want Sheriff Forrester to make this understanding something it wasn't."

I mean, I doubt it mattered anyway because Shane wasn't about to back up our story, but I kind of wished I hadn't eaten Grandma Honeycutt's crumble. I didn't know it was "strings attached" crumble. Or dirty crumble! Just like the muffin I had brought Grady. "I . . . uh, get where you're coming from." I patted her hand and took a step away. "We really should get going."

"Of course, dears, and remember, if you need anything the kitchen is always open."

Freddie waited until we were out of the dining room to whisper, "How's that crumble taste now?"

"Shut up."

Chapter Seventeen

"You're going to love this."

"Mom, I think we both know that's not true."

"Now you're just being silly."

I cracked an eye open.

"Close them."

"But why do I have to have my eyes closed to sample candy?"

"Because I don't want the appearance of it to affect your opinion of its taste."

"Now I'm really afraid."

My mother had made it home from her retreat the night before and had dragged me out onto the porch before I had even had a chance to ask her about her trip. She wanted me to sample the homemade vegan Halloween treats she was making for the trick-or-treaters—who would never come. We lived on an island. But my mother never lost hope. Every year, she waited at the end of our dock with her basket of goodies for a boatload of kids to show up. And every year it never happened. To make matters worse, she promoted her vegan candy in town. She got a lot of polite "we'll try to stop by"s, but they never meant it. Who wanted to trick-or-treat by boat for vegan candy? It was too bad really. Some of the treats weren't half bad.

The rest of the night at the apple orchard had been fine. Lots of people showed up. Lots of fun was had. I was having trouble getting past the whole pitchfork-to-the-chest incident, but the Honeycutts had just carried on like it was no big deal. And maybe it wasn't a big deal for them. Maybe they settled a lot of arguments with pitchforks, but in the cold light of day, I was thinking this was really something I should mention to Grady. Even if he couldn't do anything about it, it might help with his overall Honeycutt profile.

But the fact that Grady even needed to profile the Honeycutts was bothering me. Adam wasn't a bad guy. At least he hadn't been a bad kid. He was always wanting to help his grandparents with chores, and while he was a lot like his brothers in that he too enjoyed a good football game on the roof, he'd also been the one to slap them upside the head if it went too far. He was protective of his siblings, and he did probably know a lot more about whether Shane was good for his sister—and not that that justified pitchfork threatening, but I guess I still felt like I needed to look out for the Honeycutts.

"Okay, you ready?" my mom asked.

"I don't know," I said, feeling the sunlight through the trees dapple across my face. "What is it?"

"Just open up."

I did, and something lemony landed in my mouth. "Hmm, not bad. I like the lemon." I bit into it. It was squishy . . . like hard squishy . . . and . . . uh-oh . . . my teeth were stuck together.

"Erica?"

My eyes flew open.

"Too sticky?"

I mumbled my alarm.

"Too sticky," she repeated, and made a note on a piece of paper. "I'll go easier on the seaweed next time."

I tried to say *seaweed?* but it came out more *mea-meed?* I stuck my finger in my mouth and wiggled around until I was able to get enough leverage to pry my jaw open. "Wow," I said, taking a deep breath of the cool autumn air. "I don't think you should go with that one. You don't want any kids losing their teeth prematurely."

"Well, nothing ventured . . ." she said with a bright smile. We had the same color eyes and hair, but that was pretty much the end of our similarities. Where my hair was long and straight, hers floated around her head in a mass of curls—the kind of mass of curls that butterflies might come floating out of any second. And while, yes, my eyes were the same blue as hers, my mother's eyes were always widened in a state of perpetual wonder. Mine, on the other hand, were not. "I think you'll like the next one I'm making even more."

I scraped the lemon rubber cement from my teeth.

"Are you all right?" she asked.

"You mean aside from the lockjaw?"

She swatted me. "I just meant you look tired. You got in pretty late last night. Is everything all right at the apple orchard?"

"Yeah, it's fine. Freddie and I were just—"

"Looking into those bones you were fondling?"

"I was not *fondling* any bones," I said, squinting at her. I often looked like Robert DeNiro when I talked to my mom. Probably not flattering, but I couldn't seem to stop. And how had she heard about the bones already? The twins must have texted her or something. I would have liked to tell her myself. She didn't like it when I did things like find bodies. Probably because she was my mother.

"But you and Freddie are investigating, aren't you?"

"No, we are not. Why does everyone keep assuming that?" I slumped back into my Adirondack chair. "I don't want to have anything to do with this one. Neither does Freddie."

This time it was my mother's turn to squint skeptically. I guess I came by it honestly. "Well, that doesn't sound like you two."

"Mom, OLS is a legitimate business now. We have no desire to stick our noses into somebody else's murder business . . . at least not without getting paid."

She nodded but still looked quite skeptical as she wrapped her sweater more tightly around her body and sank back into her chair.

"What?"

"Nothing," she said in a completely phony tone.

"Mom."

She sighed. "Well, I guess I just find that hard to believe."

I shot her a suspicious side-eye. "I thought you'd be happy."

"Well, of course I'm happy that you're not getting involved with anything dangerous, but . . ."

"Grady and I are in a really good place and—"

"I'm sorry. What does Grady have to do with this?" Suddenly she was sitting straight up.

"What do you mean, what does Grady have to do with this?" I asked. "He's sheriff. There is a murder investigation going on, and—" And I stopped talking because my mother looked like she was about to blow.

"Darling, you can't be serious."

Don't let the *darling* fool you. That was a mad *darling*. My eyes darted side to side. What was going on here? It had taken a long time, but my mother had finally come around to supporting the idea of Grady and me as a couple. She had even helped bring us back together.

"I know your feelings for Grady are very strong, but if murder makes you happy—"

"Murder does not make me happy," I scoffed.

Wait a minute . . . okay, I could see where this was going now.

"Sorry." She held up her hands and closed her eyes. She was barely resisting opening a can of feminist whoop-ass on me. "Bad choice of words. If murder is your calling—"

"Murder is not my calling," I said, a little louder this time.

A blue jay cawed at me. I guess he didn't appreciate my tone.

"You know what I mean."

I folded my arms across my chest.

"Listen," she said, "I realize that your career choice has caused conflict between you and Grady, but you need to be true to yourself, and if murder—"

"Please stop saying that. It sounds very wrong." Kind of like murder and I were a couple. "And Grady's not stopping me . . ." I paused. I wasn't exactly sure where I was going with my point, and worse yet, I wasn't sure if what I wanted to say was true. Probably best to go another route. "Grady is just worried about me."

"So what?"

"So what?" I asked, blinking at her.

"I worry about you, but I would never stop you from spreading your wings so that you could fly."

Oh God, and now her arms were in the air. She looked like she was about to take flight.

"Mom, please put your arms down."

She dropped them, much like a ballerina would. "I'm sorry, but I feel very strongly about this."

"I can see that," I said. "And I hear what you are saying, but you don't have to worry. Freddie and I don't want to investigate this particular case. Murder is not my calling. And Grady is not keeping me from it. And I know you're trying to make this a women's rights thing, but it's not. Freddie and I haven't always inspired confidence in law enforcement with regard to our decision making in the past."

She didn't say anything, just looked at me.

"Seriously. I mean it. And why are you so worked up about this? Is everything okay between you and Zaki?"

Her face softened. "What do you mean? Everything between us is . . . wonderful." She said it like she really meant it, but there was also something a little pained in her voice. My mother had been single her entire adult life. Being part of a couple had to be a little weird for her. "I just worry about you."

"Well, thank you, but I am happy. You don't have to worry. Not getting involved in this investigation was my choice."

She sighed and looked away. I guess that meant she was willing to let it go. "Are you going back to the orchard tonight?"

I nodded.

"Well, be careful, darling," she said, giving herself a little shake. She kind of looked like a mother duck trying to get all of her feathers back in place. "Investigation or not, you'd be best to keep your wits about you."

I frowned at her. "Not you too."

"Not me too what?" she asked, arching an eyebrow.

"Don't tell me you believe in the Apple Witch?"

"No. Of course not," she said, "It's ridiculous. Calling women witches was just a way for men to steal property and power, but . . ."

"But?"

"Well, strange things have happened in those woods."

I sighed and adjusted the afghan around my lap.

"People are always saying *strange things happen in those woods* but they never give any examples. What strange things have happened?"

"Well, there was that fire a couple of years back."

I blinked. I wasn't really expecting her to have an example ready. But I guess that explained all the soot in the house.

"Seemed to start up out of nowhere. Or at least that's what people believed. I don't remember all the details. But I think one of the sons was charged with arson."

Huh, so that's what Grandma Honeycutt had been talking about. Not that I cared. I wasn't investigating, but . . .

I swear it was like this investigation was chasing me down. I mean, the things Freddie and I had done in the past to get information? And now leads were just falling into my lap on my very own porch. Again, a person who was investigating might be thinking that someone could have started a fire to cover up evidence. But, again, again, I was not the type of person to be interested in that sort of thing. Murder was not my calling. Hey, but Grady must have known about the fire . . . and he hadn't told me. So there *was* probably something there.

"Okay, well, I should get going," I said, folding up the blanket and pushing myself to my feet. "Can't spend the whole day sitting around eating treats."

My mother got to her feet too. "And I have to get cooking."

"Hey, maybe don't knock yourself out," I said, scratching my forehead. "You know we're just going to end up eating all the candy ourselves."

"Not this year," she said, a disturbing twinkle coming to her eye. "I have a plan."

Uh-oh. Those were words I never wanted to hear from my mother. "You do?"

"Well, I've just been spreading the word around town that I am making treats that will be both healthy and cruelty-free."

I couldn't help but smile. "Yup. That should bring the kids running."

"And allergies."

"Allergies?"

"All my treats are going to be nut-, gluten-, and dairy-free. I think I'll even make a flyer."

"Nut-, gluten-, and dairy-free?" My smile vanished. I mean, I didn't want to gorge myself on the leftover treats like I had during post-Halloweens past . . . but, yeah, I kind of did. "There won't be anything left. What are you going to give out? Hunks of sugar cane? Seaweed?"

My mother blinked. I could tell she was considering it.

"Mom, no. Definitely not. That's—"

"Bad for the teeth," she said, nodding. "I know."

"I was going to say *weird*." Man, we were never going to have trick-or-treaters come to the island. They'd be too scared. Forget the Apple Witch, my mom was going to be the vegan witch of Otter Lake.

She just smiled. "So are you off to see Grady?"

"Maybe, I—"

"That's nice." She took a long deep breath as I walked by her. "I hope you have a good time."

Hmm, if I hurried I might just be able to get off the porch before—

"And I hope Grady doesn't crush all of your dreams and your identity as a person."

So close.

Okay, so I wasn't going to see Grady. I mean, if I ran into him that might be nice. I hadn't exactly liked how we left things yesterday, but really, I was going into town to see if the general store had any hot packs for my mittens. The nights were getting really cold at the apple orchard.

And after that I might just walk by the sheriff's department . . . maybe go in and say hi.

Maybe.

I kind of wanted Grady to come to me first this time. After all, I was the one who had given him the tape, and if it was helping his investigation, then it wouldn't be out of order for him to offer me a nice thank-you. And sure, I got that he didn't like me going into the Apple Witch's house, but come on, he was not in charge of where I could and could not go . . . except for when he was acting as sheriff, I guess. He probably could tell me then, but that was neither here nor there.

I shoved my hands deep into my sweater jacket. It was another sunny day, but cold. Coming across the lake in my mother's boat had chilled me pretty much to the bone. Hey, maybe before I went to the store, I could swing by the Dawg and get some hot chocolate, then—

Splat!

What the—

"Heads up!"

Chapter Eighteen

I ducked and threw my hands over my head. A small object hit the street and burst into a million orange sticky pieces. Not too far from another mess of orange sticky pieces. I squinted at the road from my ducking position. Was that a . . . ?

I straightened back up and looked over in the direction I thought it had come from.

"Erica!" a friendly voice called out. "Sorry about that."

I spotted a man wearing safety goggles coming up from alongside a house. Actually it was his house so that all made sense. Mr. Majors. Mid to late fifties. Super-nice guy. High school teacher of physics and chemistry.

"Was that a pumpkin I saw zooming by?" I asked with a smile.

"It was," he said, waving a gloved hand in the air. "They got away from me."

"Why are you throwing pumpkins?"

"I'm not throwing pumpkins," he said. Suddenly a mad-scientist-type gleam came to his eye. "Would you like to see where the pumpkins came from?"

Strangely, or maybe not so strangely, I really did. Mr. Majors had a way of making things fun. Probably because he was a little crazy. Not bad crazy—I mean he had only set the chemistry lab on fire once, and he knew exactly what to do to put it out because he was also a volunteer firefighter, and . . .

Wait a minute. Volunteer firefighter.

Hmm, maybe he knew something about the fire that had happened in the woods at the apple orchard?

Not that I cared.

I followed Mr. Majors around the side of his house. I don't know what I was expecting to see back there, but it kind of looked like he was in the middle of amassing weaponry for a medieval siege. And maybe having a feast afterward because there were lots of root vegetables lying around, a good variety of squash, and at least thirty pumpkins.

Mr. Majors pushed the safety glasses up his forehead. "I was just making some last-minute tweaks to the catapult when it went off."

I looked over at the large wooden structure in the middle of his lawn. Not quite sure how I had missed that. I must have thought it was a swing set.

"Why do you have a pumpkin catapult?"

"It's for the tournament."

"Tournament?"

"The one the chamber of commerce is organizing," he said. "Don't tell me Otter Lake Security isn't participating?"

I blinked. "I don't think so." At least Freddie hadn't mentioned it, and he would have mentioned it. Oh, he was going to be mad if the chamber of commerce didn't invite us to something. Didn't matter what it was. He was going to be mad.

"I'm sure it was just an oversight," he said. "Do you want to try the catapult?"

"I don't know," I said. But I totally did. "It looks kind of dangerous."

"Well, certainly, but I won't aim it at the street this time," he said with a wink.

"Well, in that case . . . let's do it."

"Excellent," he said, setting off toward the machine. "I'd like to try one using pneumatic pressure next year—"

"I'm sorry, what now?" I asked, trotting after him.

"Erica," he said with a very teacherly look, "you should know this."

"Sorry." I hadn't realized there was going to be a test.

"It uses air pressure to launch the projectile, in this case a pumpkin, at high speeds, but for now the catapult will have to do." He scooped up three minipumpkins and hurried over to the machine to load them up in the cup.

"Give it a try."

"What do I do?"

"Just pull on this rope," he said, handing it to me. "But give it some force. It will release the mechanism."

"Got it."

I adjusted my stance and gave the rope a good yank. The pumpkins flew into the air. He had pointed the catapult at a stack of hay bales with a bull's-eye painted on their sides, but the pumpkins missed that target completely and hit the side of Mr. Majors's tin shed with a loud *Bang! Bang! Bang!*

My eyes shot to my old teacher to see if I was in trouble, but the only thing on his face was pure delight.

"Well, that was kind of . . . awesome." And it was. There was power that came with making loud noises.

He nodded. "I also thought about trying out a combustion-based cannon this year using flammable gas, but we wouldn't want to start any fires."

I nodded. "Mr. Majors," I suddenly found myself saying, "are you still a volunteer firefighter?"

He smiled. "Sadly, no. My knee hasn't been so good since Kenny Walters put the liquid methanol too close to the Bunsen burner. I had to vault a lab desk. Didn't quite stick the landing. But we all lived," he said with a chuckle.

"So you didn't attend the fire at the apple orchard a couple of years back?"

He looked at me with that look of polite confusion people give when they want to know what the heck you're getting at. "Well, actually, I did. That was right before I stopped."

I took a sharp breath. "Could I ask you about it?"

He frowned. "I'm not sure I should really be talking about that. It's all done now. Besides, isn't Otter Lake Security helping out over at the orchard? Why don't you just ask Adam?"

I frowned and nodded. "Actually it's Adam we're trying to help out. We were hoping that maybe Adam could get his record expunged. Grandma Honeycutt seems to think that maybe there had been some doubt about the fire being deliberately set." Oh my God. I'd just lied. I totally completely lied. To my teacher. For an investigation that I wasn't even a part of.

He shook his head. "Not much hope of that, I'm afraid."

"No? I thought it was just like a campfire that got out of control?" Another lie. It just came out of my mouth! And I had no idea why.

"Not with the amount of accelerant that was used."

"Oh, I see," I said with a nod. Well, that had kind of killed our jovial mood. "Thanks. And thanks for letting me try out the pumpkin catapult."

And just like that the mad scientist twinkle was back in his eye. "Do you want to try out the potato cannon before you go?" He pointed over to something that looked a lot like a rocket launcher.

I smiled. "You know I do."

"I haven't seen Mandy all night."

"She's fine," Freddie said, scanning the rapidly thinning crowd. "Probably just throwing up or doing something else pregnant women do."

"Keep your voice down," I whispered. "Nobody knows about the *abaybay*, remember?"

"I'm sorry. What was that?"

I didn't answer.

"Are we doing pig Latin now? Is that what that was?"

It was. It was indeed. But given his reaction, I wasn't about to confirm it.

Freddie chuckled a little then said, "Don't worry. She's probably just inside. It's cold out here."

Yup, another night of security was winding down at the apple orchard. Rhonda still wasn't able to join us because the wife in her cheating-spouse case wanted more pictures. She was having a tough time accepting the reality of the situation. But it was okay though. The crowd was a little thin tonight, probably because of the chill. We were waiting for the last few stragglers to head out so we could go home. It was weird, though, not seeing Mandy. I knew she worked the café a lot with her grandmother—they were pretty tight—but she also liked to get right out into the thick of things with her brothers whenever she could.

After Mr. Majors's place, I had picked up my hot packs then walked past the sheriff's department. I walked by a few times actually. I guess I was hoping Grady would come out, so I wouldn't have to go in, but that didn't happen. It was probably for the best anyway. I was feeling kind of guilty about my impromptu questioning of

Mr. Majors. I mean, I had been curious, and he was right there—chucking pumpkins at me; it didn't mean I was a cat in a room with a hundred doors, or however that went.

It was interesting what he had said about the fire though. So Adam *had* purposely started a fire just outside the Apple Witch's house. Why would he do that? I mean, obviously there was a voice in my head screaming something about covering up evidence, but I just didn't want to believe that. I knew the Honeycutts. They were a little on the wild side, but they weren't killers. I couldn't see Adam doing something like that . . . unless . . . unless the body did belong to Danny, and Danny had somehow hurt Mandy. Then I could see it. In fact, suddenly I was having a pretty clear flashback of him holding a pitchfork to her new boyfriend's chest. And they were just dating. But still . . .

I needed to talk to Mandy. See what more she knew.

Except I couldn't. Or shouldn't. Because I wasn't investigating.

I hadn't told Freddie about it either because that really would start a fire I couldn't control.

But, on second thought, just because I wasn't investigating, that didn't mean I couldn't talk to Mandy at all. It was only right I check in on her given what I knew. And maybe I could encourage her again to tell her family that she was pregnant so that she could get some support.

"I'm going to head over to the café to see if she's inside," I said. "You okay out here?"

Freddie shot me a look. "I guess so. I mean it's probably safer out here than it is in Grandma Honeycutt's lair."

I smiled and shook my head. "Okay, I'll see you in a bit."

I shoved my hands deep into my jacket pockets—my

hot packs had fizzled out an hour ago—and I hustled over to the café.

Unfortunately, though, when I got there, there was no Mandy to be found.

I checked the haunted barn next.

No Mandy there either. Well, at least there was no Mandy from what I could see. The flashing lights and zombie farmers screaming at me made it tricky.

I thought about giving up and heading back over to Freddie, but then I realized I hadn't checked the kids' area.

It looked deserted from a distance—which wasn't surprising given how late it was—but I figured it was still worth a shot. I walked over to the stacks of hay bales for the kids to climb on so that I could see around to the other side when . . .

Was that a voice?

Maybe Mandy was here after all.

I trotted all the way over, and walked halfway around the stack when I heard—

"We need to make a decision."

I froze. I couldn't be certain, but it sounded like it might be Brandon, the middle Honeycutt brother. And he sounded serious.

Now the right thing to do in this scenario would have been to either let them know I could hear their conversation by announcing myself, or just leave. But I wasn't doing either one of those things. And I wasn't exactly sure why. Actually who was I kidding? Both Freddie and I had a problem with eavesdropping. A problem that was often rewarded with really useful information. I should probably look into finding a way to cure that habit. Just maybe not tonight.

I leaned a little closer toward the direction of the voices.

"You're overreacting, man."

That definitely sounded like Cam.

"We can't take the chance," another voice answered. Adam?

"We need to decide."

"Decide what?"

"What are we going to do about Freddie and Erica?"

Chapter Nineteen

What are we going to do about Freddie and Erica?

I stiffened.

That was a question I never wanted to hear unless it was in regard to gifts or something like that. And this definitely wasn't. I could tell. It was said with a "this is a problem" type tone.

I peeked around the wall of hay bales super-quick. I was right. Honeycutt boys. All three of them.

"Fire them. Just tell them we don't need the security. Everything's been fine."

I peeked around again just in time to see Adam swat his youngest brother on the back of the head. "Yeah, everything's fine. Except they found Danny in the woods."

A rush of cold washed over me.

Danny.

He said it like it was a fact.

Like he knew without a doubt.

But how could he know that?

Grady said he didn't have an official ID yet.

Oh crap. Oh crap. Oh crap.

"I don't know if just firing them will solve the problem now."

"And you know they're going to bring Rhonda around more." I think it was Brandon who said that. "She's the one we really need to worry about. She's ex-law enforcement. I don't like this. We need to take care of it. The sooner the better."

"Well, if we're not going to fire them then what are we going to do?"

"We do nothing," Adam said.

"No," Brandon said. "I say go with my plan. It will be easy."

"You're just saying that because you never liked Erica."

"She was okay before . . . that day."

Oh, of course he was going to bring up *that* day. I was never going to live it down. But the whole thing was his sister's fault!

"Besides, she was always taking away my Xbox."

Because he wouldn't do his homework! And this was so not what I needed to be upset about right now! But really, I probably should have taken away his Xbox even more because it was looking like I had helped to raise a mur—

"I say we just get through Halloween," Adam said. At least I thought it was Adam. "We'll keep them close, and if they start sniffing around things they shouldn't then—"

Then what? Then what?

"Forget it, man. We're doing my thing. They'll never—"

I didn't hear the rest of that sentence because I saw something even more horrifying. It was Freddie coming out of a Porta Potti. He had spotted me, and I was almost positive that he was about to call out my name for some stupid reason, because we were already looking at each other, and I couldn't let him do that because then the

Honeycutt brothers would know that I had heard their whole conversation about what they were going to do with Freddie and Erica, and I had a feeling that conversation would have an entirely different outcome if they knew that I had heard them!

I waved my hands in big *Xs* in the air and then slit my hand across my throat like I was sawing a log.

He stopped walking.

I rushed toward him.

"What the hell is going—"

"Not here," I said, slapping my palm over his mouth, making his eyes go really big. I grabbed his arm and yanked him toward the only cover available.

Freddie dug his feet into the ground when he saw where we were headed. "You are not taking me in the corn maze."

Frick! I forgot about Freddie and his fear of corn mazes. "We do not have time for you to be afraid of stupid stuff," I hissed. "We have real stuff to be afraid of."

That got his attention.

He let me lead him through the corn gates. We took a few turns in the maze before we stopped, and I told him as quickly as I could everything I had heard. He didn't interrupt once, which was very odd for Freddie. In fact, he was pretty much frozen the entire time. And when I was through, he was still motionless. "So what do we do?"

He didn't answer.

"Freddie?"

He just blinked at me.

"Are you all right?" I shook his arm and his eyes snapped into focus. "Talk to me."

"You want me to talk to you?" he whispered.

"Yes," I whispered back.

"Fine. I'll talk." Suddenly there was a lot of rage in his eyes. "I can't believe you did this to me!"

"What?"

"Why would you tell me that?" He slapped my jacketed arm like five, six times.

"Stop hitting me," I said, swatting him back. "And of course I was going to tell you that. Why wouldn't I tell you that?"

Freddie's eyes went very wide. "Because now they have to kill us both!"

I shook my head and blinked at him.

"Two minutes ago," Freddie said, putting up three fingers before quickly correcting himself. He was really upset. "I didn't know anything. I was free to live my life. And now I know the Honeycutt boys killed Danny. So the Honeycutt boys are obviously going to have to kill not just you, but me!"

"They already thought you were a problem," I hissed. "I just gave you a heads-up. We are in this together."

"And how did we get into this mess in the first place, Erica?" Freddie asked, hands on his hips. "Did I want us to work for the Honey—"

"Would you please just focus? What are we going to do now? Should I call Grady?"

I was already reaching for my phone when Freddie swatted me again. "And tell him what? Did you hear an actual confession? He's never going to believe us."

"Sure he will."

"Eventually. Not in time." Freddie pinched his lips together and shook his head. "He never believes us in time. Grady doesn't see the value in flights of fancy. He's the opposite of that. He believes in like the crash and burn of fancy."

"You're babbling."

"Because my best friend is trying to get me killed!" Just then Freddie gasped. "Or worse yet, say Grady does believe us. Then he rushes over here to make sure his *special* friend is okay. I doubt he'd drop everything for just his regular friends, like me, and then what? He can't arrest them. They could just say that they were talking about us being around . . . was like bad for business or something. No. No. We can't tip them off that we're on to them."

"This is not something I can keep from Grady."

"Fine! Don't keep it from him. Just wait until we're off these freaking cursed lands! You told me they said they weren't going to do anything unless we were sticking our noses where they didn't belong."

"Well, Adam said that, but—"

"So fine. We don't."

"Don't what?"

"Don't stick our noses anywhere!" he yelled in the loudest whisper ever. "We just treat this like it's any other night. They're not going to kill us with people still around. We just need to make sure that we leave with the last guest."

I nodded. "Okay. Okay. We can do that."

Freddie was nodding too. "I mean, we've been in tight spots before."

"Sure we have. It's part of the job."

"We can't go running to Grady every time things get sticky. He'll never respect us as professionals."

I frowned. He was right. Grady didn't think we could handle ourselves. It was an issue. A serious issue. But a serious issue I could think more about later . . . when I wasn't in fear for my life.

"Okay," I said, "so we get out of here ASAP. Then we figure out what to do."

"Right. Exactly."

"So, we should probably get back out there," I said, jerking a thumb behind us toward the entrance of the maze.

"Probably."

Neither one of us moved.

"This is strange for me," Freddie said. "I never thought a corn maze would ever be my safe place."

"Come on," I said, taking a breath. "We can do this. Remember, just act normal. It's just a regular night. There's nothing to be afraid of."

We walked toward the entrance, stepped outside, and . . .

"Hey guys."

. . . we screamed our heads off.

"Brandon," I said with a chuckle—once I was done screaming of course. "I didn't see you there."

Freddie didn't say anything. He was too busy clutching his chest and gasping for air.

"We were just, uh, making sure nobody was left in the corn maze."

Brandon was the most average-looking of the Honeycutt boys. Not that he wasn't attractive. He just wasn't as big as his younger brother or as intimidating as his older. He looked like an average guy. Not someone you'd notice in a crowd. And yet, when you talked to him, he had almost like a smoothness to him. He always said the right thing, so it was hard to tell what he was really thinking.

"She getting to you too, Erica?" Brandon asked.

"Who? Mandy? No, I don't know anything about—"

"The Apple Witch."

"Oh," I said with a chuckle. "Yeah, I guess so." I rocked on my feet. "I guess so."

"She has a way of doing that to people," he said with a smile. "Hey, I was wondering if you guys could help me out with one last thing before you go?"

Freddie and I exchanged glances.

My immediate thought was to say *No, no, no. Absolutely not.* But what came out of my mouth was, "Um, sure."

"Sure, sure," Freddie said, with a weak thumbs-up.

"I just wanted you to come on one last run with me," Brandon said, tilting his chin over to the tractor with the large wooden trailer attached to the back.

"On the hayride?"

"Yeah, it's the kids again," he said, a look of annoyance crossing his face. "We think they're messing around in the cornfields, but I can't drive the tractor *and* chase them down."

Freddie and I just stood there nodding. Saying nothing.

"So . . . is that okay?" Brandon asked.

"Um, there aren't going to be guys with chain saws jumping out at us, right?" I asked with a nervous chuckle.

"Nah, we sent all the performers home. It's kind of been a slow night. I don't even know for sure the kids are still out there, but, you know, one of them is going to break a leg and sue us. Gotta execute the due diligence."

"Right," I said. *Execute?!* Out of all the words to use. "Got it. Well . . . sure. Let's go."

Freddie elbowed me in the ribs. Thankfully Brandon was looking the other way.

I shrugged at him. What was I supposed to say? I mean, making a run for it would definitely look suspicious, and we had just agreed that we weren't supposed to be looking suspicious!

He jerked a thumb at the tractor. "I'll meet you over there."

"We'll be right over," I said, throwing him a wave.

Once he left, I turned to Freddie, but before I could say anything, he said, "We are so about to die in a cornfield."

"You don't know—"

"So dying in a cornfield."

Chapter Twenty

"Hop on," Brandon shouted from the seat of his monster tractor.

I shot him a thumbs-up and grabbed Freddie's arm.

"But he's taking us into the field to kill us," he whispered.

"He is not taking us into the field to kill us." Yes, yes, I know what I'd heard, but I had known the Honeycutts forever. They were not killers. There had to be some sort of explanation. I just overreacted earlier because . . . of all the horror movies we'd been watching, and the thing Freddie and I had seen outside the Apple Witch's house, and the very real foot I had found in the woods, and I was letting all of that fear take over. I just needed to calm down. There could be a million reasons for why they had said what they said. Or maybe I was just in denial about the fact that I was about to die in a cornfield.

No, no, for all I knew, Grady had already ID'd the body, and there was a perfectly logical explanation for what I had overhead.

"Fine," Freddie said, hopping onto the back of the wagon. "But just so you know, if it comes down to only one of us living, I choose me." He stuck his thumb into his sternum.

"I wouldn't want it any other way," I said, climbing up beside him.

"I don't have to be the fastest in the world," Freddie went on. "I just have to be faster than you."

I found a seat on a hay bale. "I totally get it."

Freddie ran his foot along the floor. "All this hay is making the planks slippery. Keep that in mind when things get real."

"You are being ridiculous," I said, yanking at his arm to get him to sit down beside me. "We are being ridiculous. I know what I heard sounded—"

"Murderous?" Freddie offered.

"You guys ready to go?" Brandon shouted back to us.

I shot him another thumbs-up, and the tractor roared to life. A moment later we jerked forward. "It didn't sound great," I said, just loudly enough to be heard over the tractor. "But there has to be something more going on here. Brandon is not going to kill us. The Honeycutts are not killers."

"Right. But just so you know," Freddie hissed back. "The only reason I'm on this tractor right now is because I'm pretty sure the Honeycutts are hunters, and I feel like if I run, it will end for me like it did for Bambi's mom. I'd rather face my death head-on."

I whacked him on the arm. "Just stop it."

"This is not how I wanted to go, Erica."

"We are not going anywhere." Now if I could just convince my rapidly beating heart of that. Everything was happening too fast. I tried replaying the conversation I had overheard in my mind. But it didn't help. It really hadn't sounded good. And there was a body buried in the woods. But . . . but I had made these kids after-school snacks!

"Just take some deep breaths or something," I said, not sure who I was trying to reassure more, me or Freddie. "It's actually a pretty nice night."

It was. No wind. The air was crisp. There was a nice fat moon high in the sky. Of course, the tractor was just loud enough that you couldn't really hear if someone or some*thing* was about to jump out of the cornfield at you . . . but I guess that was fitting for a haunted hayride.

We bumped along in relative peace until we heard Brandon say, "What the . . ."

Suddenly the tractor jerked to a stop, and Brandon killed the engine.

"What's going on?" Freddie asked, jumping to his feet. "What's happening?"

Brandon hopped out of his seat and dropped to the ground. "I don't believe this."

Freddie and I scrambled out of the wagon.

"Where did all that come from?" I asked, staring at the makeshift barricade of branches blocking the drive.

"Must have been the kids," Brandon said, looking at me. "They're probably just pissed that we're keeping them away from the Apple Witch's house."

I saw Freddie stiffen at her name, but he didn't say anything.

I wasn't sure if I was buying Brandon's theory about the teens though. Those kids had been scared the night we found . . . the boot. I didn't see them coming back any time soon. We also knew their parents, and I was guessing they were keeping a pretty close eye on them these days.

"Were we this annoying back when we were kids?" Brandon asked me with a smile.

I chuckled. "Well, there was that time you and Cam got me to the dock, so Adam could jump out of the water wielding a machete. That was pretty . . . annoying. But the goalie mask was a nice touch."

He nodded. "You sure got us back though."

Freddie gasped. "You did something worse than that?"

I just shook my head. "I didn't mean to . . . it . . . whatever. Are we going to clear this brush or what?"

"Yeah, what are we doing just standing here?" Freddie asked with a nervous chuckle. "Let's get this stuff out of the way, so we can go home." He hustled over to the giant pile.

"I'll just run back to the barn," Brandon said. "This will be a lot quicker with a chain saw."

"Wait, what?" Freddie asked.

"A chain saw. You know, to cut through the branches?"

"I really don't think this situation warrants a chain saw, do you, Erica?" Freddie asked, taking a step back toward me.

"I . . . I . . ."

"Dudes, you're security," Brandon said, laughing. "I'll be right back. You'll be fine."

"We'll come with you," Freddie offered.

"No, someone has to stay with the tractor," Brandon said. "Last thing we need is for the teens to take it for a joyride."

Freddie shook his head. "I doubt they'd do that."

"Didn't they do exactly that with your boat?"

"Well, yeah, but . . . Erica can wait," Freddie said, taking a quick step toward Brandon. "She can watch the tractor. By herself."

I grabbed his jacket and jerked him back. "Ha ha ha. No."

"Then *we'll* go get the chain saw," Freddie said to Brandon. "You can stay here."

"Except you don't know where the chain saw is." Brandon's smile broadened. "You aren't seriously afraid, are you, man?"

"No," Freddie scoffed. "Of course not."

"Cool." And with that Brandon disappeared into the rows of corn.

I folded my arms over my chest. "We're fine, Freddie."

He matched my stance. "I know we're fine, Erica."

We waited in silence for a moment or two before I added, "Brandon is not going to kill us with a chain saw in the middle of his apple orchard if that's what you're thinking."

"I know that," Freddie said tightly. "If that's how he was planning to do it, he would have just brought the chain saw. No, what I'm thinking is that his brothers are hiding in the corn with high-powered sniper rifles."

I shot him a look. "Nobody is waiting in the corn."

Just then the corn rustled.

Freddie's eyes widened.

"Relax. That was just the wind." Except of course there was no wind. My breath quickened. But not because I was scared or anything.

"You know," Freddie said with a nod. "I think this right now might be even scarier than that time we dug up the grave."

"No way," I scoffed, my eyes darting side to side. "Are you kidding me? That was way scarier. Don't you remember that owl that kept hooting?"

"Yeah, but at least there weren't any witches."

"No, just a skeleton."

We looked at each other then fell back into silence. Both of us with our arms still folded across our chests. I kind of wanted to suggest that we stand back-to-back so that we had all directions of attack covered, but I thought there was a good chance that might add to our general level of hysteria.

"How long does it take to get a chain saw?"

I shook my head. "I don't know."

"Well, at least this hayride is a tractor one," Freddie muttered.

I frowned at him. "What do you mean?"

"Well, this would be way worse if there were horses pulling the wagon."

My frown deepened. "Why would horses be worse?"

Freddie looked at me. "Because they'd probably be all antsy right now, and doing that thing where they snort and paw at the ground."

"You're right," I said, scanning the corn. "That would be worse."

"Although their horse senses would probably tip us off to any approaching danger. We could ask them, *Are there bad men in the corn?* And they could answer by stomping their feet."

I just looked at him.

"You know, one for yes. And two for—"

"You're losing it." Just then something caught my eye. It was hard to tell in the low light, but—

"Freddie!" I shout-whispered, shaking his arm.

"What? What?"

I pointed frantically at the field. "Do you see that?"

"See what?"

"The corn!"

"I see lots of corn," he said quickly. "We are in a cornfield."

I jerked his arm around. "No, over there," I said, pointing again. "The corn. It's moving."

Yup, yup, there was no doubt. A couple of hundred yards away right near the edge of the forest, the ground had a slight slope, and the corn there was definitely rustling.

Suddenly Freddie snorted an awful lot like a scared horse might. "What is it?"

"I don't know," I said, shaking my head.

"Do you think it could be a deer or something?"

"I don't know."

"Do deer even sleep in cornfields?"

"I don't know!"

"Do you think it's a coyote?"

I swatted his arm about eight times.

"Right. Right. You don't know. We have the same information. Maybe—"

"Oh my . . ."

"Erica," Freddie said, clutching me as we both took a step back. "Tell me that isn't what I think it is."

I shook my head side to side. "It's not. It can't be."

I mean, it had been hard to see back when we were in the woods what with the fire blinding us, and all the screaming, but this . . .

This . . . I could see quite clearly, and it looked an awful lot like . . .

The Apple Witch rising up from the corn.

Chapter Twenty-one

"It can't be."

But the slant of a hood . . .

The draped arms rising up at its sides . . . like . . . like wings . . .

The unearthly fluid motion as it floated up from the corn . . .

"It's one of the Honeycutts. It has to be. They always used to pull crap like this when they were kids. They're just trying to scare us."

"It's working," Freddie moaned.

The figure rose higher in the air. It was waist-high above the corn.

"How is it doing that?"

I shook my head some more. "It's not the Apple Witch. It's not the Apple—"

"Stop saying her name!"

"No. No," I said firmly. "It's not a ghost . . . or a witch . . . or an . . ." I was going to say apple but that wasn't right. "This is not happening." I took a step toward it.

"What are you doing?!" Freddie squealed, grabbing my arm as I was just about to take another step.

"I'm going to see who that ghost really is."

"You are not! What are you, crazy?"

I yanked my arm from his grip and took another quick step.

"You stop it right now, Erica Bloom!"

"Can't. I do not believe in the Apple—"

"Stop! Stop walking!"

"It has to be done."

I was just about to launch into a run when suddenly Freddie grabbed me in a bear hug. "No! I'm not going to let you do it!"

"Let go of me!"

"No! What if you're wrong?" he grunted. "What if you pull back that hood and . . . and it's the rotten-apple face of the witch?"

"Let me go!" I shouted, wriggling against his arms. "There is no witch! I'll prove it to you."

"No! I won't let you die."

"I'm not going to die. I believe in science!" I said, kicking my legs in the air as Freddie lifted me off the ground. "I am a feminist scientist!"

"No you're not!" Freddie shouted back. "You went to school for court reporting!"

"I know it's you!" I shouted toward the ghost. "Brandon? Cam? I know it's one of you."

I kicked in the air so hard, Freddie lost his balance. We fell backward, hitting the ground hard, but he still refused to let go. "Dammit, Freddie! Let me—"

Suddenly two faces appeared above us. Brandon and Cam. And if I was not mistaken they had come from the opposite direction of the Apple Witch.

Freddie and I stopped wriggling.

"What are you two doing?" Brandon said.

Freddie's arms dropped away from me.

"Where . . ." Freddie began.

". . . is Adam?" I finished.

"Right here," another voice said, backed up by the roar of a chain saw.

Freddie and I both screamed and scurried back on our hands and feet as Adam came into view . . . with his chain saw. He clicked it off.

"Are you guys all right?"

Freddie and I scrambled to our feet.

"But . . . but if you guys are all here . . ." Freddie said, whipping his head around to look back at the patch of corn by the woods. "Who is . . ."

Empty. Gone. All still.

"I . . ." I couldn't figure out what to say. "I . . ."

"That's it!" Freddie shouted.

"What's it?" I asked.

"We're off the clock." He stomped back along the wagon trail.

I didn't move at first.

"Come on, Erica!"

The Honeycutts didn't say anything.

I ran after him.

"And we get double for tonight!"

Chapter Twenty-two

"Erica? What are you doing here?"

I straight-armed the half-open door blocking my path.

"Did something happen?"

I forced my way into the cabin slash lodge slash man-house.

"What is going on? You look like you've seen a gh—"

"No!" I pointed at Grady. Right in his face. "No. Do not say—just, no."

He froze.

I dropped my pointing finger. "We need to become closer friends, Grady."

His eyes widened. "We do?"

"Right now."

"I don't understand," he said quickly. "I thought—"

"There are some things we may never understand, Grady," I said, planting my hands on my hips and nodding. "But I need to be your friend."

He blinked a couple of times then stammered, "Okay."

"Okay?"

"Let's . . . be friends."

* * *

Happy.

That's how I woke up the next morning.

Just happy.

The room was cool—Grady always liked his place cool—but the blankets were warm and so was the man with his arms wrapped around me.

Last night had been . . .

Wow.

"You awake?" he whispered. The breath from his mouth, resting just under my ear, sent chills racing over my body. I rolled over in his arms and brought my lips to his. I couldn't believe this was happening. I was in Grady's bed . . . kissing his lips . . . snuggling in his arms. It had taken us so long to get here. I mean, yes, we had been here before, but somehow it felt different this time. Like we had actually done the impossible. We had changed as people. I had turned to Grady last night when I had needed him, not away. And he had accepted me with open arms. Without turning into Sheriff Forrester. This was just so perfec—

Suddenly he pulled back.

"What's wrong?"

"Nothing," he said, shaking his head. "This is . . . amazing. Best morning ever."

"But?"

Grady propped himself up on his elbow. "I don't know how it happened."

I rolled onto my back. Okay, maybe not all of Sheriff Forrester was gone. Which was good. Sheriff Forrester looked super-good in his uniform and had . . . cuffs.

"What happened last night?"

I shot a look over at him. "Things . . . changed last night."

Yes, a lot had changed last night. Not my belief in ghosts. That wasn't going to change any time soon, but a lot of other stuff had changed. Like our friendship, for one. And my attitude, for two. "Grady, I need to tell you something."

He brushed my bangs from my eyes with his finger. "Okay."

"I, Erica Bloom, am—" I had to stop myself because I almost said *feminist scientist* again and that wasn't right. "A private investigator." I thought about adding *pending proper licensing,* but I thought that might take away from my point, and we were talking about who I was in spirit right now.

"Okay," Grady said again. "What exactly does that mean?"

"It means," I said, getting up on my elbows, "that that is who I am. And I can't change it. Not for you. Not for anyone." Oh yeah, that felt pretty good.

"I . . . I'm not sure what's going on right now."

"I'll tell you what's going on," I said, flipping on my side to face him. "I'm investigating the apple orchard case."

"What? I thought you said—"

"I know what I said. But I'm tired of always feeling nervous about you finding out what Freddie and I are up to, so I'm officially telling you now that OLS is investigating the apple orchard case."

He tugged the sheets up closer to his chest. "Did the Honeycutts hire you?"

"Nope."

"Then why—"

I pressed my finger against his lips. "Let Mommy explain." A look of horror came to his eyes. Okay, I might have gotten carried away there. Channeled too much Freddie. I dropped my finger. "OLS needs to do this. Not just because it's what we do, but because it is the only way you and I are going to work."

Grady frowned. "I kind of thought it was the biggest problem in our relationship."

I nodded. "And that needs to change."

He shook his head. "I'm not following."

"My mother said something to me, and it took a while for it to set in, but now it has, and the way is clear."

"Erica, what the h—"

I cut him off with a look. He could feel the power. Yes, we both had changed . . . but me in particular. And that's why things were going to be different this time. For so long, I felt like I was the one trying to hold Freddie back from going too far, but now that he was sidelined by his fear of the Apple Witch, I realized that I had just been using him as a cover. An excuse. Truth was, I wanted to investigate. I wanted to find out what happened to Danny. I wanted to follow this through to the end. "I can't change who I am, Grady. And if you truly care about me, you won't want me to."

"Of course I don't want you to change," he said. "But I'm sheriff . . . and you and Freddie . . . you do things . . . like rob graves and—"

"You really have to let that one go," I said, patting his hand. "I've been giving it a lot of thought"—you know, in between our friend sessions last night and sleep—"and you're right. Freddie and I need to walk the straight and narrow." I would have said Rhonda too, but she already was following the rules . . . or law . . . whatever.

"Well, good because—"

"But," I said sharply. "You need to start trusting me more, and—"

"Erica, I—"

"*And* respect me and the entire OLS team as professionals."

He didn't say anything, but his face dropped a little. Like he couldn't quite believe I was asking that of him, but he didn't want to be too dramatic about it because that might be insulting.

"It's the only way this is going to work," I said, gesturing back and forth between us.

I waited a really tense moment as Grady thought things over. Finally he said, "You're right."

"Excellent!" I launched myself toward him.

"But," he said, putting a finger between our lips, "you need to mean it when you say you won't do anything illegal."

"No problem," I said, closing my eyes and going in for—

His finger was still there.

"I mean it, Erica. It's not fair to ask me to put my job at risk—"

I leaned back. "We're not going to put your job at risk. We don't have to break any laws to—"

He scoffed a little. "Right."

"What does that *right* mean?" I said, mimicking his scoff.

He just shook his head.

"Do you really think that OLS can't solve a mystery without breaking—no, *bending* some laws?" I asked.

"Well, *bending some laws* has kind of been your go-to move when things get sticky."

"It has not," I snapped, although I was already skimming through all of my memories to see if I could really stand by that.

"Okay," he said with a chuckle.

I slapped the mattress. "Oh my God, that's what you've been telling yourself, isn't it?"

He raised a frowny eyebrow.

I pushed him on the pectoral muscle. Oh, hard. Nice. "You think we have caught murderers before you because we break the law to do it."

His eyes darted side to side. "Um, yeah."

"Well, I'll tell you what, Mr. Sheriff, I'm about to prove you wrong."

He squinted at me.

"In fact, why don't we make this a little more interesting?"

He blinked. "Last night was already the most interesting night of my life."

"I don't mean *that*," I said, pushing him on the chest again. I couldn't seem to stop doing that. "I mean, we're agreed that we have to start doing things differently, right?"

"Right."

"So maybe instead of fighting our whole way through this investigation, we should make a bet."

"A bet?"

"Yeah, I bet you that OLS can find out who killed *Danny* before OLPD can without breaking a single law." I said *Danny* with extra emphasis to show him that yes, I already knew who the victim was.

"Really," he said, no reaction to the Danny thing.

"Yes, really."

He smiled. "You're on."

"Awesome."

"Terrific."

"Wait," I said. "Before we officially start, can you tell me if you told anyone that Danny was actually the owner of the boot I found?"

"That's privileged police information."

"Of course it is."

We smiled at one another.

"Well," I said, taking a deep breath. "Now that that's all settled, I should probably get going. OLS is about to have an early-morning meeting to discuss our latest case."

Suddenly Grady's arm was wrapped around my back

and he was pulling me back into him. "Does that meeting have to happen right now?"

"Um . . ."

"'Cause I think our friendship could use some more work. There have been a lot of developments as of late."

"You're just trying to distract me with your masculine wiles, and . . ." The thought rolled away with Grady's lips on my neck.

Chapter Twenty-three

"Hey guys, I'm here! And I brought Freddie!"

Freddie and I blinked at each other with confusion. We were sitting in his gourmet kitchen—that rarely got used to cook anything—waiting for Rhonda so that we could start our early-morning emergency OLS team meeting. Okay, well, maybe it wasn't that early, but it was early enough. Grady and I had had a couple of issues to work out. Three to be precise.

"I'm right here," Freddie said as Rhonda came into the room.

"I mean, I brought Freddy Krueger. *A Nightmare on Elm Street*," she said, laughing and holding a DVD in the air. "I know it's a little early in the day, but if we don't get watching then we're never going to—"

"Oh no, no, no," Freddie said. "We will not be watching any horror movies."

The hand dropped to her side. "What? Why not?"

"Because my life is now a scary movie thanks to Erica."

Rhonda smiled. "Freddie, are you still freaking out about the Apple Witch?"

"No, I am freaking out about the freaking *you know who* and the freaking *you know who*'s descendants who now want to kill me, thanks to Erica."

I looked at him. "Will you please stop ending every sentence with *thanks to Erica*?"

"I would, but I can't because I'm too scared, thanks—"

"To Erica," I finished for him.

"What is going on with you two?" Rhonda asked. "Freddie, did you have too much Halloween candy again? You know the sugar makes—"

"I did not eat too much candy," Freddie said, slapping the counter, sending a tidal wave of mini-chocolate-bar wrappers cascading to the floor. He whipped his hand up and pointed at her. "Not one word."

We filled Rhonda in on everything that happened. When we were through all she said was, "Whoa."

"So you're the ex-cop," Freddie said. "What do we do? I don't want to die. And I'm pretty sure the—*you know who* now has my scent."

I frowned at him. I mean, even if the Apple Witch was real—which she was not—I don't think she'd be able to smell anything but her rotten-apple face. I mean, think about it.

"Well, you should definitely tell Grady," Rhonda said. "Not that he can do much about it."

"Forget about Grady. He's not part of this. He has his investigation, we have ours." When I said that we told Rhonda everything, I didn't mention the part where Grady and I . . . reconnected. I didn't tell Freddie that part either.

"Whoa. Whoa. Whoa," Freddie said. "You just said *investigation*. Since when is this an investigation? We agreed there would be no investigation."

"Well . . ." I said, chewing on the corner of my thumbnail.

"No. No. No," Freddie said. "Remember? You said *at least we're on the same page about something.*" He said it in a very obnoxious high-pitched girly voice.

"Well . . ."

"I like where this is going," Rhonda said, sitting up in her seat. "Erica, please tell me you have switched your vote."

"Well . . ."

Suddenly, a mini chocolate bar came out of nowhere and bounced off my chest. "Erica, what are you doing?"

I held up my hands just in case Freddie decided to bombard me with more chocolate. "I'm changing my vote."

"Yes!" Rhonda hissed.

"What?" Freddie shouted. "No! Erica, you were there. You saw the witch. If the Honeycutt boys don't kill us, she will."

"If the Honeycutt boys wanted to kill us," I said, "they could have easily done it last night and they didn't."

"No. No. N—"

"Yes. Yes. Yes," Rhonda said. "While your happiness is very important to us, Freddie, OLS is a democracy—" She was cut off by the chocolate flying in her direction. "Seriously, you need to lay off the candy. Oh, and I didn't say it earlier because I didn't want to interrupt the flow of your story, but the whole town knows it was Danny buried in the woods. I heard at the grocery store yesterday. That girl Krystal was packing my groceries and—"

"Everybody knows?" I asked.

"Well, maybe not everybody," she said with a little shrug. "Just everybody with friends." Which was everybody. Otter Lake was too small not to be friendly.

"See?" I said to Freddie. "I told you the Honeycutts weren't killers."

"But you said you heard them threaten us," he said.

"I believe your exact words were *What are we going to do about Freddie and Erica?*"

"I know," I said. "But that could mean a lot of different things."

"What is going on with you?" Freddie asked. "Why do you want to do this so badly all of a sudden? What about Grady?"

"What about Grady?" I repeated as casually as I could. "This is about OLS. Rhonda was right. We don't ignore murders that happen in our town."

"That's right!" Rhonda shouted, pounding the table with her fist. "Hear! Hear!"

I put my hand on my chest. "People look to us to feel safe. It's our duty."

"You have never cared about duty before," Freddie said, frowning at me. "In fact, I don't think I have ever heard the word *duty* come out of your mouth."

"Duty," Rhonda said with a snicker. Then she caught the look on our faces and shrugged. "What? Somebody had to say it. You were all thinking it."

"I don't believe this," Freddie said, shoving another mini chocolate bar into his mouth. "We are going to get ourselves killed, and for what? We're not even getting paid."

"We've never been paid for any of the murders we've solved," I said.

"But we're a legit business now and—"

"Oh!" I put my finger in the air. "That's another thing. Everything we do while investigating this crime has to be on the up-and-up."

Rhonda and Freddie both threw me confused looks this time.

I folded my arms over my chest. "I was just putting it out there as a reminder." Part of me wanted to tell them I had made a bet with Grady after spending the night at his place, but . . . actually, no. No part of me wanted to tell them that. Especially not Freddie. Not when he was this candy-angry. They would have so many opinions . . . and it was still really new.

"I don't like this," Freddie said, grimacing with disgust. "But what about the . . . *you know who*?"

"The Apple Witch?" I asked.

That resulted in another mini-chocolate-bar bombardment. "Yes! You saw her too last night. You can't deny that."

"I saw a person dressed as the Apple Witch."

Freddie threw his hands in the air in a pretty crazy pattern. "Levitating above a cornfield."

"Yes, levitating above— Okay, well, maybe not levitating above the cornfield. They probably had a step stool or something."

"We saw all three Honeycutt brothers, so who was it out in that field?"

"I don't know," I said. I mean, the thought had occurred to me that it could have been any number of people—including Mandy—but I hadn't settled on anyone who made a lot of sense. "It's all part of the mystery. That we are going to solve."

"So where do we start?" Rhonda asked.

"Wait," Freddie said, leaning back while gripping the edge of the island's counter. "We're seriously doing this?"

"We seriously are," I said with a nod.

"We're a democracy," Rhonda threw in.

"Fine," he said, smacking the stone surface. "Fine. I give up. But if we're really doing this then we're doing it the right way."

I frowned. "What does that mean exactly?"

"Forget all your useless feelings about the Honeycutts not being killers. The body was found on their property. We know Adam has a violent streak . . ."

And an arson streak. I had been conveniently forgetting about that. Freddie was going to go nuts when he heard that. I'd wait maybe until he was a bit calmer.

". . . and Danny had a personal, romantic connection with the family. And we all know romance leads to murder. At least in heterosexual couples."

Rhonda and I exchanged glances. Seemed a small point to argue right now though.

"So, given all these irrefutable facts, there is only one course of action. We need to question them. One by one."

"I don't think they are going to agree to that," Rhonda said.

"Yeah, that's why we can't let them know that's what we're doing."

"Huh?"

"We question them without them even knowing they are being questioned, maybe tomorrow. At say a recreational event where they wouldn't even suspect—"

"Oh no," I said. "You're not thinking . . ."

"Hey, this is what your democracy looks like," Freddie said.

"What?" Rhonda asked. "What is going on?"

I looked at her and sighed. "We are going paintballing."

Chapter Twenty-four

"This was seriously the best you could do?" I looked down at my burlap jacket and pants with the hay sticking out of the cuffs.

"Don't you even start with me. Cam said it was a costume thing," Freddie said. "We don't want to draw attention to ourselves, so we had to come in costume."

That's right. We were paintballing. First thing in the morning. The absolute last thing I had ever wanted to do. Especially in costume.

We had parked in the apple orchard's main lot where we normally did, and there were a lot of cars, but we hadn't come across any people yet. Maybe they had all gone to take a nap in the barn. That's what I was planning on doing if given half a chance.

"Besides," Freddie went on, "this way we don't look threatening. And you know what, Miss Judgey Judge? Next time, you get the costumes with absolutely no notice. We're lucky I offered to store all of Mrs. Mathers's old theater gear." Mrs. Mathers was the drama teacher at the high school. These costumes were left over from last year's production. "And you have nothing to complain about. At least you can move in your outfit."

I looked over at Freddie's silver-painted . . . I want to say cardboard-boxed torso? It didn't look very comfortable.

"But why couldn't you have gotten me Dorothy's costume?" I asked. "I can rock pigtails."

Freddie chuckled. "Okay."

"I like my costume," Rhonda said, shaking her mane. "It's warm, and I feel fierce."

I looked her over. "You're supposed to feel cowardly."

"A leopard can't change its stripes."

Freddie squinted at her. "You just broke something deep in my brain."

I chuckled. "Okay, so where exactly are we going?"

"The Web site said the first five-minute . . . *battle,* I guess, is taking place at the east cornfield. It's like a capture-the-flag type of deal," Freddie said.

Rhonda pointed in the direction of the rising sun. "I think it's just behind that barn."

"And you're sure each round is just five minutes?" I asked.

"If you weren't planning on believing me," Freddie said, "you could have checked the Web site yourself."

"True," I said with a nod. "And you're sure there are dead zones we can just hide out in where nobody can shoot us?"

"That's right," Rhonda said. "But you also don't win that way."

I chuckled. "Yeah, surviving is a win."

"Okay," Freddie said, holding up his hands, "so let's stick to the plan. Rhonda is on Adam. I'm on—"

"Why am I on Adam again?" Rhonda asked.

Freddie let out a frustrated sigh. "We've been over

this. You're on Adam because he's the scariest, and until Erica and I actually go to the jujitsu club—"

"Jujitsu," I said in a super-cool voice.

Freddie sighed. "And we can't go until she stops saying the name like that. You're the only one who has any self-defense training."

"Got it," Rhonda said with a nod.

"But keep him away from pitchforks."

"Acknowledged."

"Now, as I was saying," Freddie went on. "Rhonda is on Adam. I'm on Brandon. And Erica is on Cam because he likes her, and maybe in a surprise twist they'll fall in love and—"

"Just stop," I said, shaking my head. "The babysitter thing is not happening." Besides, I had enough *friends*.

"So, remember," Freddie said, clapping his hands together. "No one goes off with any of the brothers alone. We're just gathering information today. Getting a feel for each of them. I did some research last night and—"

I frowned. "What kind of research? Research on the brothers?"

"No, research on birth order."

"What?"

"I couldn't sleep," Freddie said, shaking his head. "Too much chocolate. Besides, I thought you'd like it that I was doing research. It is science and all."

"Okay," I said, kicking a rock. "What Web site did you look this up on?"

"Does it matter?"

"Oh, it matters."

He sighed. "I think it might have been like one of those science journals that psychologists write in."

"Uh-huh," I said. "Name one science journal that—"

"Fine. It was *Men's Health* magazine. Are you happy?"

I smiled. "A little bit."

"They do their research, and what I found out was very interesting."

"Okay. Let's hear it," Rhonda said.

"Firstborns tend to be ambitious, reliable, cautious, and controlling."

I shook my head. "Adam didn't look all that cautious the other night with the pitchfork at Shane's chest."

"Actually, I think he looked really cautious," Freddie said. "He walked right up to the line of murder but didn't cross it. Can you say you've ever been able to do that?"

I frowned. "No?"

"That's because you're not a firstborn."

I frowned some more. "I think technically I am."

"No, you are an only child like me," the Tin Man said, patting his box chest. "It's completely different."

"And explains so much," Rhonda said.

"Okay, next you have your middle child," Freddie went on. "In this case Brandon. Middle children tend to be the peacemakers of the family. They bridge the gap between the oldest and youngest child. They also tend to be the sneakiest."

"Is that the scientific term?" I asked.

"Oh, if you only had a brain," Freddie grumbled.

I looked at him. "You've been waiting all morning to say that, haven't you?"

"Anyway, the youngest child, well, they are the rebellious, attention-seeking ones in the family. They tend to be outgoing and somewhat uncomplicated."

"That does sound like Cam," Rhonda said.

"But isn't Mandy technically the baby of the family?" I asked.

"She's a girl. She doesn't count."

"I dare you to say that on Twitter."

"You know what I mean."

"No, I don't."

"Actually, I hate to jump on the Erica bandwagon," Rhonda began, "but . . ."

"What's wrong with the Erica bandwagon?" I asked.

"Nothing," she said quickly. "But I think using this theory of yours could be dangerous, Freddie."

"What?"

"Well, when I was in training they were always warning us to let the evidence guide the investigation. Not the other way around," Rhonda said in an authoritative voice. "If we look at these brothers as being certain types, it will skew how we pursue this thing."

"I see," Freddie said.

"Aw, come on," she said, bumping his shoulder with her own. "Don't be like that."

"No, no, it's fine," he said lightly. "I mean it stings a little after the whole democracy thing, but at least now I know what happened to my missing heart."

I rolled my eyes.

"My partners stomped it into a million little mushy pieces."

"Can we please just get on with this?" I asked.

"You're so gung-ho lately," Rhonda said. "What is going on with you?"

I scratched at some straw popping out my sleeve. "I just know that OLS can do this. And really, the whole paintballing thing shouldn't be that big of a deal. I just want to get on with it." It had nothing to do with the bet I had made with the town's sheriff who also happened to be my very close friend.

"Yeah," Rhonda said with a nod. "Maybe it will even be fun."

We had just walked the length of the barn and got our first glimpse of the playing field.

"What the . . ."

Rhonda clutched her tail. "I would like to go home now."

"What is going on?" Freddie asked. "Why are we the only ones in costumes?"

"No. No. They're wearing costumes," I said with a hard swallow. "That side has smiling skull paintball masks. And that side has . . . yup, zombie paintball masks."

Chapter Twenty-five

"This is just great," Freddie said. "I brought a Scarecrow and a Cowardly Lion to the paintball apocalypse."

The three of us just stared at the horrifying tableau waiting for us in the field backlit by the sun. Even worse? The skulls and zombies were starting to look back at us. It was only a couple at first, but it didn't take long before all of their terrifying faces were turning in our direction.

"You know what? I'm just going to say it," Freddie said.

Rhonda sniffed. "Say what?"

"I hate Halloween. I hate the costumes. I hate the scary movies. I hate the . . . pumpkins. You know what I want to do in the fall?"

"What?" Rhonda asked again. God only knows why.

"I want to eat butterscotch cookies, and . . . and make art with fall leaves . . . in a room full of kindergarteners."

"Oh. Me too," Rhonda said. "That sounds like fun."

Suddenly I spotted three enormous zombies headed our way. It was really hard to resist the urge to run. "Come on, guys," I said, trying to keep my voice steady. "We've got a job to do."

"Is our job dying?" Freddie asked. "Because three horsemen are coming."

The zombies pulled up their masks. Adam. Brandon. Cam. All three were laughing.

"You guys look great," Brandon said. "We're glad you could make it."

"Yeah, thanks for the heads-up about the costumes," Freddie said.

Cam punched him on the shoulder. "Sorry, man. I couldn't resist. We brought guns for you though."

Adam handed us each a gun. "You all know what you're doing with these, right?"

"Absolutely," I said, looking at the weapon in my hand. It could have been a remote control to launch a space shuttle for all I knew. Although I doubted they used remote controls to launch space shuttles.

"We thought you might need these too." Cam passed us some helmets with goggles. They weren't the cool zombie or skeleton ones, but you know, they were something.

"Okay, well, it's the regular rules," Brandon said. "Make sure you keep your masks on until the round is over, and if you get hit, leave the field."

All three of us nodded.

"And have fun," Adam said in a voice I wasn't sure I liked all that much. "I know we will."

"Don't you worry about us," I said. "We're going to have so much fun." Then all of a sudden I was shouting, "O-L-S! O-L-S!"

It didn't catch on.

All three brothers just stared at me, before Adam said, "Actually, Freddie and Rhonda, you're on Team Skulls. Erica, you're a Zombie."

Freddie chuckled. "That's what Grady said."

I shot him a look. "What does that even mean?"

He shook his head quickly. "I don't know. I'm really scared."

"Here," Rhonda said, digging into the top of her costume. "I brought these just in case." She passed Freddie some candy. "Now's the time to harness the anger."

"Candy does not make me angry!" he shouted.

"That's the spirit," she said, punching him on the other arm.

Just then something caught my eye. Mandy and Shane huddled over by a row of Honey Crisp trees. It was hard to be certain, but I was guessing by the way Mandy had her arms folded over her chest and, well, by the way Shane was flailing his hands around, that they were having a pretty intense conversation. Maybe a *baby* type conversation. Oh boy . . . and now Shane was stomping off. That couldn't be good.

"Um, guys?" I said, still looking over at the trees. "I'll catch up with all of you in a bit. I just want to say hi to Mandy."

"But Erica—" Freddie called after me.

Too late. I was already trotting my Scarecrow self away.

Oh crap, it looked like Mandy was crying. She had her hand over her face.

"Mandy," I called out, still a good distance away. I didn't want to startle her.

She quickly wiped her cheeks.

"Erica, hey, I didn't think you guys would actually come to this thing," she said, forcing a smile.

"Neither did we. Are you okay?"

"Yeah," she said, taking a hard swallow. "I'm fine. What's going on?"

"Well, we haven't actually talked since—"

"The outbuilding. Yeah." She nodded tightly. "I was kind of hoping you and Freddie could forget that whole

thing ever happened. It was just the lack of sleep talking."

"I saw Shane leave. Is everything—"

"We broke up," she said with another nod. "It's better
this way. He's going away on a fishing trip, so I'm going
to tell my brothers everything while he's gone."

"Oh no," I said, reaching for her arm. "But did you tell
Shane about—"

"Erica, I know you mean well," she said, shaking her
head some more. "But . . . can we drop it?"

I released the breath I hadn't realized I was holding.
"I . . . I just don't like seeing you like this, and I know
things have to be even harder now that we know . . . who
it was in the woods."

She looked at me with fresh tears in her eyes. "Yeah,
I guess Danny never made it to Las Vegas after all." She
bit her lip and shook her head. "It really sucks. You know
he didn't have any family. He grew up in the system. And
while he might not have been the best boyfriend, it kills
me to think that he was . . . out there the whole time, and
I didn't even look for him. Nobody looked for him." She
crossed her arms and clutched her elbows. "How sad is
that?"

"Mandy, I promise you. I'm going to find out what happened to Danny. You don't have to worry—"

"Please, Erica. You want to help? Just forget everything I said." And with that she walked away.

I almost chased after her, but I didn't want to push.
Besides, I was still a pregnancy genie. Any reasonable
request had to be granted. I could give her some space,
but I wasn't about to forget everything. I couldn't. Too
much had happened. I also couldn't forget that Mandy
was a Honeycutt, and I was pretty sure she would do
anything to protect her family if she needed to. She may
not know for sure if her brothers were involved with

Danny's death, but I was starting to think she at least suspected . . . something.

I headed back toward the herd of zombies, throwing a little wave at the first group of the undead. I got a couple of nods and waves back. It was possible I knew them . . . you know, when they were still alive.

Cam trotted over to me with his mask up. "Hey, Erica, you don't have to look so freaked. Just stick with me, you'll be fine."

"Are you sure?" I asked, looking around. "Everyone here seems like they take this very seriously."

"Nah, it's all in good fun," he said with a smile. He suddenly looked so earnest. Like the little boy I used to babysit again. It was killing me to think he could have been involved in Danny's death. "When the air horn sounds we're just going to run for that wooden wall over there," he said with a point. "That's the dead zone. They can't shoot you there."

If only there was a way I could just start over there.

"Once we reach the zone, if you want, you can stay there. The rest of us will head on. No shame."

"Cool."

"But get ready because we're about to—"

The air horn blasted.

"Run!"

Chapter Twenty-six

Run?

I wasn't ready to run.

I didn't even know how to work my gun!

This was all happening too fast.

I ran over the plowed field as fast as my hay legs would carry me.

Whompf! Whompf! Whompf!

Whoa! Paintballs! Paintballs everywhere!

Why?

Why was I doing this? Suddenly I couldn't seem to remember.

And why did people do this for fun? This wasn't fun.

Thankfully, though, I guess I wasn't seen as much of a threat because I hadn't been hit yet. In fact, I was almost at the wall. How the heck had that happened? I could see why these rounds were only five minutes. It's amazing how time changes when paint is flying around you.

Maybe I could make it to the dead zone without being hit. That would be a win for me. I didn't need to capture any stinking flag.

I pumped my legs and arms with everything that I had in me. I was going to make it. I was actually going to make—

Whompf!

"Son of a—"

Pain exploded in my thigh as I rolled to the ground. Feet thudded past me as a neon-yellow ball exploded a foot from my face. I needed to get out of here. Army-crawl! It was my best chance to get to the dead zone without getting hit again.

I dug my elbows and knees into the dirt. Just a little farther. Just a little—

Suddenly someone grabbed my arms and pulled me the last few feet until I was safely behind the plywood.

"Cam?!" I yelled.

"Yeah?" he said, smiling.

"That really hurt!"

"Stings, doesn't it?"

"Why do you guys like this so much?"

He just laughed some more.

"Okay," I said with a groan. "Well, that was interesting, but I'm out. You go on ahead," I said, shooing him on. I could always find time to ask him questions later.

"No, you're still in," Cam said, pointing to where I was clutching my leg. "The paintball didn't explode."

"What?" I shrieked. I looked down at my burlap pants. Not even a drop of paint. "What kind of stupid rule is that?"

He laughed again. I was glad this was so entertaining for him.

"You know what?" I said, pulling off my helmet. "I'm just going to stay here. You can go on without me."

Whompf!

What the . . . ? I thought they weren't supposed to shoot at us when we were in the dead zone?

"Put your helmet back on," Cam said, reaching for me.

Whompf!

Cam looked around trying to find the shooter while I struggled to get the helmet back over my head, but my hands weren't working. All the adrenaline and—

Whompf!

I was yelling again. Yelling lots of obscenities. Not because of the pain though.

"Erica?" Cam said, grabbing my arms. I knew he was right in front of me, but I couldn't see him. All I could see was the color blue. "Are you okay?"

"I can't see anything. The paint . . ."

"I am so sorry. Let's get you out of here."

I let him lift me to my feet and lead me from the field. I didn't have a choice.

So much for not going anywhere with a brother alone.

Chapter Twenty-seven

"Are you okay?"

I blinked a few times. "I think so." The paintball had hit me in the shoulder actually. It was the splatter that got me.

"Have a seat," Cam said. "I've got some bottled water here somewhere."

Cam had led me . . . over to some sort of building. Again, it was kind of hard to see. My sight was starting to come back to me though. At least in my left eye. My right had taken the brunt, and I wasn't quite ready to open it aside from a quick blink. I shuffled over to some boxes. Huh, was that a wooden beer crate? That could work.

"No, not there," he said, rushing over. "There's a bench over here."

Well, why hadn't he said that in the first place? I couldn't see anything.

He took me by the arm and led me over to the bench. "Hey, where are we?" I squinted around the room with my good eye—too big to be a shed, but with tin walls. Uh-oh. And the wall across from me had a counter running its length with drawers underneath. I knew that wall. Oh no. I looked up at Cam as best I could. "Are we . . . ?"

"My grandfather's workshop. Where the whole thing went down."

I looked around again. Yup, this right here was where Mandy and I had pulled our epic revenge prank that went so wrong. I still didn't think Cam was a killer, but if he was, this would definitely be the spot he would choose to do the deed. Or at least it was where I would choose if I were going to kill me, but I wasn't going to kill me. And neither was Cam. And that was, you know, that.

"Okay," he said, twisting the cap off a bottle of water. "Tilt your head back and try to keep your eyes open."

I did as I was told and—

"Holy frickin' crapfish!" I shouted. "That's worse than the paintball." I think the force of the water had flipped my eyelids back.

Cam laughed. "You know, you can swear in front of me. I'm not eight anymore."

"Right," I said with a chuckle. "I guess I keep forgetting that."

"I'm really sorry," Cam said, kicking a bolt across the floor. "That shouldn't have happened. Once you had been hit, nobody should have been shooting at you. Especially with your mask off."

"Did you see who it was?"

He shook his head. "I'll find out though." He passed me a cloth he had dampened with what was left of the bottle of water. "I guess the apple orchard hasn't exactly been the best job for you guys, huh?"

"Hey, we're always happy for work."

"I just mean . . . first there was the body. Then, well, I heard about what happened in the loft the other night between Adam and Shane."

I chuckled. "Oh yeah, that. I take it your brother is not a big fan of Shane's."

"No, it's fine. They're friends," Cam said, leaning against the counter. "He just didn't know Shane was with Mandy. And Shane's a good guy, but it's just . . . he can't always keep it in his pants."

I scrubbed my cheek gently with the cloth. "Oh."

"Mandy's never been good at picking winners." He reached over to a minifridge on the floor. "You want a beer?"

Part of me did because of all the stinging in my shoulder and thigh, but I needed to keep my wits about me. Who knew where the next paintball might be coming from? "No, I'm good," I said. "Didn't she used to date . . . Danny?" God, why was I bringing this up in a creepy old workshop with no witnesses around? Oh right, probably because I was a private investigator and this was what private investigators did. At least, that had been the point I had been trying to make with Grady. It had seemed a lot less scary in bed.

"As I said, Mandy's dated a lot of losers." Cam walked over to the counter, leaned his back against it, and folded his arms over his chest.

And just like that the mood had changed completely. We weren't old friends reminiscing, and we both knew it.

"You know," he said suddenly, "I wouldn't blame you guys if you just bagged off."

I frowned. "You mean from the tournament?"

"I mean from everything," he said, twisting the cap off a bottle. "This job has to suck. I would totally get it if OLS wanted to bail."

"Oh no, we're cool," I said carefully. Carefully, because I didn't want him to know that my heart was suddenly beating about a hundred times faster. The first time he had said it, I didn't think that much of it. But now I was really getting the impression that he wanted us gone, and I was pretty sure that he wasn't even trying to be subtle. "I mean, it's been a lot of fun hanging out at the orchard again. Unless there is some reason you guys—"

"No, not all." He took a long swig of beer. "It's awesome having you and Freddie around." He chuckled. "He really is afraid of the Apple Witch, isn't he?"

Oh, that chuckle of his was not the carefree chuckle he had earlier. "Yeah, Freddie's always been a bit superstitious." I squinted at him. "But be honest with me."

He raised his brow in question.

"Are you sure you didn't see anything in the cornfield that night?"

"Nope," Cam said, shaking his head. He snapped his fingers. "I guess I missed the Apple Witch again."

"So you're not a believer?"

"Well, some pretty messed-up things have happened at the orchard, but no, I'm not a believer." Cam suddenly brightened. "But you already know all about those messed-up things, don't you?"

I froze. Suddenly the conversation of the three brothers behind the hay bales flashed through my mind. Was he testing me? Trying to find out what I knew?

"The prank? When we were kids?"

"Oh, yeah, that was messed up. I had no idea—"

"It's all cool," he said. "It was a good one." He grimaced with mock terror. "I don't think I've ever been that scared."

Suddenly the door burst open.

"Erica!" the Tin Man shouted.

"Freddie?"

"I got the flag!" he shouted, holding up a piece of cloth.

"No you didn't."

"Sure I did," he said, shaking it at me. "It's right here."

I looked him up and down. "But you're covered in paint."

Freddie looked down at his front. "Okay, fine. It was a team effort. I had to do a *Full Metal Jacket* thing, so Rhonda could get the flag. But she totally wouldn't have been able to do it without me. And she said I could keep it for a souvenir." He looked back and forth between Cam and me. "Everything all right in here?"

"Yup," I said with a nod. "Cam has been taking good care of me."

Chapter Twenty-eight

"Ow. Ow. Ow. Pass me the popcorn," I said, lightly smacking the edge of the table with my good hand. Actually my other hand was okay, but it was attached to the arm that was attached to my very sore shoulder.

"Can't. Broken."

"Come on, Freddie. Just slide it down the table with your foot. I can't reach."

"I really can't."

Suddenly a voice came from the phone propped up on the table facing the TV. "Freddie," it cajoled.

Despite my pain, a satisfied smile spread across my face. The voice was Sean's, Freddie's boyfriend. He often half watched movies with us while studying. It helped them keep their long-distance love alive. I liked it too. Freddie had to be nice—or at least nicer—when Sean was around, so now he had to pass me the popcorn. He knew it too because he mouthed the words *you suck* out of Sean's sight line then slid the popcorn in my direction.

"Thank you, Freddie," I said sweetly. "Thank you, Se—" I had to stop talking for a moment because of the woman screaming on the TV. I turned to Rhonda. "Can you turn it down a little?"

"No way," she said, tossing some popcorn in her mouth. "That ruins the experience. You have to feel the fear."

I sighed. Yup, Rhonda had somehow managed to pop another horror movie in. Actually, I know how she did it. Freddie and I were too weak to fight, and Sean was just so nice, he supported everyone's dreams—even Rhonda's thirty-one days of horror.

We had all survived our paintball experience. Some of us better than others. Rhonda, for example, had not been hit. Not even once. I guess her police training had helped her out. And now she and Freddie were sitting on the couch whereas I was on the floor in a beanbag chair. Not quite sure how that happened. Even Freddie's mini French bulldog, Stanley, had a good spot on the couch. But again, in fairness, he was eight thousand years old.

I stretched my arm out again and wiggled my fingers trying to reach my beer. Just short. I dropped my arm and flung my head back. I'd ask Sean to ask Freddie to pass it to me in a minute, but in the meantime, there were some things we needed to discuss about the day's events— murderous leprechaun on the TV screen or not. Well, at least Freddie and I could discuss them. Rhonda was too busy watching the movie, and Sean had an exam on hormones and glands or something that he needed to study for. "Anyway, I'm telling you, I still don't see Cam as a killer, but I definitely got the vibe that he was warning us off investigating."

"What exactly did he say?" Freddie asked with a groan as he shifted positions.

"Just that he'd totally get it if OLS wanted to bail on this job."

"Yeah, but how did he say it?"

"What do you mean how did he say it? He just said

that he would understand if we wanted to bail on this job, given the body, and Adam threatening Shane with the pitchfork, and now the paintball."

"But was he saying it in a threatening voice?"

"No, not like that," I said, shaking my head, staring at the ceiling. "I mean, he didn't push it."

"What did you say?" Rhonda asked in a super-interested voice before switching to something much darker and adding, "Is what I would be asking you if we weren't watching a movie!"

I ignored that last part and just answered the question. "That we were fine," I said with a half shrug that shot pain through my body. "Happy for the work. That kind of thing." I turned to Rhonda. "What were your impressions of Adam?"

"You know, it worries me when you guys go after murderers," Sean suddenly piped up from the phone.

"It's fine, baby," Freddie said. "You don't have to worry. Focus on your test." He said it in a really sweet tone, but he rolled his eyes at me, once again out of Sean's sight line of course. It was all for show though. I knew Freddie was so into Sean that it scared the crap out of him, and that sometimes led to bad behavior. Thankfully, Sean was pretty patient with Freddie—probably because he was just as into him.

"No," the phone answered, "I want to hear what Rhonda has to say about this guy."

Rhonda sighed and paused the movie. "Fierce competitor. Military precision on the field. Worthy adversary." She pressed the remote to restart the movie.

"But do you think he could kill someone?" Freddie asked.

She sighed—with more annoyance this time—and paused the movie again. "Absolutely. With the blink of an eye, but . . ." She frowned at the man on the TV screen, frozen, mid-death. "I can't really see him committing a crime of passion, and I can't see him involving his family. If he were going to kill someone, he'd do it himself, and he wouldn't drag anyone else into it."

"I don't know about the passion thing," Freddie grumbled. "You didn't see him with the pitchfork to Shane's chest. That seemed like a pretty passionate act."

"Pitchfork?" Sean repeated in an alarmed voice.

Freddie made an uh-oh face. "It wasn't . . . a real pitchfork."

"Freddie," the voice said in a warning tone.

"Baby, we've talked about this."

"I know we've talked about this, but—"

"And you shouldn't be worrying about me. You've got a big exam tomorrow, and you really need to study," he said, leaning forward and reaching for his phone. "I'm just going to put you on mute for one min—"

"Freddie! Don't you put me on—"

"Love you, baby. There," Freddie said, tapping his screen then putting the phone facedown on the table. "I really do love that man, but— What?" he asked, looking at me. Probably noting my horrified face. "He knows I gotta be me."

I shook my head.

"I'll make it up to him. Now where were we?"

Okay, regardless of how into Sean Freddie was, sometimes I really did worry that he and I were going to die alone . . . together. Neither of us knew what we were doing when it came to relationships. "Um, what were your impressions of Brandon?"

Rhonda got the movie going again.

"Oh, he's a sketchy one," Freddie said. "Everything he says is perfect. Slick. Sneaky . . . just like my research said he would be."

"Huh."

"It's like trying to pin down Jell-O. He's not going to make any stupid mistakes. Oh! Oh!" Freddie said, pushing himself up in the couch again. "And you know what else?"

"I give up," Rhonda said, stopping the movie and throwing the remote on the couch. "We're never going to get through all seven *Leprechaun* movies at this rate."

"It's a Halloween miracle," Freddie shouted, throwing his hands in the air. "But what I was going to say, was that Brandon totally did not seem surprised when my gun jammed."

Rhonda and I exchanged looks. "So you think they gave us defective guns?"

"It's possible," Freddie said. "They want us gone. Why not make the experience as unpleasant as possible?"

"So, what's next?" Rhonda asked.

"I know! I know!" I said excitedly—then groaned. That was too much enthusiasm for my injured state.

Rhonda and Freddie were staring at me still groaning on the beanbag chair.

"What? I know," I said. "Cam said that Mandy always picked losers for boyfriends."

"Okay."

"He kind of implied that they all cheated."

"Again, okay."

I raised my eyebrows. "So who did Danny cheat with?"

Rhonda frowned. "I don't know. Who?"

"No," I said. "I don't know the answer."

Rhonda shook her head. "I don't either."

"I know you don't know either," I said. "I mean, we have to find out."

"Oh," Rhonda said in a very knowing tone.

"And how are we going to do that?" Freddie asked.

"Well, we need to ask around or something," I said, throwing my head back again. "I can't do all the work here. You guys need to help out."

"You mean like Mandy's friends?" Rhonda asked.

"It's not a big town," I said. "We just have to talk to the early-twenties age group."

"Ew," Freddie said. "I hate early-twenty-somethings almost as much as I hate teenagers. I think I was born old."

I tried to straighten up in my beanbag chair, but the beans shifted, and I slid right back down. "Where do all the early-twenties people hang out these days?"

"The same place they've always hung out," Rhonda said. "That club on Highway 9."

"What club on Highway 9?"

Freddie looked at me. "We didn't start going there until after you left town. You need ID to get in."

"What's it called?"

"The Palace," Rhonda and Freddie said at the same time.

"The Palace?"

"That right there," Freddie said, pointing to my face. "That nose curl you're doing to indicate disgust. You're going to want to save that look."

"Why? What for?"

Rhonda grimaced then said, "The Palace is like a strange mix of the clubs from the Jersey Shore and an angler's pro shop."

I shook my head. "I'm having trouble picturing that."

"It's hard to understand even when you're there."

From the corner of my eye, I could see Rhonda was already looking at her phone. "Says on their Web page they're having a Halloween bash tomorrow night."

"We could go after the orchard," I said . . . to the ceiling. I still couldn't manage to get up. Suddenly my phone buzzed. I grabbed it from where it was resting on my lap and looked at the number. "Shut up. Shut up. Grady's calling."

"You're not going to lie to him, are you?" Freddie asked.

"Are *you* seriously going to try to give *me* relationship advice right now?" I said, throwing a pointed look to the phone on the table.

"What? I'm looking out for him. He needs to study."

"And no," I said. "I'm not going to lie to him."

"But you're not going to tell the truth, right?" Rhonda asked. "You know about his triggers."

"I know all about his trigger—"

Freddie snickered before I could make it plural.

"I told you Grady and I are in a good place." And that was still all I wanted to tell them. What had happened between Grady and me had happened so unexpectedly. Well, maybe not that unexpectedly given that we had been talking about taking our relationship to the next level, but whatever. It was all so new. I wanted to be sure I knew exactly what it was we were doing—and that we weren't going to screw it up epically—before I told anyone. "Hey—" I cleared my throat. I started off at a way too girly pitch there. "Hey, you," I said in a much more friendly and less of a "we just slept together" tone.

"Hey. I've been trying to get a hold of you," Grady said. "What have you been up to? Following up leads? Looking under rocks? Getting ready to lose our little bet?"

"Whoa," I said. "There will be no losing—" I suddenly remembered that Freddie and Rhonda were staring at me. "Um, there will be no losing of our friendship."

"I take it you're not alone," Grady said with a chuckle.

"No, Freddie and Rhonda are here. Well, actually we're all at Freddie's watching a movie."

"And I take it they don't know about—"

"Nope. Nope. Kind of want to keep it that way."

"Are you lying to him about the investigation?" Rhonda whispered pretty loudly.

I shook my head at her.

"But you are lying to them," Grady said with a chuckle. I guess he overheard Rhonda's whisper.

"No. No," I said, lightly scratching the back of my head. "I'm just—"

"She's lying to him," Freddie said.

"I like being on this side of the equation," my phone said.

"Okay, everybody stop talking," I said. I was getting pretty confused about who I was lying to and why. "Grady, what do you want?" I didn't mean to say it like that, but I was really overstimulated.

"Oh nothing," he said. "Just to let you know that I am getting all sorts of new forensics reports in for the investigation. You know, because I am sheriff—"

"Yeah, yeah, yeah," I said. I couldn't help but smile. He sounded happy. This bet thing was way better than all the fighting we used to do. "You're sheriff."

"She's definitely lying," Freddie said.

"So I guess I just wanted to say good luck and happy movie watching."

"Just because we're watching a movie doesn't mean we're not—" Rhonda and Freddie were still looking at me. "Going to want pizza later."

"What?"

I covered my face with my hand. "I don't know. I gotta go."

"Oh, but Erica?"

"Uh-huh."

"The other night was—"

"Awesome," I said, and quickly ended the call. Lord only knew if he started talking about that, well, there'd be no way I could hide it from Freddie and Rhonda. Not with all the blushing I'd be doing.

"So are you in trouble with Grady?" Rhonda asked.

"No. No," I said with an awkward chuckle. "More like he's in trouble with me, know what I'm saying?"

"No, what are you saying?" Freddie asked, while taking a quick peek at the screen of his phone. I guess he didn't like what he saw there, so he quickly put it back down and muttered, "It will be fine. I'll do a search for apology gifts later," before looking back at me.

"I'm saying . . ." I said, shaking my head, hoping a good lie would pop into my head. "Put in the fourth Leprechaun movie, Rhonda. I've been dying to see that one."

"Leprechaun in Space?"

"That's the one," I said with a finger wag that quickly lost its energy. "Can't wait."

The next morning I borrowed my mom's boat and headed into town. I was meeting up with Freddie and Rhonda to discuss costume options for our clubbing experience later on and had some time to kill. I thought now might be a good time to read up on the Apple Witch. I mean, obviously, I didn't believe she existed, but someone wanted us to believe she did. The most likely option was that it was the Honeycutts trying to scare us off. I didn't know who they enlisted to dress up as the witch and hide out in that cornfield, but I was determined to find out, so it couldn't hurt to find out as much as possible about the legend. Of course, there was the awkward problem of the librarian who probably didn't want me hanging around Freddie anymore.

I trotted up the library steps and boldly walked inside.

"Erica Bloom, I thought I rescinded your library privileges."

"What?" I squeaked. I was trying to keep my voice low. It was a library after all. "I didn't think you were serious. Is that actually a thing?"

"You abused library equipment."

I heard a couple of snickers. Huh, the preteen boys were back at the computers. This was so unfair.

"But Freddie told you, we didn't know what was on the tape. Come on, Mrs. Robinson."

"Well, I suppose I could reinstate your status if you were willing to sign a code-of-conduct form." She slid a piece of paper across her counter.

"Sure," I said.

"That I will then post on the corkboard by the front door."

My jaw dropped, but I grabbed a pen from her little cup of pens—a mug actually that said, *When in doubt ask a Librarian*. "This is a public shaming, is it?"

"I need to be sure you won't do it again."

"Did Freddie have to sign the form?" I asked, looking from my paper up at her.

"That is not your business."

He so didn't have to sign the form.

I glanced over the paper then quickly signed my name at the bottom. I slid the paper back to her.

"Wonderful," she said. "Now is there something I can do for you?"

I would have just taken the book I had seen on the table last time we had been in, but it was gone.

"I, uh, was looking for some information." I suddenly realized that asking her straight-out about the Apple Witch maybe wasn't the greatest idea. It would spread pretty quickly through town and then everybody would know we were investigating, and it wouldn't take long for that information to get back to the apple orchard. Best to keep it light and breezy.

"You've come to the right place," she said. "What kind of information are you looking for?"

I scratched my temple. "Just, uh, town history and stuff."

"Anything in particular?" she prodded. I could tell by the look on her face that she didn't think I was a suitable playmate for her adopted son.

"No. No," I said, chewing my lip. "I'm just kind of interested in all of it. I mean, I've lived in this town most of my life and know so little about it."

"Well, I have a wonderful book on early New Hampshire towns. It's in the reference section," she said, coming around the counter. "Follow—"

"Um, well, actually," I said, putting my finger in the air. "You know what would be more fun? And seasonal?"

She smiled and raised her eyebrows in question.

"I guess because it's Halloween and all," I said with an "I'm about to suggest something crazy" shrug. "I think it might be fun to read up on some ghost stories."

"Oh, I have a delightful book just in on Jebediah Moore. He was a sea captain—"

Oh for the love of— "I want to know about the Apple Witch. We're working at the apple orchard, and I was curious." I chuckled a little. "I just didn't want anyone to think I believed—"

"Erica," Mrs. Robinson said, smile dropping from her face. "The Apple Witch is not a laughing matter."

The intensity of her look stopped me from answering for a moment. "I'm sorry. I didn't mean to . . . I don't really believe in ghosts."

"Strange things have happened in the woods around the apple orchard."

It took everything in me not to sigh. "I've . . . heard."

She dropped her glasses down her nose, so she could

look me in the eye. "And the story, the story of . . . that poor woman is one filled with torment and pain."

I blinked. "That poor woman?"

"You do know Dorit Honeycutt's story, don't you?"

"Wait. Is that the . . . was she really the ancestor of the Honeycutts?"

"Oh yes," Mrs. Robinson said with a nod. "God rest her soul."

"Well, I don't really know much. Freddie seems to think that she goes after young women in the woods. But I swear the twins told me at some point that it's men that she . . ." I didn't know exactly what she did to men, so I just made a scary face.

"She had reason to hate both," Mrs. Robinson said with very wide eyes. "Follow me."

A moment later we were in the far back corner of the library.

"Let me see. Let me see. I've already checked out one copy, but . . . here," she said, tipping a book by its top edge from the stack to slide it free. "This has all the answers you're looking for."

I nodded and took the worn book in my hands.

"Now you read it cover to cover," she said.

"Right. Sure."

"And you promise me you'll read it before you go into the woods again."

"Okay."

She nodded, seemingly satisfied with that response, and she led me back to the counter and checked out the book for me without any more trouble. I thanked her and headed for the door.

Well, all in all that hadn't been too bad. Code-of-conduct notices notwithstanding. I pushed the door of the library open and—

"Brandon?"

Chapter Twenty-nine

"Hey, Erica."

Yup, Brandon Honeycutt. What a coincidence. He was wearing a green canvas jacket, not unlike Grady's, and had his hands shoved deep in his jeans pockets. It was a casual look. Down-to-earth. Kind of terrifying. Maybe it was because he was standing right at the foot of the stairs. There was no easy way I could get around him.

"Hey."

He smiled. It was friendly enough, but I wouldn't call it warm. "We're just running into each other all over the place."

"Yeah," I said with a chuckle. I dropped my foot onto the first step hoping that would cause him to make room for me to pass, but, nope, he wasn't budging. I brought it back up.

"Whatcha got there?" he asked, tilting his head to read the spine of my book.

"This?" I slapped my other hand over the book. "Oh, it's nothing. Girl stuff."

He frowned in question. "Girl stuff?"

"You know, sex with billionaires . . . in exotic

locations." It wasn't my usual reading, but Rhonda had told me it was a pretty big deal.

"Are you sure? Because I could have sworn . . ." Brandon tilted his head again to look at the book in my hand. "Yup, yup, we have that book. New Hampshire ghost stories. It has a big section on the Apple Witch."

"What?" I said in a super-high voice. "Mrs. Robinson must have given me the wrong one." I looked over my shoulder back toward the library. That was right at my back. Because I couldn't get down the stairs. "Do you believe that? I think she needs a new prescription for her glasses."

"Don't tell me Freddie really is getting to you with all his ghost stuff," he said, putting one foot up on the edge of the bottom step.

"No, no . . . no." I had tried to think of something more plausible right there. It just didn't come out.

"Right," he said with a laugh. "Well, I was hoping to run into you."

"You were?" I mean, the question just popped out of my mouth, but I was thinking it was a good one. Brandon hadn't been heading into the library while I was heading out. It was actually feeling a lot like he was waiting for me. And if he was waiting for me, then he knew I had gone in, which meant he had either seen me by chance or . . . he was following me.

"Yeah," he said with a smile that was supposed to communicate that he was surprised that I was surprised he'd want to run into me. Well, I was surprised! I was indeed. "I spotted you from the Dawg," he said, jerking his thumb back in the restaurant's direction, "and I just wanted to make sure you were okay after the whole paintball thing."

Huh, I see. He was a slick one. And possibly psychic.

I definitely didn't remember him being this way as a child. "Oh yeah, I'm fine. It was no big deal."

"Good. Good," he said, not moving his stupid foot from that bottom step. "You know we all care about you."

"What?"

"Yeah, you were totally our favorite babysitter. We all think you're awesome."

Liar. Liar. Pants on freaking fire. I hadn't forgotten his Xbox comment.

"We just all felt so bad when you got hurt."

I did not believe that at all. Especially not from him. And the creepiest part of all was that he wasn't even really trying to hide it. It was like he wanted me to know that he was lying. Which I guess would make sense if this whole conversation was . . . what? A warning? A threat? I was thinking more and more our running into each other wasn't a coincidence at all.

"That's so nice."

"Yeah," he said, looking away and taking a deep breath. "So will we still be seeing you guys at the orchard? I mean, it's almost Halloween, we'd understand if, you know, you wanted to cut it short."

This was it. He was offering me my out. But we both knew it was more than that.

"Are you kidding me? Leave you shorthanded right before Halloween?" I walked down the steps, forcing him to move. "You're not getting rid of us that easily."

Chapter Thirty

"This is fun!"

"What?"

"I said . . . this . . . is . . . fun!"

"What?"

I shook my head. No way I was going to be able to make myself heard over the thumping music. It didn't help that Freddie was wearing a mask that covered his entire head. So instead of shouting again, I jabbed a thumb over to the far side of the club. We were too close to the speakers to have any sort of communication.

Freddie, or Darth, nodded then he cut us a path through the crowd with his red lightsaber. Once again, we'd missed the boat in the costume department. Everybody here was dressed in hunting camouflage. Some were dressed in sexy camouflage. And I had spotted more than a few sexy deer.

Once we made it to the other side, Freddie propped up his mask and said, "I didn't think it was possible for me to hate this place any more than I already did, but I do."

"Oh cheer up," I said, elbowing him. "We've never gone clubbing together. This is a first."

"We are too old to go clubbing."

"No we're not."

"We have passed the clubbing window," he said. "And just so you know, when the kids look at you, they are not imagining the gold bikini Carrie Fisher. They're picturing the bad guy's mom."

I frowned and adjusted my side buns. I was fine with that. It beat being a sexy deer, and, you know, being mounted on somebody's wall. That sounded all kinds of wrong in my head. "Maybe we should just stick to talking about the reason why we came here in the first place. Work."

"No, no, no," Freddie said, wagging a black-gloved finger in the air. "Work is something you get paid for. We are not getting paid for this, so it is not work."

"Then what would you like to call it?"

"Tomfoolery."

I sighed. "Have I mentioned you're being a real good sport about losing the vote?"

"Thank you," Freddie said . . . without any sarcasm?

I gave my head a shake. "Okay, so how are we going to infiltrate this—"

"Hey guys!"

"Chewbacca!"

Chewbacca and I high-fived.

"You look awesome," I said.

"Thanks," Rhonda replied, pulling up her mask. "It's hot in here though." We had gone to a costume shop this time to deck ourselves out. Rhonda got Chewbacca because she was the tallest of the three of us.

"Rhonda. Thank God," Freddie said. "Erica's not letting me have any fun."

"What? What are you talk—" He rolled his eyes. Oh, he was just teasing me.

Rhonda leaned toward me and said, "He been into the candy again?"

"I think so."

She nodded and leaned back. She then slapped her furry hands together and said, "Now this is what I'm talking about. Undercover work. I love it."

"We're not undercover," Freddie said. "We are questioning people. We are only doing it in costume because it is this wretched holiday."

Rhonda planted her hands on her hips. "You ate the rockets this time, didn't you? They're straight sugar, Freddie. You know you can't handle straight—"

"Okay, okay," I shouted. "Let's just focus, so Freddie can go home."

"Does that mean you and I are going to stay and par-tay?" Rhonda said.

I shrugged. "Maybe." I felt like I'd missed this whole part of the Otter Lake experience.

"High-five," Rhonda said, raising her paw in the air.

I slapped it again.

Freddie raised his hand in the air, but not to high-five us; I think he was trying to crush our throats like his namesake did in the movies.

"Come on, Freddie," I said. "This . . . this is what we do. You know that. You're always the first one who wants to go after murderers."

"Flesh-and-blood murderers. Not supernatural murderers."

"This is a flesh-and-blood murderer," I shouted. Thank God I was in a very loud club because that might have made me stand out otherwise. "You know that deep down. And I didn't want to say it before, because I was trying to protect your feelings, but this flesh-and-blood murderer, I think, is maybe trying to make a fool of you."

Freddie frowned. "What's this now?"

I shrugged. "The entire town is talking about how afraid you are of the Apple Witch. And when I say talking . . ." I made a cringey face. "I mean laughing." I had no idea if that was true, but if we were going to solve this crime, we needed Freddie at his best. And we needed to solve this crime. Not just because I had a bet to win with Grady, but I needed to know what was going on at the orchard. More importantly, Mandy needed to know. I knew the first trimester was hard on women, but she was not looking so great last I'd seen her.

"Nobody is . . . laughing," Freddie said, but the way his eyebrows were twitching I could tell he wasn't sure.

I shrugged. "If you say so."

"You know, you're being weird about this whole thing," Freddie said with an angry finger point. "You're always the one who wants to put the brakes on investigations. Always worried about *what Grady will think*." He made a weird girly voice for that last bit. "So what is going on? And when did you start looking so happy?"

I froze. "I don't look happy."

"Uh-huh."

"Could we please just get on with this?" furry Rhonda asked. "Because I am so going to take this party to the next galaxy." She let out a yell that I guess was supposed to sound like Chewbacca. The crowd liked it.

"Let's do it," I said.

"Freddie?"

"Fine. But only because we're already here," he said. "And I am not happy about it." He flipped his Darth Vader mask down.

"Okay," I said, rubbing my hands together. "Let's start mingling."

We all went our separate ways, cutting our own paths through the crowd.

Where to start? Where to start? I thought I recognized a lot of faces—it was hard to tell with all the camo makeup—but I couldn't remember a lot of names. Maybe I just needed to start up random conversations with people. Maybe with the three young men staring at me. Oh, and now that they caught me looking at them, all three were raising their beers. This was going to be easier than I thought.

"Hey guys," I said, walking up. Unfortunately, the closer I got, the drunker they looked.

"Hey," one of the guys said, leaning on his buddy. "Are you Erica Bloom?"

"And . . . good-bye." I spun back around. I was guessing by their goofy laughter they knew me from the Raspberry Social where I flashed everyone holding the town mascot. They probably would have been about twelve at the time. Probably made an impression.

"Good choice," a young woman standing at a pedestal table beside me said.

"Oh, I . . . was it?"

"Yeah, you don't want to talk to those three. They had an Erica Bloom fan club back in eighth grade. I'm not sure they could handle meeting their idol," she said with a cute nose wrinkle. "I like the costume by the way."

"Yeah, we obviously didn't read the Web site well enough. I didn't realize this was a hunter-deer party." But hey, wait a minute. I eyed the young woman in front of me. She wasn't a hunter . . . or a deer. "You weren't in the mood to dress up?"

"Whatever do you mean?" she asked with mock horror. "You don't like my costume?" She straightened up and held her flannel shirt open. Underneath she wore a black T-shirt with a sign stapled to the front. It said NO HUNTING. TRESPASSERS WILL BE PROSECUTED.

I laughed. "Cute. I like it."

"Thanks," she said with a happy shrug. "So, what's the famous Erica Bloom doing at the Palace? I'm pretty sure this isn't your usual stomping ground."

I smiled. "I know I don't know you, but this, uh, doesn't really seem like your kind of place either." I gestured to the sign on her shirt.

"Yeah, I grew up with all these knuckleheads though. We can't help but love each other. Besides, there isn't much else to do in Otter Lake."

"I get it."

"Didn't you move to Chicago for a while?" she asked, before taking a sip of her beer.

"I did. I did. But Otter Lake pulled me back."

She huffed a laugh. "Like a giant black hole."

I laughed. Wow, I really liked this person. I kind of felt bad about the fact that I was about to hit her up for information. But I had to. That's what Grady would do, and I was every bit the professional he was. "Um—"

"Your mother runs Earth, Moon, and Stars, doesn't she?" she suddenly asked.

Or we could just chat a bit more. "Yes, yes, she does."

"That is so cool."

"You think so?" Nobody from Otter Lake had ever said that before.

"She's a vegan too, isn't she?"

I nodded. "Yup, she's making enough vegan candy for the whole town. Not that any trick-or-treaters ever come to the island."

She laughed. "Your mom's my hero."

Yet another statement I had never heard uttered among the citizenry of Otter Lake. I couldn't tell if she meant that or not. "It would make her happy to hear you say that." I looked around the club to see if Freddie and Rhonda were doing a better job of getting information out of people, and . . . oh well, would you look at that. Chewie was jumping up and down in a crowd of people on the dance floor while Freddie was trying to get his lightsaber back from a group of hunters. Guess this was all on me.

She smiled. "Hey, you were also a hero of mine back in the day. Going topless to stick it to the patriarchy." She raised a fist in the air.

"Yeah, that's not exactly what happened."

"Still, you were so brav—"

"I can't do this," I said. "I came up to talk to you because I wanted information on some people you might know given your relative age and the small size of Otter Lake."

"Oh," she said, taking a bewildered sip of beer. "Okay. Thank you for telling me?"

"It's just you seem cool, and I didn't want you to say these nice things without knowing my ulterior motives."

"Huh," she said, putting her beer back on the table. "Well, I've never been one for much foreplay. So you probably want to know what I know about Mandy, and by extension Danny."

I shrugged. "Kind of."

She rolled her black-makeupped eyes. "I know Mandy was dating him, and I know he was trying to date everyone else."

"Really?"

"Oh yeah, dude totally tried to get me in bed with his whole ghost-hunting shtick."

"I take it, it didn't work."

"No, it didn't. He tried to convince everyone that he was like this legit paranormal investigator, but I'm pretty sure he was just a dude with a camcorder. And taking grainy video of shadows in the woods doesn't really do it for me, you know?"

"Did it work on anyone else?"

She shook her head. "Well, yeah, but I know what you're thinking, and the person Danny actually managed to screw around with . . . she's . . . well, there's no way she had anything to do with Danny's death."

"You sound pretty sure."

"I am," she said, nodding her head to the beat of the music.

"Well, I'd still like to talk to her. Where can I find her?"

She smiled. "At the post office. Monday to Friday. Nine to four."

Chapter Thirty-one

"I drank too much."

"Yes, yes you did."

"When did it all change?" Rhonda asked, putting her forehead down on her hands. "I used to be able to go out every night of the week."

"Twenty-six," Freddie said, taking a sip of coffee. "I never had a hangover before twenty-six."

"Hey, at least we got a lead out of it," I said brightly.

Just then Big Don put a plate in front of me. Oh yeah, the Lumberjack's Breakfast. Two eggs, two pieces of bacon, two sausages, hash browns, toast, and a piece of pecan pie. Okay, fine, the pecan pie was a side order. Big Don made really good pecan pie. And I needed my strength. We had a big day in front of us once we finished having breakfast at the Dawg.

"I still can't believe that Becca Davies was involved with Danny," Freddie said.

"I'm not surprised," Rhonda said. It was hard to hear her. Her face was still on the table. "Her mother put a lot of pressure on her growing up."

I broke off a piece of my toast. "Oh yeah?"

"Well, I mean her father's the reverend, and I think her mom wanted her to be this perfect example of . . . perfection for the community." Rhonda groaned. I think that observation took a lot out of her.

"We need to figure out who's going to talk to Becca," Freddie said.

"Why don't we all just go in?" I mumbled through some bacon.

"I'm not going to do it," Rhonda said. "Especially after last night. I spent too much on alcohol."

"Yeah, I hear you," Freddie said.

"I don't understand," I mumbled some more.

"Have you been starving to death and we just didn't notice?" Freddie asked. "Don't talk with your mouth full."

"Sorry," I mumbled.

"Becca sells products," Rhonda said from the table.

I swallowed hard. "Products? I thought she worked at the post office. What kind of products does she sell?"

"She does both. She works at the post office and sells products. Kitchen products. Candles. Bulbs. Tupperware."

I frowned. "Light bulbs?"

"No, like bulbs you plant in your garden." Rhonda groaned. "Come on, Erica. Get with the program. I can't use extra words to explain . . . the things."

Rhonda really wasn't doing well. "So she's like one of those women who throw lingerie parties out of her home?" I'd been to one of those back in Chicago. I learned more than I ever wanted to know about my co-workers' love for thongs.

"Lingerie?" Freddie said with a chuckle. "Oh no, no, no, no."

"Not Becca," Rhonda added.

"She would be disowned," Freddie said. "By her mother. Not Reverend Davies. He's cool."

"And she's got something to prove," Rhonda said. "Her mother was the top-selling Avon lady for all of New Hampshire for something like fifteen . . ."

I assumed the end of that sentence was *years*. "Okay, but I don't see why you just can't say no?"

"Guilt," Freddie said.

"Guilt?"

"Absentee church guilt," he said with a sigh.

"Oh," I said, eyeing my food. It was really unfair that Freddie wouldn't let me eat and talk at the same time. "Wait, you still go to church?"

"No, of course not," Freddie said. "But I still feel guilty about not going to church."

"Then why don't you just go to church?" I asked.

"Because it's on Sunday," Freddie said in a tone that spoke to the fact that I should already know this. "In the morning. Besides, I'm not sure I believe in . . . you know, all of it."

"Then why do you feel guilty?" I asked.

"Oh my God!" Rhonda shouted from the table. "Freddie, why are you even . . . she can't understand this." She flopped a hand in my direction.

"You're right," Freddie said, taking another sip of coffee. He then looked back at me. "It's not your fault. You were raised heathen."

"Hey." I wasn't entirely sure why I said that. I was raised heathen. But I believed in . . . stuff. "Okay, well, as the heathen, I'll question Becca." I picked up my own coffee mug. "I don't have any guilt—"

Just then the door opened.

A manly silhouette filled up the threshold of the door, sunlight blazing behind him.

I knew that manly silhouette . . . and that sheriff's hat. Grady Forrester.

He stepped inside. Deputy Amos right behind him.

"Erica?" Freddie said, snapping his fingers in my face. "Are you okay? It's just your friend Grady."

"I know it's just my friend Grady," I said with a scoff. Not sure I pulled the scoff off though. I was too overwhelmed by memories of the other night . . . and some of that overwhelmedness might have affected my delivery.

Grady smiled at me, but walked right on past, toward the bar, nodding to each citizen he passed. "Hey Don," he said in a super-loud voice. "I'm going to need your biggest coffee. Amos too."

"Oh yeah?" Don said. "Been hard at it, Sheriff?"

Grady turned from Don and leaned his back against the bar to face me. Amos tried to copy the move, but his elbow slipped off the edge. "Lots happening."

"You had a break in the case?" Don asked, passing him the coffee.

Grady turned to reach for it, but kept his eyes on me. "I'd say we're close to breaking this thing wide open."

"What is going on right now?" Freddie asked, looking between the two of us. "What is this?"

Even Rhonda lifted her head to shoot me a quizzical look.

"Don," I said, getting to my feet. "I think I'm going to need a refill too. Lots of people to talk to today. People you might never suspect."

Grady chuckled. "Oh, I don't know about that, Erica. I suspect a lot of people of a lot of things."

"Oh, I don't know about that," I said, hiking up my jeans for some unknown reason. "I've been places." Like the Palace. "I've done things." Like wear a Princess Leia costume. "That you would never imagine." All true.

"How interesting," Grady said, with a nod. He swung his gaze to his deputy. "Amos, when did you say that forensics report was coming in?"

"What report, boss?"

"You know," he said, shooting him a look. "The one that should have all the answers we need?"

"Oh . . . um . . . any minute."

"Any minute," Grady said with a nod and way too much satisfaction. "Well then, I guess we should get going."

I lowered back down into my seat. Grady walked toward the door but made a sudden stop at our table. "We missed you at the tournament this morning."

"What tournament?" Freddie asked.

Oh crap, I had forgotten about the tournament, and that meant I hadn't had a chance to warn Freddie that we had not been invited to a chamber of commerce tournament. Grady was playing dirty now.

"You weren't invit— Oh I see," Grady said with a totally fake nod. "I'm sure it was just an oversight."

"What tournament?" Freddie repeated.

"Amos?" Grady called out.

"Yeah, boss."

Grady jumped. He hadn't realized Amos was standing so close behind him. "Show Freddie the trophy."

Out of nowhere, Amos took out what looked to be a bronzed potato trophy and put it on the table.

Oh, you have got to be kidding me. I shook my head at Grady. He didn't smile or anything, but his eyes danced with glee.

"It was just a seasonal skills tournament the chamber of commerce put together for Otter Lake businesses. The sheriff's department won for overall highest score. I doubt OLS would be into it, Freddie. You guys don't like trophies, do you?"

"No, we don't," I said, once again jumping to my feet. Too bad Freddie looked like he was about to cry. "And a trophy proves nothing. It certainly doesn't mean the sheriff's department is the best . . . at anything."

Grady shrugged and polished the potato with his sleeve. "All the same, I think I have a nice spot to put this back at the department. It's a big shelf. Has room for more . . . wins."

"Really," I said with a nod. "I have a feeling it might be lonely for a while."

A small twinge of fear came to Grady's eye. Uh-oh, I just meant that he wasn't going to win the bet. Not that I would punish him by withholding—well, you know. Then I'd just be punishing myself!

"That would be so sad for my . . . potato, Erica," Grady said. "Do you really think it's going to be all alone?"

I held my position for as long as I could, but then said, "No, there's no reason for all the potatoes to be sad."

"Oh," he said, smile returning to his face. "Good."

"Yes, it is," I agreed and sat back down.

"Well, good-bye," Grady said, tipping his hat.

I shot him a little two-fingered salute.

The door shut behind Grady and Amos but still nobody was talking. Nope, just silence, until—

"Oh my God, you two had sex!" Freddie shouted. "And you didn't tell me!"

I closed my eyes. Unfortunately, that didn't stop my ears from hearing somebody say, "Well, it's about time. That friend thing was annoying."

Somebody else answered, "Yeah, I'm not sure this potato thing is going to be any better."

Chapter Thirty-two

"I don't believe this."

Freddie was stomping down the sidewalk. I had to practically skip to keep up with him.

"I'm sorry," I said. "I know I probably should have told you, but it's just so new and—"

"Are you seriously talking about you and Grady right now?" Freddie asked.

I stopped walking. "Wait, what are you talking about?"

Freddie stopped too. "About the fact that we weren't invited to the chamber of commerce potato, pumpkin tournament or whatever it's called. We are so going next year. And we are so winning." He started stomping away again, but I could hear him muttering, "I'll give that trophy a proper home . . ."

I skipped after him again. "Would you slow down? We need to wait for Rhonda." She was about half a block back.

Freddie stopped and put his hands on his hips. "Well, she did drink like a Wookiee last night," he said with a sigh. "Now, getting back to the you-and-Grady thing . . ."

I knew he wouldn't let it go for long.

"Don't get me wrong," he said, putting up his hands. "I'm really happy for you, but here's the thing I don't understand."

I waited.

"You slept together."

"Yes."

"But we're still investigating."

"Yes."

"And that's what I don't understand," he said. "I thought sleeping with Grady meant you would lose all of your investigative powers? Like Rapunzel cutting her hair off or something." He looked away from me long enough to wave at Mrs. Shank walking down the other side of the street with her dog. "How is this working here?"

I waved at Mrs. Shank too. Not waving at your neighbor was a pretty serious offense in Otter Lake. We had too much going on to deal with a PR nightmare like that. "Oh well, I just told Grady straight-out that if we were going to work as a couple then he needed to respect me and OLS."

"Wow," Freddie said. "And he was okay with that?"

"Yes," I said.

"That is so mature," Freddie said, blinking like he couldn't believe it. "I didn't think you guys had it in you."

"Yup," I said, and quickly got walking again. I didn't want to face any follow-up questions.

"But what was all that other stuff about the sheriff's department being the best?" Freddie asked, chasing after me.

I sighed. I knew that wasn't going to work. "Well, in addition to taking our relationship to the next level . . ." I put my hand to my mouth and chewed on the side of the thumbnail. "We may have also made a bit of a bet."

"What kind of a bet?" Freddie asked, looking perhaps

even a little more upset than he had just moments ago over the chamber of commerce insult.

"That OLS could solve this mystery before OLPD," I mumbled.

"Are you serious?"

"I know. I know," I said, dropping my hand from my mouth. "It wasn't the most mature move in the world, but Grady's always like, *You and Freddie don't think things through. You and Freddie are going to get yourselves arrested. You and Freddie are going to get yourselves killed.*"

"Oh my God, it's so annoying when he does that," Freddie said. "I would have slept with him too just to get him to shut up."

"I know, right?" I said, glad I was winning him over. "But the bigger point is that our relationship is never going to work unless he accepts what you and I do."

Freddie nodded. "Preach."

"And the only way he's going to do that is if we prove we really are good at this. That we haven't just gotten lucky and broken the law a lot."

"Okay," Freddie said. "But what are the stakes?"

Oh crap. I was hoping he was going to forget that part. I kind of had. See, Grady and I had come up with some stakes—in between friend sessions—but outside of Grady's room, well, those stakes seemed kind of serious . . . and presumptuous for me to be making without consulting my partners. "Well," I said. "If we discover the murderer, Grady has to put out a full-page ad in the paper thanking Otter Lake Security."

Freddie smiled. "I like it. I like it. And if we lose?"

I made a face.

"Erica . . ."

"Then we have to cut the lawn of the sheriff's department all summer," I said quickly.

"Okay, well, that's not—"

"And . . ."

Freddie frowned.

"Clean any dog droppings from the K-9 unit they have coming in once a week for training."

"I see."

I grimaced again. "I know I should have talked to you and Rhonda first, but it was kind of a spur-of-the-moment thing and—"

Freddie stopped walking and looked at me. "Erica?"

"Yes?"

"I don't think I've ever loved you more."

"What?"

"Oh yeah," he said, putting his hand in the air. "Don't leave me hanging."

I jumped in the air and slapped his palm.

"We are so going to win this thing!" he shouted. "Yah! But we have to put this investigation into overdrive. Oh my God! Halloween is tomorrow, and—"

"Wait," a sad voice called out from behind us.

"Maybe we shouldn't tell Rhonda yet, though," Freddie said. "I don't think her mind can handle any new information."

"Rhonda," I said as she staggered up to us. "Maybe you should just go on home. I don't think you're up for this today."

"No. No, I'm fine," she said, bringing the back of her hand to her mouth as she burped silently. "I want to help. And I'm really curious about what Becca has to say."

"Well, if you're sure . . ."

"I'm sure."

We walked on to the post office.

When we were almost there, Freddie said, "Now, unless you want to end up with your Tupperware stocks being taken to a new level, I suggest you have your excuses ready."

I frowned at him. "I think I'll be fine."

"You say that now . . ."

Just as I was about to walk in Mrs. Krammer came out. "I knew it."

I smiled at her. "Knew what?"

"I should have just driven the five hours to deliver my nephew's birthday gift. The gas would have been cheaper."

"See?" Freddie said. "That is what I'm talking about."

I smiled. This was ridiculous. I walked past all the little windowed boxes to get to the inner sanctum of the post office.

"Hi," I said to the sweet-looking girl behind the counter. She had her dark hair styled in a pixie cut that accentuated her big hazel eyes. "You must be Becca."

"And you're Erica Bloom. I've never seen you in church," she said with a sweet voice to match . . . her face. "But I was at the Raspberry Social." She suddenly looked sad. "I've prayed for you a lot." She nodded reassuringly.

"Oh," I said with a smile. "Thank you." It was hard to be offended. She said it so earnestly . . . and in that ultrafeminine voice some women had. It would have been like being offended by a baby bunny or something.

"I pray for your mother too."

I smiled again. Too much earnestness could be annoying though.

"Can I help you with something?" she asked.

"Oh no, not exactly," I said, walking up to the counter. "I mean, yes—"

I was cut off by a strange burbling noise.

Becca leaned over and picked up a baby girl. "This is Angel. She's helping out today."

"She's adorable." She really was. She looked like a curly-haired Gerber baby.

"I'm not really supposed to have her here, but my sitter's sick, and no one else could cover for me."

"Right. Of course." *And* suddenly this was becoming a whole lot more awkward given what I needed to ask her about. "So . . . um," I said, rocking on my feet. "If you have a moment, I was wondering if I could ask you a few questions." I was skipping the rapport building this time. Left me feeling too dirty. And I had really liked . . . that girl I met at the bar whose name I hadn't even bothered to ask for.

"Does this have something to do with Otter Lake Security?" she asked, her voice becoming even more baby-like.

"Kind of," I said, scratching my temple, before just pulling off my wool hat. "We've been helping out at the apple orchard and—"

Becca stood up pretty abruptly. "I'm going to need to put Angel down for her nap."

"Here?" I asked.

"She can sleep anywhere," she said with a nervous smile. "There's a playpen in the back."

"But don't you have to be at the desk?" I asked.

"I'll hear the door if anyone comes in."

"Are you just saying all this to get rid of me?"

That sweet smile came back to her face.

"Look, Becca, it's okay. I'm not here to judge you. I'm just trying to find out what happened in those woods."

Her face trembled a bit. "Why would I know anything about that?"

I grimaced. "Because you were seeing Danny?"

"Who told you that?" she whispered. "I wasn't seeing Danny. I've been with my husband since the ninth grade."

"Oh. I didn't realize." Actually, I kind of did know

that. The nameless girl at the bar had mentioned something about everyone knowing Becca was messing around with Danny . . . except her boyfriend. "So, of course, you were never seeing Danny."

Her cheeks burned, but she dropped back into her seat, baby still in her arms. "Is . . . Sheriff Forrester going to ask me about this too?"

"I think there's a good chance if I was able to find out about the thing that didn't happen that he will be able to too." I mean, he wishes. He was no Erica Bloom. But it was possible.

"But . . ." She looked like she might start to cry. "No one will understand."

Man, I was really not having a good time with questioning lately. First, I had made friends with a girl in a bar on totally false pretenses, and now I was going to make a mom cry in front of her baby. "I could maybe understand," I said gently. "You know, I could see— hypothetically, of course—how a person might hook up with another person if, say, they had only ever dated one other person seriously."

Both she and the baby just stared at me with their baby eyes.

"I wouldn't judge that person, but I could see how a husband might."

"Especially a husband who was as sweet and generous as mine. He would never understand what might lead a woman to fall under the spell of a man like Danny." She placed her baby gently back on the blanket she had laid on the floor. The girl immediately picked up one of the toys there and shoved it in her mouth.

"A man like Danny?" I prodded.

"The way he would look at you." Suddenly her eyes were far away . . . and much less innocent looking. "You knew he was thinking about all the things he could do to you."

Oh jeez. Okay.

"Things your husband would never dream of because he respects you like he respects his own mother, and his back never quite healed from that football injury, and anything too vigorous sets it off in spasm. Not Danny though. His back was like rubber and—"

"Okay," I said, putting my hands up. "I understand."

Her eyes dropped back to mine. "It was only once or twice," she pleaded in her wispy voice. "Well, maybe like a handful of times. We used to meet at the house of the Apple Witch. Danny liked all the dark things. He was kind of a lost soul. All alone in the world."

I nodded. "Right."

"But his pain was like a drug. And I was an addict."

Crap, I had lost her again.

"And I had nothing against Mandy, but I would have tied her to a train track if it meant I could have—" She cut herself off again. "Danny wanted Mandy though. Danny and Mandy, doesn't the sound of it just make you want to be sick?"

I felt my eyes go wide. "Um, so, did you ever think of telling Mandy about you and Danny?"

"I couldn't," she said. "Danny made sure of that."

Just then I felt a tug at my jeans. Oh wow, baby looking at me. She must have crawled under the counter. There was a baby-sized space there. I stooped to pick her up. I was guessing that's what she wanted. I didn't really speak baby. "And how exactly did he do that?"

"He had lots of tapes of us. At first, he just wanted me to dress up as the Apple Witch to make some videos for his Web cast. He had this old camcorder thing. But then it went further. A lot further. I wanted us to be together.

It was crazy—my husband is the best man I know—but I was under Danny's spell. Danny didn't want that, though. He said if I told anyone about us the entire town would see the tapes." Becca's eyes darted over my face. "You don't look surprised."

"I . . . uh." I looked down at the baby, who was trying to stick her fingers in my mouth. I kind of wanted to cover her ears for this next part. "I may have come across a tape. Grady has it now."

"What?" Becca's face went white. "Was it just the one tape?"

I nodded.

"But where did you find it? Danny had this old-fashioned-looking beer crate that he used to keep them in." Her eyes darted over my face. "You've seen it."

"I don't know," I said, thinking back to the paintball tournament when Cam had taken me to his grandfather's workshop. "Maybe."

"At the orchard?"

"There were lots of boxes in one of the outbuildings, but I don't know anything for sure."

"This . . . this is going to ruin everything," Becca said, shaking her head. "Sheriff Forrester has a tape?"

I nodded.

"But I had nothing to do with Danny's death! You're talking to the wrong person."

Chapter Thirty-three

"Who should I be talking to then?"

I shot Becca a sideways glance—which I guess my baby friend didn't like, because wet baby fingers trailed down my cheek. I looked down at the baby. She gave me a big gummy smile.

"Cam."

"Why Cam?"

"Look, after Danny disappeared, I tried to track him down, but he wasn't answering my calls or texts. William and I had gotten engaged, and the thought of those tapes just being out there . . . it was driving me crazy. I wanted to make sure he destroyed the tapes, but Danny was gone. I saw those pictures he took in Vegas on his Facebook, and I thought it was over. But a weird thing happened a couple weeks after that."

Just then the baby squawked. I looked down at her, trying to figure out what that sound meant.

"Try bouncing her on your hip," Becca said.

I jiggled around a bit before I found a rhythm that worked.

"Anyway, it wasn't weird then . . . but now that we know Danny never made it to Vegas . . ."

We didn't know that for sure. It was possible he went to Vegas and came back, but now didn't seem the time to derail her.

"I think Cam went to Vegas."

"What?" I stopped bouncing and the baby squawked at me again. Wow, these things were demanding.

"He kept getting these flyers in the mail from this hotel in Vegas. It wasn't like a sponsored mailing because he was the only one getting them." She ran her hands through her hair. "I noticed because every time I saw anything having to do with Vegas, I'd remember Danny . . . then the tapes and . . ."

Yeah, I could see how that might stick in her mind. "But there could be a lot of reasons for why Cam was getting Vegas mail. He just could have signed up for something online."

"Except I asked him about it one day, you know, really casually. Said I noticed he was getting all these flyers."

"And?"

"He was really weird about it. Said he had no idea what I was talking about. Kind of like I did," she said, fiddling with an elastic band, "at the beginning of this conversation."

"So, you think Cam went to Vegas after Danny was already . . . gone, and he was the one who posted those pictures? Using Danny's phone?"

"Yes," she said, dropping the elastic. "That way it would ping off whatever towers, and everyone would believe he was in Vegas, and no one would look for him. It would at least buy time."

It would. Danny didn't have family. Mandy thought he wanted nothing to do with her. Nobody would be looking for him. At least not in Otter Lake.

"That's who the police should be focusing on," Becca said.

"You know you are going to have to tell Grady this at some point."

"I can't," she said, shaking her head. "And you can't either. Promise me."

"I can't promise you that," I said, looking down at her daughter . . . for understanding, I guess. "A man is dead."

"I'll deny I told you anything. I'll say you're just making it all up for . . . like your business."

I wasn't worried. Grady would believe me. I mean, he'd probably believe me more if we hadn't made this bet, but he'd believe me.

"I think maybe you're going to want to talk to your husband before it comes out. It will be better if he hears it from you. You weren't married at the time, and you have this beautiful baby. He might be more understanding than you think. Just maybe don't tell him about Danny's rubber back and all that stuff."

Her shoulders slumped as her eyes drifted to the floor.

"I think I should probably be going now."

She nodded. It was the saddest nod I had ever seen.

"Oh, this belongs with you," I said, turning back around. I had almost walked right out with this thing. I passed Becca her baby—who took one look at her mother's face and suddenly looked just as sad. "Oh no . . ." I said. "Don't do that."

Tears came to both their eyes.

"No, no, no," I said. "There has to be something I can do."

A minute or two later, I walked out of the post office with a piece of paper in my hand.

"What's that?" Freddie asked, jutting his chin at the paper.

"It's . . . a baby-basket-of-the-month subscription."

Rhonda and Freddie burst out laughing.

"Oh, shut up. The both of you."

After the post office, we all decided to go to our separate homes. We obviously couldn't just ask Cam outright if he had taken Danny's phone to Vegas to snap pictures to make people believe that he was still alive, because if he hadn't killed Danny himself—he was covering up for someone who did, so asking him a question like that seemed . . . dangerous. We were going to meet up later to brainstorm ideas of what to do with this information. Again, Halloween was tomorrow. We wouldn't have an excuse to be at the apple orchard after that. We were running out of time. In the meantime, though, I had a date with the Apple Witch.

The dark clouds had rolled in just as I had made it back to the island in my mother's boat. I quickly snapped the boat's cover on, and hurried up to the lodge. Just as I had shut the door behind me the rain began to fall in heavy sheets. Our brainstorming meeting later might have to be over the phone.

"Mom?" I called out.

No answer.

I wandered over to the kitchen, and yup, she'd left a note on the table.

Visiting with the twins.

Well, I was guessing it was going to be a long visit unless she wanted to get soaked.

Seeing as I had the place to myself, I decided I might as well make myself a cozy reading nook in the main room. I got in my jammies because it was a stormy-fall-jammies kind of day, and got a fire going in the fireplace. Once that was all done, I made myself a cup of Earl Grey and settled into the armchair closest to the fire with an afghan on my lap. I grabbed the library book from the side table. "Time to spill your secrets, witch."

I flipped a couple of pages. Hmm, headless horseman . . . nope. Werewolf of Nantucket? Definitely not.

Just then I peeked over the top of my book at the pair of eyes staring at me.

Caesar. My fur brother and archnemesis. "Came for the fire, did you?"

I could practically hear him thinking, *It wasn't for the company.*

"Well, okay," I said. "But don't sleep too close. Remember what happened last time."

Last time Caesar and I had shared a fire, we had used some really dry wood that had crackled and popped quite a bit as it burned. I didn't think it was a problem until I saw a thin pillar of smoke rise up from the cat's enormous body. A spark had landed on him. He didn't even notice . . . well, at least not until I started smacking his side trying to put it out. You can imagine how well that went over. My mother had bought another screen since then, but I couldn't take any chances. If I lit the cat on fire again, my mother would never let me use the fireplace.

I got back to flipping through my library book as Caesar capsized himself on the floor.

Nothing.

Nothing . . .

Aha! Apple Witch.

My eyes scanned the page. Okay, background information on New Hampshire, historical context, and . . . bingo.

There have been many versions of the Apple Witch story told over the years ranging from the grotesque to

*the ridiculous. The real story was far less fanciful, but
just as tragic. Perhaps even more so.*

I brought my tea to my lips. Huh, that was kind of a
depressing start. Maybe—ow, frick. Too hot.

*Dorit Honeycutt was married at a young age to the
proprietor of the Honeycutt apple orchards. Unhappily
so. It was believed that Jacob Honeycutt was a cruel and
impatient man, and soon tired of his young wife. For
many years, Dorit was unable to have any children,
which angered her husband. As a result, Jacob set his
eye on another young woman, Margarete Sinclair, and
made very little pretense of hiding his affection. It seemed
most of the town knew that Jacob wished to be rid of his
wife, but divorces were uncommon and difficult to pro-
cure. Then, at perhaps the most inopportune of times,
Dorit Honeycutt found herself with child. Any hope she
had that this would soften her husband's feelings toward
her quickly faded. Whatever his motivation, Jacob was
more determined than ever to have the young Margarete
Sinclair to be his wife.*

Huh, maybe the *young* had something to do with it.
What a jerk.

*As soon as Dorit delivered her baby son, Jacob had
her committed to a sanitarium and filed for divorce.*

Well, he was just wasting no time.

*This is where the story of the Apple Witch has di-
verged into many a strange and fanciful tale. One point
on which the majority of stories agree is that Dorit Honeycutt somehow did manage to get back to New Hampshire by train, then traveled by foot to her home on the
edge of the White Mountains. Apparently Dorit was spotted by several of the townspeople and inevitably Jacob
Honeycutt was told of her return, and her intention to
reunite with her child.*

Some say upon hearing of his wife's escape from the

sanitarium, Jacob sent a search party of seven men into the forest on a particularly cold and tempestuous night to capture his former wife. In this version of the story, none of the men returned the next morning. Three days later one of the men was found alive but in dire condition. He spoke of a terrible demon in the woods that killed each of the men in the most horrible of ways. Impalement. Fire. Drowning. The account was outrageous, yet none of the bodies were found. The man died shortly after telling his tale.

Yup, that's the way I had heard the story. The Apple Witch, or Dorit—I kind of felt like we were on a first-name basis now—had turned Rambo and slaughtered men in the woods for her revenge.

Others say that Dorit was able to make it into town the night before her husband's marriage—not to be reunited with her child but to seek revenge on his new bride, the woman she believed had seduced her husband and was responsible for her admission to the sanitarium. The fiancée had gone to sleep the night before her wedding in the best of health. Yet the next morning, she was found frozen atop her bedsheets fully dressed in her bridal gown. The windows of her room were left open, and footprints were found in the mud outside the house. A sleeping tincture was found on the young bride's dresser, although her mother claimed her daughter had never taken such a remedy before and was averse to taking any sort of medicine. This particular version has a further unfortunate tragic turn. The young Margarete Sinclair had been caring for Dorit's baby since her husband had her sent away, and the child also perished, frozen, in a crib at the side of Margarete's bed. It is said that Dorit's ghost wails are for her child that she had mistakenly killed.

Whoa, okay, so that one was definitely more in line

with Freddie's version of events, but way more sad. I wasn't entirely buying it though. How did she get the girl to drink the tincture without anyone knowing? What, did she knock on her window? Sounded a little Snow White to me. And how do you not notice a baby? I guess maybe if it was on the floor on the far side of the bed or—I was getting carried away. Probably because I was mad about the tragic turn. I hated it when books made me sad.

Perhaps the saddest story of all . . .

Well, great. Just great.

. . . has the most truth to it. In an attempt to be reunited with her child, Dorit set off into the woods to return to the apple orchards, became disoriented in the storm, and succumbed to the elements. Never to hold her only child.

I slammed the book shut, making Caesar jump.

That wasn't a good story. Or at least it wasn't a fair one.

I chewed the corner of my thumbnail and stared at the flames dancing in the fireplace.

I couldn't imagine what it would be like to give birth, only to be torn from the baby and thrown into a sanitarium because my husband wanted to marry the new girl in town. Then to find a way out of the sanitarium, struggle to make it back to your child only to succumb to the elements in the woods? I knew these woods in October. That would truly be a horrible way to go.

Well, this . . . this . . . was infuriating. If by some crazy possibility Dorit had managed to come back as a ghost, well, I was totally in support of her right to haunt.

"Erica?"

"What?" I shouted angrily before whipping around. "Oh . . . I'm sorry. I didn't hear you guys come in."

My mother and the twins stared at me from the front entryway. They looked cute all dressed up in their slickers.

"Everything okay?" my mother asked carefully.

"It's fine," I said, rubbing a hand over my face. "I'm just enraged about something that happened like a hundred and fifty years ago."

They were still staring at me.

"I was just reading about the Apple— No, no, I will not say that anymore and not for all the ridiculous reasons you guys and Freddie give. Her name was Dorit Honeycutt."

"Oh," all three of them said, pulling off their raincoats.

"She really got a raw deal, you know," I said, launching into the story. When I was through, Kit Kat said, "Hey, think of it this way, if she had been born a hundred and fifty years earlier, she would have been burned at the stake."

"How is that better?"

"A sanitarium shows progress."

"I can't even," I said, throwing my hands in the air and spinning away.

Kit Kat came over and patted me on the shoulder. "Settle down there, honey."

"I know," I said, looking at her. "It's just the story was really sad. She just wanted her ba—"

"We will never settle down!" my mother suddenly shouted from across the room. "The Bloom women never settle down!"

"Here we go," Tweety said with a sigh before wandering off to the kitchen. "Do you see what you've started?"

My mother wasn't going to the kitchen though. Oh no, she was sweeping across the room to embrace me. I barely had time to widen my eyes before I was locked in her embrace.

"I have never been prouder of you, darling."

"Really?" Kit Kat asked . . . from somewhere. I

couldn't see what with all of my mother's hair covering my face.

"Really," my mother exclaimed.

"Not even when she saved that real estate girl's life?"

"Candace?" I mumbled.

"Yeah, that's the one."

"No," my mother said, rocking me side to side. "Well, of course I was proud of her then. My girl is amazing. But this . . . this . . ."

"What did I do?" I asked, spitting out her hair.

She gripped my shoulders and pushed me out so that she could face me. "You have found the feminist fire within."

I frowned. "Please . . . I've always had at least a candle burning."

"Not like this. I've never heard you speak so passionately."

"Okay, well—"

"You know what we should do?" my mother said, the flames from the fireplace reflecting in her eyes. "We need to petition the town to reclaim Dorit Honeycutt as a hero."

"Oh," I said. "That's an idea." I was somewhat worried about the paperwork involved. I did not love paperwork.

"We need to expose this twisted Apple Witch story to the light of day. Show the men that we aren't going to take it anymore. We could march outside the town hall. I'll get Zaki to bring us warm drinks, and—"

"Whoa. Whoa. Whoa," Tweety said. "I like the . . . *you know who* stories."

"Yeah," her sister said. "Maybe *like* is the wrong word. But a town needs stories . . . legends . . . it builds community."

"At the expense of a poor woman's memory."

"Ow. Ow. Mom," I said, prying her hands from my shoulders. She was gripping me pretty tight. She had yoga strength in those hands.

"I don't think you've thought this through, Summer," Kit Kat said. "What are mothers supposed to threaten their children with when they're misbehaving if there's no witch?"

"Yeah," Tweety added. "You can't just go ripping apart a town's culture."

"Of course we can," my mother said. "That's what some of us were born to do!"

"Not on our watch."

I closed my eyes and shook my head. This was my fault. Why couldn't I just stick to easy things? Like solving murders.

"The woman has been gone for a hundred and fifty years," Tweety said. "If I were her, I'd be happy if people were still talking about me that long after the fact!"

"Exactly," Kit Kat said with a point. "I *want* little kids to throw their sheets over their heads in terror when they think of me for years to come." She looked at me. "Not your kid though, Erica. And when are we going to get our baby? How's it going with Grady? We're not getting any young—"

"Okay," I said, holding my hands up in defeat. "I think this conversation has run its course."

"All right. All right," Tweety said, settling into a chair. "You don't have to shout."

I looked at her. "But I wasn't shouting."

"No," my mother said suddenly, shaking me again. "You shout if you want to."

"But I don't want to shout," I said. "And I wasn't shouting."

"Of course you do," my mother said, patting my shoulder. "And yes, you were."

My mouth dropped open. I had no idea how to answer that.

"Hey Erica," Kit Kat said. "We were going to play three-handed euchre, but now that you're here we can have a proper game. You in?"

My mouth was still open, but I couldn't seem to remember how to make a sound.

"Yeah, yeah," Tweety said. "It will be like our own little coven. In honor of the . . . Dorit Honeycutt."

My mother twirled her fingers excitedly in the air. "I'll make us our own little witch's brew. Perfect for a stormy fall day."

And I guess we were all friends again.

"Don't worry," Kit Kat whispered at me. "Whatever she makes us, I've got my flask." She patted her chest pocket and gave me a knowing nod.

I blinked. Euchre and gin.

Huh, if only all the world's problems could be solved so easily.

"So," Tweety said, leading my mother to the kitchen. "I guess things between you and Zaki are still going pretty well."

"They are," she said, beaming. "You know I really feel like he completes me."

Suddenly everything went still.

My mother's face dropped.

Had she just said that a *man* completes her?

"I mean, I was already *whole*. I don't need a man to make me feel complete. You guys know that better than anyone. I've never needed a man for anything."

Except for maybe warm drinks on picket lines . . . and maybe my conception, but now probably wasn't the time to bring that up.

"I just meant—"

"We know what you meant, honey," Kit Kat said gently. "It's okay."

Tweety patted her on the shoulder. "And don't worry, we won't tell anyone."

"You can keep your feminist card."

Okay, the euchre had been pretty fun, but now I was lying in bed staring at the ceiling, listening to the wind throw icy rain against my window. I was right. We had to postpone our OLS meeting. No way I was going to cross the lake in this kind of weather. Didn't mean I couldn't brainstorm by myself though. We needed to figure out some way to prove Cam went to Vegas during the week those pictures were taken on Danny's phone. I could see why he would have had to go right away. Danny's phone service would have eventually been cut off, so he wouldn't have had much time to waste. That didn't mean the phone wasn't still on the apple orchard property though. Grady had no idea how lucky he was with his ability to get search warrants and stuff.

If Cam *had* gone to Vegas to make it look like Danny was alive, well, then that raised a whole bunch of other questions. Was Cam acting alone? Or were his brothers helping him? The way they had been talking at the orchard, it certainly made it seem like whatever was going on, they were in it together. Maybe one of the other brothers had killed Danny, and Cam was just helping with the cover-up. Which also made me wonder how much Mandy knew. She had to have known that Cam went to Vegas, didn't she? And now that she knew Danny was dead . . . her mind must be spinning the way mine was, but she, of course, had a lot more at stake.

The whole thing just made me so sad. I did not want to believe that any of those kids I had known could be responsible for taking a life, but they sure were acting guilty. But again, if I was sad, I could only imagine what Mandy was going through. Of course, in my darkest of thoughts, I had even wondered if Mandy was capable of such an act. I mean, she certainly had motive. Danny was cheating on her. But she knew that I was close to Grady, so why draw me into this if she was guilty? Unless she thought she could get information from me that way. Maybe she had made up all of her fears about the Apple Witch just to see what I knew? Either way, she was genuinely upset and stressed, and that couldn't be good for the baby. This needed to come to a resolution.

I couldn't just lie here and think about it anymore.

But there was one thing I could do.

I grabbed my phone.

A moment later, a voice answered, "Hey, I wasn't expecting to hear from you. I thought you'd be busy shaking down—"

"Yeah, can we put the whole bet thing on hold for a moment?" I said, putting my hand on my forehead.

"Absolutely," Grady said, concern tingeing his voice. "What's going on?"

"I'm just . . ." I shook my head. "This is all too important to mess around with."

"I agree."

"So I wanted you to know that I went to see Becca Anderson at the post office today."

Grady didn't say anything, just waited for me to continue.

I bit the corner of my lip and looked at the rain hitting my window. "She mentioned that Cam might have gone to Vegas in the weeks after Danny disappeared, or, I guess, was murdered. And somebody took pictures in Vegas and put them on Danny's Facebook page, probably using his phone, so I just thought you should know."

A moment passed.

"Thank you."

I don't know what I was expecting him to say, but that was really nice. "You're welcome. The whole bet thing—"

"I know. I know," Grady said. "It's probably going to take some time to feel our way through this, and if this . . . relationship lasts as long as I know I want it to, these issues are probably going to come up a lot."

"I want it to, too," I said with a big stupid nod that no one could see. "I mean, the relationship. I want it to last."

"I'm glad."

"And I think we can figure it out," I said, using my fingers to rake my hair back from my face. "We just have to keep communicating and trying new ways to . . . get along."

Grady chuckled. "The bet thing was actually kind of . . ."

"Hot?"

"Yeah, that," he said. I could hear the smile in his voice. "I'm glad you trusted me with that information though."

I took a deep breath. "What can I say? This cat likes to dress up like a white knight."

"What?"

"Sorry. Nothing. It's a Rhonda-and-me thing."

"But you know," Grady said in a playful voice, "just so OLS and OLPD are on equal footing going forward . . ."

I propped myself up on my elbow. "Yes?"

"Well, you might find it interesting to hear that Cam may not have been the only one to travel to Vegas in the weeks after Danny died."

"Seriously?"

"Yup."

"Who? Who else went to Vegas?"

Grady chuckled. "You sound like an owl."

"Don't you toy with me, Grady Forrester." I was pointing this time—again, for absolutely no one to see.

"Becca Anderson."

"Becca?" My Becca? The post office Becca? Whose
baby I held while she told me all about her theories
of Cam going to Vegas? "That little . . . minx. I've got
to go."

"You need to call Freddie?"

"I need to call Freddie."

Chapter Thirty-four

"Okay, let's get this emergency meeting started," Freddie said, clapping his hands together. "Happy Halloween everyone. Rhonda, glad to see you back in the land of the living. Erica, good work last night, but where's the cappuccino? It's your turn to make it."

I threw my head back against my chair. "Again?"

"Do it."

I dragged myself up and headed over to Freddie's cappuccino maker that probably cost as much as a small car. It was a gift from his poppo. Actually I could probably use the caffeine. Freddie and I were up pretty late discussing the latest tidbit of information we had about Becca. Unfortunately, we didn't get very far with it. We just kept going round and round in the same circles. We had a new suspect, but no proof of anything, and no clear course of action to take to lead us to proof. Hence the emergency meeting.

"Well, it's good to see you in a better mood, Freddie," Rhonda said. "I thought we were never going to get you on board with this investigation."

"Oh, I'm on board," Freddie said. "Ever since Erica told me about the bet, I—"

"What bet?" Rhonda asked.

I cringed and tried to make myself invisible over by the cappuccino while Freddie filled Rhonda in. When he was through, Rhonda said, "And what about me in all this?" Loudly. You know, loud enough for it to reach me in my hiding spot.

"What about . . . you?" I asked with a smile while handing her a cappuccino.

"Did you think about the redhead in this situation?"

"Of course I did." Maybe not in the exact moment Grady and I were discussing it. I was kind of overwhelmed with all my lusty competitive feelings. "Actually, that sounded oddly specific. I'm not entirely sure what you're getting at."

"Yard work? I freckle, Erica. A lot." Rhonda took a sip of her cappuccino. "Mmm, this is good. Do you want me to get skin cancer?"

"Of course I don't want you to get skin cancer," I said, passing Freddie his minicup. "I just thought—"

"I'm just messing with you," she said, laughing.

"You are?"

"I love the idea," she said, taking another sip and looking at me over her cup. "This is my moment."

I frowned with confusion. I looked at Freddie but he just shrugged. "What moment?"

"You know, that moment when you're walking down the street with your hot new boyfriend and you run into the ex that dumped you? You smile and wave, but really in your head you're saying *suck it*."

"I see."

"But we can't lose this thing," she said, shaking her head quickly, making her red curls shudder. "I was serious about the freckling. I can't mow lawns all summer."

"It's okay," I said. "Grady and I talked last night, and if we really wanted to get out of the bet—"

"Nobody is getting out of the bet," Freddie suddenly shouted.

"Whoa," I said. "I'm going to take that cappuccino back if you don't settle down, mister."

He clutched it to his chest. "I'm just saying," he said in a much quieter voice. "Nobody is getting out of the bet."

"Listen, it was just a silly thing Grady and I made up because we're trying to figure out how to make all of this work, and, really, the important thing—"

"I'm sorry," Freddie said. "This whole thing stopped being about just you and Grady when you dragged all of OLS into it."

"I was going to say—"

"You heard Rhonda," Freddie said, pointing at her. "She needs her hot-new-boyfriend moment."

"I was going to say—"

"And what about me?" Freddie said, patting his chest. "I swear, I am going to kill Andy over at the chamber of commerce if he keeps excluding OLS from town events. That should have been our potato trophy. And you know what would force him to recognize OLS as a legitimate business?"

"Oh, I know!" Rhonda said, putting up her hand. "A full-page ad in the town paper from the sheriff thanking us."

"Ding. Ding. Ding. Ding. Ding," Freddie said. "Give that girl a prize!"

Rhonda smiled happily and took another sip of her cappuccino.

I rolled my eyes. "I was going to say this is really about finding justice for Danny, and—"

"Oh God," Freddie moaned. "I hate it when you dead-shame me."

"And Mandy and her baby."

He threw his hands in the air. "Oh sure, pile a baby on top."

Rhonda snickered.

"At least," I said, "we are all finally, *finally,* on the same page about finding Danny's killer. The truth needs to come to light."

"Hear. Hear." Freddie said, thumping the kitchen table, which was also our conference table.

"And," I said, "we also need to expose the truth about the Apple Witch."

"No. No," Freddie shouted.

"Oh yes," I said, pointing at him. "We are going to prove to this town once and for all that the Apple Witch is not roaming the woods of Otter Lake killing unsuspecting young men. It's time to move out of the dark ages."

"Right," Freddie said. "I would just like to point out that the other night when we actually saw the . . . you know who—"

"We did not see the Apple Witch. We saw someone dressed up as the Apple Witch."

"You weren't all"—he waved his hands in the air— *"Hey! Hey you, witch! You don't exist!"*

"Yes I was!" I was jolted so badly by what he said that I spilled some cappuccino on my hand. "I so was! When you were holding me in that bear hug?"

"You were holding Erica in a bear hug?" Rhonda asked, frowning at Freddie.

"I saved her life," he said with a dismissive head shake. "It was no big thing."

"The Apple Witch doesn't exist," I said, putting my cappuccino safely down on the table and folding my arms over my chest. "And I'm going to prove it."

"And how are you going to do that?" Freddie asked.

"I," I said, pausing a moment for dramatic effect, "am going to Scooby-Doo that thing."

Freddie dropped his chin to his chest. "You're going to do what now?"

"I am going to Scooby-Doo that ghost."

Freddie looked to Rhonda.

"She means she's going to take its hood off, and say, *Oh look, it's old Mr. Johnson from down by the river.* And he's going to be all like, *And I would have gotten away with it too if it weren't for you meddling kids.*"

I pointed at Rhonda. "She gets it."

Freddie closed his eyes and pinched the bridge of his nose like I had somehow given him an instant migraine. "Okay, why don't we just table that for another meeting, and focus on the murder at hand."

"I'm sorry, but someone dressing up as the Apple Witch and trying to scare us obviously does have something to do with the murder. The Honeycutts and Grady were the only ones who knew we were going to be at the Apple Witch's house that first night—"

"So, one of them is a murderer," Rhonda said with a nod.

"Well, not necessarily," I said. "Maybe—"

"Oh my God, Erica," Freddie said. "I get that you feel protective over the Honeycutt children, but all the evidence has been pointing in their direction. Occam's razor. If it looks like a duck and quacks like a duck, then it's obviously a Honeycutt."

I rolled my eyes. I hated it when Freddie used Occam's razor.

"We need to focus our efforts on them."

"But what about the Becca lead?" I tried.

"I'm sorry," he said. "But I'm not feeling it, and we

have limited time to solve this before Grady does, so I say we take the chance and put all our eggs in one basket. Rhonda?"

"Agreed," Rhonda said.

I blinked at them. "What?"

"How do you like your democracy now?" Freddie said.

"I—"

"No time for that," Freddie said. "So, I've been giving it some thought, and that family is never going to turn against one another."

I just crossed my arms over my chest again.

"But Erica almost heard them confess the other night when they were talking to one another."

"So?" Rhonda asked. She had an excited gleam in her eye.

"Well, I was thinking," Freddie said. "If we could get them in the same room at the same time, then that might happen again. With us overhearing of course. I'd actually like to tape it, but Erica handcuffed us with this whole 'everything has to be legal' business."

"But . . . but . . ." I clutched my forehead. There was just so much wrong with this plan. "First of all, there is no guarantee that they are just going to randomly confess because they're all in the same room with one another."

"I know," Freddie said, wagging a finger. "We're going to have to rattle their cages somehow."

"And second of all," I said. "If we can't secretly tape it—which we can't because of New Hampshire law"— we had found that out on a previous case. Both parties have to give permission for a conversation to be taped in New Hampshire, otherwise it's inadmissible—"what's the point? It will just be their word against ours in a court of law. And it will look like we were just some desperate

PI team trying to entrap them to win a bet against the town sheriff."

"Erica, Erica, Erica . . ." Freddie said in that tone of his that made me insane.

"Ooooh," Rhonda said, smiling and fidgeting in her seat. "This is about to get good."

"We won't be relying on the overheard confession."

"We won't?"

"No," he said. "You see, we will overhear them talking about the crime, then when they confess, we'll pop out, and the guilty party will willingly confess in order to protect the rest of the family."

"Or they just kill us," Rhonda said, eyes widening. "Bad plan, Freddie. Bad plan."

"We could have an escape route planned," he said. "And maybe Grady standing by."

"But what if they all killed Danny?" I asked.

"I doubt they all killed him," Freddie said. "Like all at the same time? That would be weird. I mean, I know they're close, but that's just weird."

"I don't know," Rhonda said, tilting her head side to side as though considering the scenario. "If I was going to kill someone, I think I'd want you guys there with me."

"Aww," I said. "That's so—"

"Stop talking!" Freddie snapped. "You're ruining my moment here. Regardless of whether they all killed Danny together as a bonding experience or not, they will still confess because they will want to protect Mandy. She'll look guilty too if they don't. It was her cheating boyfriend."

I shook my head. "This . . . this plan is crazy."

Freddie sighed. "Of course it's crazy. When hasn't one of our plans been crazy?"

"I'm not sure that makes it okay," Rhonda said.

"It's worth a try," Freddie said. "Look, it's Halloween, and after tonight we won't have access to the apple orchard anymore. This is our best shot. The only thing I haven't quite figured out is how to get them all in the same room at the same time and where it should be."

Suddenly my cappuccino wasn't sitting too well in my stomach. "I . . . I might have an idea on that front."

Freddie raised an eyebrow. "You do?"

I nodded.

My partners stared at me, waiting.

I scratched my temple. "I may . . . have done something a little like that to the Honeycutt boys once before."

"Oh my God!" Freddie shouted. "Is this the thing? From when you were babysitting?"

I nodded.

Freddie put his chin on his hands. "I'm all ears."

I sighed. This really wasn't a story that I wanted to tell, but . . . it might help. "Well, it all started when—"

"Hang on," he suddenly said, holding up a hand. "I'm going to get us snacks." He jumped up again from the table. "I feel like it's Christmas in October!"

Chapter Thirty-five

"Okay, let me start by saying I'm not proud of this."

"I love it when stories start that way," Freddie said, shooting Rhonda a smile.

She nodded excitedly.

"No, no, really," I said, clutching my cold cappuccino cup. "It's not that big of a deal. It's just . . ."

"Just tell the story!"

It had taken Freddie about fifteen minutes to get us sufficiently snack ready. We had an interesting mix of popcorn, ready-made bacon, and frozen mango chunks. Freddie had thought he might try a smoothie cleanse not too long ago, and had bought three two-pound bags of mangos. He didn't make it far past the first smoothie.

"Okay, but first—"

Freddie groaned.

"Rhonda needs to have context for this," I said, looking at him. "She needs to know that the Honeycutt boys were always playing practical jokes on me."

"Yes, yes," Freddie said. "They dressed up like Jason from *Friday the 13th* and jumped out of the lake at you with the machete."

"Seriously?" Rhonda asked. "They did that?"

"Yes," I said with perhaps a little too much vehemence. I was already feeling the need to defend myself. "Cam and Brandon came running up to me and said Adam was drowning in that little pond by their house, and when I went down to the dock, Adam pops up with a hockey mask and a machete and it was all—" I threw my hands in the air and made a halfhearted screaming sound.

"That's awful," Rhonda said, leaning back in her seat. "But you have to admire their commitment to the prank."

"And that was just one of the tricks they pulled on me. One time, at night, they suggested we play hide-and-seek, and that I be *it*," I said, putting my hand to my chest. "And they said I had to count in the closet, so—"

"That should have been your first clue," Freddie said.

"But once I was in there," I went on, ignoring him, "they locked me in, and turned off the power to the entire house."

"But . . . why?" Rhonda asked. "Why were they doing these things to you? Were you a mean babysitter?"

"No, I was not a mean babysitter," I said. "And I always felt like they really liked me. But, you know, their parents had died. I thought they were just acting out. But see, the thing is, they would never let Mandy help out with any of the planning or enacting of the pranks because she was the youngest, and a girl or whatever, so she came up with the idea that—"

"You should get them back," Rhonda said, nodding sympathetically. It was nice, but suddenly I kind of felt like this was Rhonda's cop routine to get confessions out of people. "So what did you two do, Erica?"

Yup, yup, this definitely felt like an interrogation-type question.

"Okay, well, first Mandy wanted to be the one to scare them," I said, picking apart a piece of bacon on my plate.

We were getting to the thick of it. It was hard to look Rhonda in the eye. "So she dressed up in this little clown outfit she had and—"

"Oh God, I hate clowns," Freddie said, slapping his hands over his ears.

"And I put a bunch of clown makeup on her."

Freddie squeaked.

"It was cute makeup. She looked adorable actually. She was barely seven," I said with a shrug. "Then she was going to hide in her grandfather's workshop. I was supposed to pretend like I couldn't find her and lead them there and she was going to jump out and scare them."

Freddie dropped his hands from his ears. "That doesn't sound very scary."

"It wasn't supposed to be," I said, throwing my hands up in the air, sending little bits of bacon onto my lap. Freddie shot me a look, but we both knew Stanley would get around to licking them up later. "But Mandy had plans to take it a little bit further."

"Uh-oh," Rhonda said.

"Yeah," I said with a sigh. "I guess pranking runs in the Honeycutt DNA. But I didn't know that at the time. So anyway, I convinced the boys that I couldn't find their sister. You know, I told them I looked at the tree fort, and down by the river, I got them all really worried, and then I told them the only place I hadn't looked was their grandfather's workshop."

"Like poor little lambs to the s—"

"Shut up," I said, pointing at Freddie. "Well, by this time, the boys are all worried . . . and the sun was going down. It was one of those cold windy evenings, where the leaves rustle across the ground, and I'm starting to feel really guilty, but again, it was just supposed to be their cute little sister jumping out at them."

"So?" Rhonda said.

"So we all run over to the workshop. It's all dark inside, but one of them brought a flashlight. I let them go in first obviously . . . but no Mandy jumps out at us." I shook my head. It was like I was right back in the moment. "Instead, we see what looks like Mandy kneeling over in the corner of the room with her back to us. I swear to God, it looked just like her from behind. It was wearing her snow jacket. Her hat. But it was super-still." I took a deep breath. "Anyway, I can tell the boys are freaked, and actually I'm kind of freaked out too because it was just so real and unnatural at the same time. So Cam calls out Mandy's name but nothing happens. Then Adam goes up really slowly and—"

"Oh God," Freddie moaned.

"And he reaches his hand out, and drops it on what he thinks is his sister's shoulder and . . ."

"And?" Rhonda asked, grabbing my hand.

"The head rolled off."

"The head rolled off?!" Freddie shouted.

"Rolled right off. Mandy had rigged it that way. Said she had seen it on TV. But even though it was a doll, it just looked so real."

"Oh God," Freddie said, shaking his head. "I hate dolls too."

"I can see why you didn't want to tell this story," Rhonda said, patting my hand.

"It gets worse," I said miserably.

Her eyes widened. "Worse?"

I nodded.

"What happened?"

"Well, so the head falls off, and we all start screaming, and I'm sure if we had a second or two to realize it was a doll, we all would have started laughing, but . . ."

"But what?" Freddie asked, quickly standing up then sitting back down again just as fast.

"But then Mandy jumped out," I said, shaking my head. "There was this stack of scarecrows in the corner—"

"Scarecrows too?" Freddie moaned.

"I didn't realize she was hidden in them, so she jumps out and—"

"It was just cute little Mandy," Rhonda said. "Tell me it was just cute little Mandy, Erica?"

"It was," I said, nodding. "It was. Except . . ."

"Except what?"

"All of the makeup I had put on her . . . smeared. I don't know if she did it herself or when she was hiding . . ." I shook my head. "Anyway I had used a lot of red, for the lips and the cheeks, and it looked kind of like . . ."

"Kind of like?"

"Blood," I said, swirling my hand around my face. "It looked like blood."

"Good God," Freddie said, clutching his chest.

"And . . . she didn't just jump out and say boo or anything . . ."

"I'm afraid to ask . . ." Rhonda said, shaking her head.

"She came out leaping toward us in this like side-to-side jumping-jack dance, and she was like shouting in this real singsongy voice . . ."

"Not the little-kid voice," Freddie whined.

"She kept shrieking the same thing over and over again."

"What did she say, Erica?" Rhonda asked. "What did she say?"

I looked up at her. *"Mandy Apple! Mandy Apple! Mandy Apple!"*

"What?" Freddie jumped up and his chair fell over on the floor. "What the hell is that supposed to mean?"

"I don't know," I said. "I guess it was like a pet name

her grandparents had given her. But with the doll, and the makeup, and the shrieking . . ."

"And what did the boys do, Erica?" Rhonda said, gripping my hand.

I nodded. "Adam, he started crying."

"Not Adam," Freddie said. "He's the brave one."

"Brandon . . . Brandon, he wet himself."

Rhonda gasped. "But he's always so in control."

"Cam . . . he just rocked on the floor in the fetal position."

"Erica!" Freddie shouted.

"I know!" I shook my head with my hands pressed to the sides of my head.

"You're . . . you're lucky Grady's not here right now," he said, jabbing a finger into the table, "because he would have to arrest you."

"It was supposed to be funny! And cute. And I really think it would have been if, you know, the head hadn't fallen off . . . and the red makeup was just . . . We couldn't have known."

"Well," Freddie said, nodding. "I think it's a pretty safe bet that they've all grown up to be serial killers. Way to go."

"I—"

"And why haven't we been investigating Mandy this entire time?" Freddie said. "She obviously did it! What kind of seven-year-old—"

"No, no, she was so upset when she saw how upset her brothers were. She had seen it on TV," I said, throwing my hands in the air. "I was the . . . teenager in charge. I should have stopped it sooner."

We fell into silence and averted our gazes from one another.

Finally, Freddie said, "Well, that was a horrible story." He picked his chair up off the floor. "I was wrong. This isn't like Christmas in October. I'm going to have nightmares tonight because of you."

"And . . . and I'm confused," Rhonda said. "What does the story have to do with our plan exactly?"

"Well, I'm just saying if we want to get all three brothers in a room at the same time, where we can overhear their conversation, and rattle their cages at the same time then . . ." I couldn't finish the thought. I could only shake my head. "We could maybe get them in that room again. With notes. That's how Mandy got me to meet her. And there's a small window. We could leave it open a crack, so we could hear what they are saying from outside, and . . . I know they'd come if they somehow thought Mandy needed them."

"I'm never leaving you alone with my children," Freddie said, shaking his head. "Not even for a second."

"I know. I know. It was ridiculous to even bring it up. I—"

"Oh no," Freddie said. "We're totally doing it."

"Doing what?" Rhonda asked.

"Going with Erica's plan," Freddie said, gesturing toward me.

"It wasn't just my plan. You said—"

"Oh no," Freddie said. "This is your baby. Your twisted, twisted baby."

"It was Mandy who—"

"Don't blame it on the child," he said, sneering.

My hands dropped into my lap. "I'm just saying, we don't have to use my plan. We could—"

"Nope," Freddie said, getting to his feet. "We're out of time. We're doing it. Now, I'm going to take a shower then we'll work out the details." He knocked on the table with his knuckles. "Good meeting."

Chapter Thirty-six

"Whoa, Mom."

"Isn't it impressive?" my mother said, swirling her arms in the cool October air. She was standing on our dock wearing a cute homespuny orange sweater with a knitted pumpkin hat. She was also surrounded by lots of wooden crates with homemade vegan Halloween treats on top. To top it off she had a lawn chair with a blanket, lots of lanterns, and one big jack-o'-lantern.

"I really think this might be the year we get trick-or-treaters," she said, clutching her hands to her chest.

I frowned. "So you've gone full *if you build it, they will come,* huh?"

"What's that, dear?"

My mother never had been into movies. "I just hope you're not too disappointed if . . . nobody shows."

"Of course I won't be disappointed."

I didn't know about that. She had put in an awful lot of work. But this was not something that I could control. Especially not tonight. Rhonda, Freddie, and I had spent the rest of the day working out the details for tonight, and those details were . . . not at all inspiring.

Making things even worse was the fact that Freddie was constantly bringing up how horrified he was with my story. And what was this nonsense about him not leaving me alone with his children? One, he didn't have children, and two, we both knew he would be begging for Auntie Erica to babysit his kids if he did have them. I was a very . . . experienced babysitter. I knew exactly what *not* to do.

"You're off to the apple orchard now?"

I nodded.

"Well, be careful." She looked very worried for a woman wearing a pumpkin hat. "I completely agree with you on the Dorit Honeycutt story, but with the body they found, and it being Halloween, well, you never know what people might do."

I almost said *don't worry,* but seeing as I was very, very worried, that didn't seem right. I just settled for, "Okay." And I gave her a hug.

"And call me later if you're going to be late or you decide to stay at Freddie's."

"Got it," I said, getting in her boat. She was already untying the rope from the dock for me.

"And I hope you get some trick-or-treaters tonight," I called out as I eased the boat away from the dock.

She shot me a double thumbs-up.

Freddie picked me up from the marina to drive me to the apple orchard. Rhonda was supposed to meet us there.

We were both pretty keyed up. Well, I knew I was, and by the way Freddie was drumming the beat to some unheard song on the steering wheel, I was guessing he was too.

"The notes are done, right?" I asked.

"You've already asked me that," Freddie said. "And the answer is still yes."

"All three of them?"

"Yes," Freddie said with way more annoyance than was called for. "Did you call Grady?"

"Not yet," I said.

"What? Why not? It was your one job."

I nodded and took a breath. "I know it was . . . but, I don't know, we're just doing so well, and—"

"Do it now," Freddie said, taking his eyes from the road to shoot me a pretty ferocious look. "If this thing goes sideways, I want Grady there to rescue me with his excessive handsomeness and gun."

I shook my head.

He flicked his eyes to the phone in my hand. "Call him."

I looked at the phone in my hand and frowned. "But I don't want to lie to him."

"Then don't," Freddie said. "Just invite him to meet you at the orchard when the gates close."

"That is still lying by omission."

"Please," Freddie drawled. "Lying by omission is nothing. Nobody ever got fried for lying by omission."

"Yeah, but I betcha they got dumped though."

"It's not like this is his first day on the job with you. He knows who we are and what we do. Call him."

"Fine," I said, swiping at my phone then bringing it to my ear. "It's ringing."

Freddie waited a moment then looked over at me.

"It's still ringing," I said. "Wait—voice mail." I waited for the beep and said, "Hey, Grady."

Freddie waved a hand in the air and mouthed the words *more girly.*

"Hey Grady." I tried again at a much higher pitch that felt very, very wrong. I dropped back down to my normal speaking voice and said, "I was just wondering, if you weren't doing anything tonight—"

Freddie backhanded me on the arm.

Ow, I mouthed.

"We need him there," Freddie hissed. "This isn't optional."

"Sorry about that," I said into my phone. "I was actually really hoping that you could meet me tonight at the apple—"

Freddie whacked me again.

What? I mouthed again, but this time my facial expression totally let him know I was yelling it.

More girly, he mouthed again, and this time he was twirling a finger around in his imaginary hair, I guess, and batting his eyelids.

"*That* is going to give *me* nightmares. I'm sorry. Again," I said into my phone. "Freddie's distracting me. Um, I was wondering if you could meet me at the apple orchard when it closes tonight. Hope you can. Bye."

I ended the call, and mentally started a countdown in my head.

Three . . . two . . . one.

"That was terrible," Freddie said.

I just shook my head against the seat of the car.

"There was zero sexual urgency in that," Freddie said. "We'll be lucky if he gets back to you before tomorrow, when we're, like, dead."

"Do you want to call him back?" I offered Freddie my phone. "Maybe you can do a better job with the whole sexual urgency thing."

"With Grady?" Freddie said. "Don't be disgusting. That's like hitting on somebody's dad."

I just shook my head some more.

A moment later, Freddie turned the Jimmy and drove through the wooden posts that marked the entrance to the apple orchard.

"Hey, look," he said with a point. "There's Rhonda."

I spotted her getting out of her Jeep Wrangler.

"Perfect," he said, pulling into the spot beside her. "We can all get on our costumes right here before we go in."

I whipped my gaze over to him. "More costumes?"

He smiled. "Well, it is Halloween."

Chapter Thirty-seven

"I'm not sure how I feel about this."

"I thought you'd be happy," Freddie said. "You were the one who said you wanted to be Dorothy at the paintball tournament. This is like Dorothy."

"It's just a lot of skirt," I said, looking down at the many, many folds of red gingham with an apron on top.

"You are impossible to please," Freddie said, hiking his ax up on his shoulder.

"Hey, at least you're not wearing the nightgown," Rhonda said. "And that red hooded cloak looks very warm."

That was true. It was warm. I just wasn't sure how fast I'd be able to run in all this clothing. Not that I would need to run for my life or anything. Hopefully.

Yup, that's right. I was Little Red Riding Hood. Rhonda was the wolf, so she was wearing a granny nightie and cap with wolf ears sticking out of the top. She also had a plastic wolf snout and fangs that had an elastic string that went around the back of her head to keep it in place. And Freddie was the huntsman, which really just comprised of him wearing jeans, a red flannel shirt, black suspenders, and knit cap. He actually kind of looked like a cute hipster. He just needed the handlebar mustache.

I held up my basket to Freddie. "I'll trade you this for your ax?"

"No tradesies," he said. "Besides, it's not a real ax."

"Still, it might come in handy," Rhonda said.

"Which is why I chose it," he said. "Now we all know the plan, right?"

"Such as it is," I grumbled.

"Oh cheer up," Rhonda said, elbowing me. "This just might work."

"I know. I know," I said. "It's just that it's Halloween . . . and a lot could go wrong." I was almost going to bring up the fact that I was dressed like a brainless victim—seriously, who can't tell the difference between their grandmother and a wolf?—but Freddie didn't deserve any more grief about the costumes. I mean, God forbid he'd make me choose them next time . . . if there was a next time.

"Okay, so let's do this thing," Freddie said. "It's time OLS got the respect it deserved."

"And a murder victim got his justice," Rhonda said.

"That too."

We started off toward the entrance gate to the orchard. I had my doubts about the whole justice thing. I was still holding on to the hope that the Honeycutts hadn't committed this murder, but they did obviously know something, and if we could find out what that was, then maybe we could figure out the rest.

"Remember," Freddie said as we got closer. "We need to act like this is just any other night."

"Right," Rhonda and I said at the same time.

"Let's start with you two not talking in unison," Freddie went on. "You don't do that on a normal night, and I just pictured those creepy twins in the movie *The Shining*. Thanks a lot, Rhonda."

"Come and play with us, Freddie," Rhonda said in an eerie voice.

"No, no, no!"

I snickered.

"There will be absolutely none of that."

"Actually, I agree," I said. "We need on-the-case Freddie tonight. Not the Halloween Freddie we've been dealing with all month."

"Okay, okay," Rhonda said.

We were just about to go under the vine-covered archway that led to the main part of the orchard when Freddie said, "Does everyone have their note?"

"Check," Rhonda and I both said again. I tagged on a quick, "Sorry," before Freddie could say anything.

"Okay, well, in that case . . ."

All three of us looked over toward the apple orchard.

"Go, team."

Chapter Thirty-eight

This was going to be fine.

Piece of cake really.

I mean, sure, several hours had passed, the gates were going to close soon, and I still hadn't done my job, but it was going to be fine. The job part wasn't really that hard. All I had to do was act like it was any other night at the apple orchard . . . and somehow slip a note to Adam without him seeing me, and make sure he read it, again without him seeing me.

We had drawn the names out of a hat this time to see who got which brother. I got Adam. Obviously. The big scary one. Who could swing through barns on ropes. There wasn't a lot about him that reminded me of the preteen boy I once knew. But, you know, I was sure everything would be . . .

Just then a teenage girl went screaming past me. She had a zombie with a machete chasing her.

. . . fine.

I twisted the handle of my basket as I walked toward the haunted barn. I had put it off as long as I could, but it was getting pretty late. The crowd was already thinning out. There hadn't been a lot of families here tonight, for obvious trick-or-treating reasons, but there were lots of teenagers. But even they were starting to head home. Rhonda and Freddie had probably already delivered their notes. We had split up, so that we'd draw less attention to ourselves. I just needed to get this done.

I kept on walking toward the barn looming in front of me.

And yes, that was the other unfortunate part about getting Adam. The haunted barn. It was Adam's favorite event to work. See, Brandon was driving the tractor for the hayride again tonight and that came with a lot of responsibility. I mean you couldn't just have teenagers falling off. Cam was supposed to be keeping an eye on all the zombie entertainers and troubleshooting any problems. Mandy was covering the café and supervising the gate. But Adam . . . he was in the barn. With a chain saw. It didn't have a chain of course. He just used it as an obstacle for the terrified guests to get through. But I got the impression he enjoyed it.

So this left me with the problem of getting to Adam, in his hiding spot in an old stall, without him seeing me. The building itself was an old horse barn with two rows of stalls. The Honeycutts had set up in every fourth or fifth stall a horror-show-type display with actors. They had hired a private group of traveling monsters, I guess, to pull it off. Guests had to walk down one side and up the other before they could get out. Adam was waiting at the very back of the barn at the halfway point. I did have one idea about how to get to him unnoticed, and I was really hoping it would work because . . . well, I just had one idea.

There was a window at the side of the barn that only had wood shutters blocking it. If I crawled through that, I was thinking it would put me at around the midpoint of the first hallway of horrors. Yes, Freddie and I had done a walk-through. It had seemed important for security. Every time one of the zombie entertainers jumped out at us, Freddie threatened to destroy him or her. Repeatedly. I'm not exactly sure what he meant by that, and I don't think the entertainers did either because it didn't stop them. Anyway, I was thinking that if I crawled through the window, I would end up just about at the maniac-surgeon display. Don't ask what a maniac surgeon was doing with an operating room in a barn, but there was one, and I really wanted to get by him unnoticed. This whole plan was pretty shaky as it was, but if Adam knew for sure it was me delivering the note then, for sure, the whole thing would fall apart.

No sense in worrying about all the things that could go wrong at this point though.

I pulled my hood over my head so my face was mostly covered and hurried over to the side of the barn. Thankfully, this wasn't a busy part of the orchard. I put my basket on the ground and pried the wooden shutters of the window open. The rusted hinges screamed in protest, but I doubt anyone but me heard them. There was a lot of screaming going on in the barn.

I got up on my toes and peeked through the window. Yup, the operating room was one stall over to my left. They had walled it off with plywood, but through the slats, I could see the evil doctor scratching his nose quickly before the next guests came his way. They were a good ways back. Maybe at the medieval torture chamber judging by the screams, and they had to make it through the graveyard after that.

If I hurried, I could get in, crawl past the doctor, and get to Adam before they were on me.

There was, however, one other minor problem. Well, maybe two.

The window was really high.

And I did not have a lot of upper-body strength.

But it was okay. I just needed one good jump to get me up there, and then gravity would do the rest on the other side.

Okay. Go time.

I rubbed my hands together and planted them on the stone ledge of the window. I took a deep breath, bent my knees, and hiked myself skyward, grunting something that sounded a little bit like *Hup!*

Half a second later, my feet were back on the ground.

Well, that hadn't worked at all.

Right.

I planted my fists on my hips and contemplated the wall in front of me. Maybe if I gripped the ledge and planted my feet against the wall, I could push myself up using my lower-body strength.

I rubbed my hands together again and gripped the ledge above me. This time, instead of the *Hup!* I thought a countdown might help.

"Three . . . two . . . on— Ow!"

Son of—

My foot had slipped, and my knee hit the wall.

Well, all right then. That apparently wasn't going to work either.

I replanted my hands on my hips and stared at the wall, gritting my teeth. This obviously was not going to be easy. I needed a step stool or someth—

"Hey, Red!"

I yelped at the voice behind me.

"Whatcha doing?" a near-identical voice to the first one called out.

I collapsed against the wall, clutching my heart, and stared at the twins approaching me. They both were wearing gray hats and black pants, but Kit Kat had a white shirt on with a black *S* stitched to the front, and Tweety wore a black shirt with a white *P*. Salt and Pepper. They had been wearing the same costume at least as long as I had been alive.

"You guys scared me," I panted out.

"You know, there is a door back there," Kit Kat said, jerking a thumb behind her.

"Yeah, it might be easier than breaking in," her sister added.

I nodded. "I am aware."

"Then what are you doing?"

I didn't answer. I wouldn't be able to think up a lie that they would believe in time, but, really, adding more people to this really shaky plan didn't seem wise either, so there was really nothing for me to say. Oh! But maybe I could distract them. "What are you guys doing here? I thought you were afraid of the App—"

"Whoa. Whoa. Hey," Tweety answered. "Do not say her name on her home turf."

"What, are you trying to get us killed?" Kit Kat added. "And what else were we supposed to do tonight? You know the island's not getting any trick-or-treaters, no matter how many vegan rubber cement balls your mother makes."

"And that does not answer the question of what you are doing here," Tweety finished.

I knew it had been a long shot. I just shook my head.

"Oh," Kit Kat said, eyes widening. "It's an OLS thing!"

Tweety leaned toward me and whispered, "Is the killer in the barn?"

I still refused to answer. And why? Why was this happening right now? Did I not have enough to deal with?

"Come on," Kit Kat said. "Tell us what's happening."

I shook my head again. No. No. No.

"We hate it when you freeze us out."

I shook my head some more.

"Tell us what's happening, and we'll give you a boost?"

My head stopped shaking. I did need a boost.

I cleared my throat. "Okay, what if you give me a boost, and I tell you everything . . . tomorrow."

"Tomorrow?" Kit Kat whined, looking at her sister.

"Yeah, I don't like that either," Tweety said.

"It's the best you're going to get."

The twins looked at each other, shared a telepathetic moment, then nodded.

"Okay, great," I said. "Now help me up."

We all jostled around for position before finally settling on Kit and Tweety gripping each other's wrists to form a step right beneath the window.

I stepped forward and clutched their shoulders for balance before gingerly placing my foot on their forearms. Before I put any weight on them I said, "I'm not like going to break your wrists, am I?"

They both shot me a disgusted look.

"What? I was just checking," I said. "Okay, here I go. One . . . two . . . three!" Just as I hiked myself up, Tweety yelped, "Ow! Ow! Ow!

"Oh my God, Tweety!" I dropped back down. "Are you ok—"

I cut myself off when she started cackling.

"Sorry. Sorry. Couldn't resist," she chuckled.

"Hilarious," her sister chortled.

I just stared at them. And they wondered why I didn't let them in on plans?

"Come on." Tweety gestured to the window with her chin. "Get back up there."

"Are you going to be serious this time?"

"As a heart attack."

That didn't make me feel any better—she'd probably

fake that next time—but I shot her a warning look and regripped her and Kit Kat's shoulders. "Okay, so on the count of three. One . . . two . . ."

"Three!" The twins grunted and launched me into the air.

Oh crap. I was supposed to say *three*!

Luckily, though, instinct kicked in and I landed on the windowsill with my belly. "Oof!"

Just then I felt the twins pushing my feet up.

"Slow down!" I hissed. I was tilting forward into the barn at an alarming rate. "I'm going to—"

This was going to hurt.

I tumbled into the barn and fell hard on my shoulder.

Son of a—

Okay, yeah, that had hurt.

"Erica?"

"I'm fine. I'm fine," I half whispered back. Yes, it was noisy in the barn, but I still didn't want the surgeon to hear me.

"Do you want us to wait for you?" Tweety called back.

"Yeah, yeah," I said, untangling myself from all of my skirts and my cloak. Which was easier said than done. "I may need help getting back out." The floor of the barn was a little higher than the ground outside, but it still might be tricky.

"How long are you going to be?" Kit Kat asked.

"I don't know," I hissed out the window. "Just wait for me."

"But are you going to be like a really long time?" Kit Kat asked, scratching her cheek. "It's kind of cold out here, and—"

"I don't know how long I'm going to be. But you said you wanted to help, so . . . just wait." Weren't these two just giving me a hard time about freezing them out of plans?

They didn't answer, just frowned.

"You two are going to wait, right?"

"Sure, sure," Tweety said.

"That was not reassuring."

She rolled her eyes. "Fine. We'll wait."

"But hurry up," Kit Kat added. "We want to get candy apples before they're all gone."

I shot them one last look before I whirled back around.

Okay, go time.

I dropped to my hands and knees and crawled my way out of the stall toward the main hallway. Once I got to the threshold, I peeked out and looked from left to right. All clear. But the next batch of kids was definitely at the graveyard. I needed to hurry. I crawled out, keeping as close to the wall as I could. Because all the exhibits were in stalls, the barrier protecting me from sight was about waist-high. I figured I should be able to crawl right on past the operating room without the good doctor ever noticing me. I had to make sure he didn't hear though . . . which I didn't think would be too much of a problem because he was singing . . . yup, yup, that was definitely "Roxanne." Couldn't blame the guy; the scaring-teenagers bit had to get pretty old after a while.

Slowly. Slowly.

Just a little farther.

Suddenly, I froze.

The singing had stopped.

Uh-oh.

I slowly looked up at the undead doctor with the head mirror staring down at me.

"Hey."

"Hey."

Chapter Thirty-nine

"I . . . like your . . . missing cheek," I said. "I mean, makeup." Yup, he had one of those rubber open wounds on his face. "Very realistic."

"Thanks."

"I'm just doing a security sweep," I said, still looking up at him. It was hard on the neck.

"On your hands and knees?"

"I'm trying to keep a low profile," I said with an awkward chuckle. "Get it? Low profile?"

"Sure," he said somewhat skeptically.

I smiled. "Well, I guess I'll see you around."

He nodded then disappeared.

Okay, well, that had been unfortunate, but he didn't look like he was in any hurry to report me to anyone, so I just needed to carry on.

I scurried forward, which was not easy; the hallway was cobblestone. Very hard on the knees. And I kept getting tangled up in my skirts.

Now, if I could just remember what stall came next. The zombie prison? Or the witches' coven? Didn't matter. I could hear the kids catching up behind me. I needed to hustle. I really didn't want them noticing me. I propped myself up on my toes so that I could move faster, but . . . man, was I out of shape. Okay yeah, the zombie prison was next. I could hear them talking about the . . . makeup?

"Dude, it's not the makeup that gave you that rash. You need to see a doctor."

Yup, I was going to speed right by that.

Witches were next. I could hear them talking too.

"I swear, if one more of these brats makes fun of my witch's cackle—"

"I know. I know."

"It's like this generation doesn't appreciate the classics."

"I know."

Okay, made it past them.

Next stop?

Chain saw Adam.

Oh boy. I'd forgotten how dark it was at the end of the barn. I mean, it was a haunted barn, so it should be scary . . . but this was pretty scary.

It was quiet too. It was hard to hear the shouts from the teens once I had made the turn to the hallway that joined the two sides. And I hadn't realized it, but there had been background music with scary noises and people screaming the whole time, but I could barely hear it now. And it had been so comforting.

I can do this.

I dropped back down to my knees and moved really slowly.

Almost there.

Almost there.

Wait! There he was.

It was hard to tell in the low, low light, but the door that covered Adam's stall was open just a crack. Unlike the other exhibits, he came all the way out of his stall to chase people to the other side of the barn. It was just a crack, but I could see him, sitting on a milk crate, maybe? With his back against the wall. Chain saw in hand. Hockey mask over his face. Jeebus. It looked like the same one he had used to frighten me back in the day.

Now, how the heck was I going to do this?

I couldn't creep any closer. He was facing my direction. He would see me for sure. I was half tempted to just stretch out and slide it across the floor so it was right in front of his stall, but it was so dark in here, there was a good chance he wouldn't see it.

Excited screams sounded behind me.

Frick! I was running out of time.

What was I going to do?

I quickly pulled my note out from the pocket of my skirt and laid it on the brick in front of me. My hands were shaking, but I folded it in half then started folding the edges.

Please let this work. Please let this work.

The kids were coming. In fact they were almost on me. But I wanted them to come now. I had to time this just right.

I got up on my knees and aimed my missile at Adam.

The teens were almost at the end of the hallway and . . .

Almost. Almost . . .

Now!

Just as the teens turned the final corner, I shot my paper airplane at Adam.

I waited just long enough to hear him say, "What the—" before I jumped to my feet and plowed my way through the group of teenagers.

"Hey!" Adam shouted.

But there was no way he could see me, I had already turned the corner.

I was worried he was going to chase me, but I heard one of the kids say, "Dude, you're not scary."

Then the chain saw started up.

That's right. Nothing to see here. You've got a job to do, Adam.

I speed-walked my way back through. Sure, all the paid entertainers would see me, but I pulled my hood down low over my head, so maybe they wouldn't recognize me. And Adam hadn't seen me in costume . . . yet. And maybe there were other Little Red Riding Hoods here tonight. Whatever, that had taken a lot out of me. I was too scared to care anymore. The whole plan could fall apart. I didn't mind mowing lawns really. And I had faith that Grady would catch the killer. Eventually. I just wanted out of this freaking barn!

A witch's cackle startled me out of my speed-walk, but I quickly caught myself.

"Thank you!" the witch called after me. "That is the appropriate reaction."

I shot her a thumbs-up.

Uh-oh . . . was that chain saw sound getting louder?

Maybe Adam was coming for me after all!

I sped up my speed-walk to a loping jog.

I didn't even look at the zombies as I passed them. They were back to discussing rashes. Although one of them did shout, "What's the matter, Red? The wolf after you?"

It felt like it. Yes, it certainly did.

That chain saw was definitely getting louder.

I shot the doctor a wave as I zoomed past. Didn't stop to see if he noticed. And pushed my way through another bunch of teens. They all started screaming. Probably because there was a man with a chain saw chasing me.

I then slingshotted myself into the empty stall where I had come in.

The saw was even louder.

Please let Kit Kat and Tweety still be there.

Please let Kit Kat and Tweety still be there.

I launched myself at the window.

And . . . that had to be what internal damage felt like. I had hit the window with such force, I couldn't slow myself down enough to brake my fall off the other side. This was going to hurt even more than the first time.

I closed my eyes, and . . .

Someone caught me. Actually two someones. Tweety had one arm. Kit Kat the other. They pulled me through the window. I hit the ground, but not as hard as it would have been if they hadn't been there.

"Erica," Kit Kat began. "What took you so—"

I slapped a hand over her mouth, before jerking both her and her sister down so that we were well below the barn window.

The chain saw was coming closer . . . closer . . .

. . . and it just kept on going. I collapsed against the barn. He hadn't seen me go into the empty stall.

"Erica," Kit Kat said a moment later, "was that person with the chain saw chasing you?"

I nodded.

All three of us exchanged looks.

"Well," Kit Kat said, "that was fun."

"What's next?" Tweety asked.

Chapter Forty

"I don't think I can do this," I said quickly. "The barn was really scary."

"Come on, Erica," Rhonda said, eyes round with sympathy. "You just have to try. It will be all right."

I shook my head. "I don't think it will be all right. I think I am going to throw up."

"No you're not," she said, patting my hand. "Just try."

I brought the spoon to my mouth.

"So?" Rhonda asked.

"It's good," I said with a small nod. "It's good. I'm okay."

So after I had completed my mission at the barn, it was time for phase two. It took me a while to lose the twins, but there was really only room for me, Rhonda, and Freddie in phase two. Explaining this to the twins didn't achieve the result I was hoping for, though, so I had to buy them candy apples. That did the trick. Once I had them squared away, I met up with Rhonda and Freddie and we headed for the café.

The café was not part of phase two. We actually had a little time to kill before phase two, and Rhonda thought some apple crumble might help calm my nerves. Plus, it was the least likely place we would run into the brothers. They were all too busy.

The gates were closing in about fifteen minutes, so the place was sprinkled with tired-looking parents waiting to drive their kids home.

I actually kind of felt bad that we were in here neglecting our security duties, but, you know, for what we had planned next, I had already decided that we weren't going to charge the Honeycutts for security services this time around.

"I hate this," Freddie said, looking around. "This café is just as creepy as the dining room."

It wasn't. It actually looked like an old-fashioned country kitchen, just with lots of little tables and crafts everywhere.

"How is this creepy?" Rhonda asked.

"I feel like we're in the part of the horror movie where we've just killed ten zombies but fifty more are out there, and we've just walked into a grocery store, and Muzak is playing, like 'The Girl from Ipanema' or something, and the bored checkout girl is staring at us with her jaw dropped because we're all covered in zombie blood and mud. It's just all too surreal."

I swallowed the crumble in my mouth and looked at Rhonda. "We really can't do thirty-one horror movies in thirty-one days next year."

She nodded. "I think I see that now."

"So," I said after taking another mouthful, "you guys delivered your notes?"

"Yup," Rhonda said, pulling up her wolf snout so that it was resting on her forehead. "I dropped mine on the seat of the tractor when Brandon took a five-minute break. I saw him read it when he got back."

I looked at Freddie. "How did it go with Cam?"

"Too easy," Freddie said, eyes on the door that led to the kitchen. He was probably worried that Grandma Honeycutt was going to appear. But as far as I could tell, she wasn't around tonight. They just had two teen girls working the café. There hadn't been any sign of Mandy either.

"What did you do?" I asked him.

"I wrapped the note around a chocolate bar with an elastic band, and threw it at him. I was hiding in a bush."

"He didn't come looking for you?"

"Nah," Freddie said. "I think he was just happy about the chocolate. Ate the whole bar before he read the note."

I nodded. "You guys had it way easier than me."

"Oh, come on," Rhonda said. "Adam doesn't actually have a chain on that saw."

"You weren't in that barn," I said, shaking my head. "You don't know what it was like." I shoved three spoonfuls of apple crumble into my mouth in rapid succession.

So the notes were delivered. I guess we were actually doing this.

All three notes said the same thing.

I know what you did.

Meet me in the workshop after the gates close if you want to help your sister.

Tell no one.

We wanted it to be vague so that the brothers could fill in the blanks with whatever story made the most sense to them. I didn't feel great about the whole thing. But the brothers were keeping secrets, and all the evidence did seem to point at them. Again, I just did not want to believe they could kill someone and bury him in the woods and just carry on with their apple growing like nothing had ever happened, but I guess we were about to find out if I was right about that.

"We'd better get going," Freddie said, pushing himself to his feet. "We don't want to run into Grady."

I shoved the last bite of crumble into my mouth. "We don't even know if he's coming. He hasn't called. He hasn't texted."

Freddie shook his head. "Would it have killed you to . . ." Freddie twirled his imaginary girl hair again.

"Yes," I said, getting to my feet. "Yes, it would have."

"What's going on?" Rhonda asked.

"It's not important," I said, heading for the door. "I'm just saying we maybe shouldn't count on Grady being around if things get hairy."

We walked back out into the night. It suddenly felt a whole lot colder. And spookier. The place was really starting to clear out.

"Things aren't going to get hairy," Rhonda said. "Let's just hear what the brothers say. If they confess but the situation feels too dangerous, we don't confront them. At least not tonight."

"I like that plan," I said, pulling my hood back over my head.

Freddie moved in front of us, walking backward. "And the bet with Grady didn't have anything to do with an arrest. We just have to find out who the killer is. Let's leave the legalities to him."

"Yeah," I said. "Yeah. And after that, we can figure out how best to help Mandy." I mean, I could see why she didn't want to tell her family about her pregnancy if they had killed her last boyfriend.

"Okay, let's cut through here." We needed to head toward the workshop the back way through the trees. "And we should be quiet now. In case the brothers are around."

We traipsed as quietly as we could through the forest—not easy in the dark—and a little while later we were positioned in the woods at the back of the workshop. Waiting.

Minutes ticked by at a ridiculously slow pace.

"Maybe . . . maybe the brothers compared notes," I whispered. *Ha, compared notes. Like literally. Get a hold of yourself, Erica.* "And they're not coming."

Nobody said anything.

A moment later, Rhonda gripped my wrist. "I think I see something."

I peered into the darkness. There was someone coming up to the building. By the build, my guess was that it was Adam.

We stayed deathly quiet as he went into the workshop.

Now we just needed two more brothers.

It wasn't long before we spotted the other two coming across the lawn. There was no mistaking Cam's giant silhouette and that had to be Brandon with him.

We could hear them open the door to the workshop, but we still didn't move.

We had obviously gotten these three to come here by incredibly suspicious means. They were bound to be on guard, and sure enough, a minute or two after Cam and Brandon had joined their brother, Adam was walking the perimeter of the building.

We crouched even lower to the ground as he walked toward the treeline. I think all three of us stopped breathing as he walked by us, not once, but twice. Finally, he seemed satisfied and went back around to the front.

We waited until we heard the door of the workshop open and shut, then I whispered, "Okay, come on." We hurried up to the back wall. Freddie had cracked the back window earlier in the night, so we could listen. We jockeyed for position under the window.

"So how long are we going to wait?" one of the brothers said. I think it was Cam.

"I don't know, but I don't like this." That was definitely Brandon.

"Just stop talking," Adam said. "This is definitely some sort of setup."

"But somebody knows, man." Yup, that was Cam, and he was starting to freak out.

"We don't know that," Brandon said.

"Did you even read the note?"

"Of course I read the note."

"So?"

"We've come this far," Adam said. "We stay the course."

"Do you think it was Erica?"

My eyes widened, and I looked back and forth between Freddie and Rhonda. They were purposely avoiding my gaze. Yeah, I wouldn't want to know me right now either.

"Of course it was Erica," Adam said. "Who else would choose this place? She's messing with us."

"I don't think Erica's like that," Cam said.

I knew Cam was my favorite.

"She's like a private investigator," Adam said. "Of course she's like that. I knew we should have gotten rid of them. We never should have hired them in the first place."

"Hey," Cam said. "I just wanted them to keep the kids away from the woods so that nobody would find . . . anything. It's not my fault they didn't get to those kids in time. I mean, what were the odds of them finding that boot anyway?"

"Have you been checking the spot every week like I told you to?" Adam asked.

"I did!" Cam shouted. "I . . . I just may have had some trouble remembering where the spot was."

"Doesn't matter now," Brandon said. "We've all made

mistakes. We should have just fired them after the whole thing blew up, but I thought they were completely inept."

"They've solved tons of murders," Adam said.

I smiled. Couldn't help myself.

"By dumb luck."

Well, that wasn't very nice— Oh wait, and he just said they solved tons of murders! Implying that this too was a murder that we had solved! Oh God! It was the Honeycutts! I looked back and forth between Rhonda and Freddie again. By the look on both of their faces this time, they had already figured that out.

Okay, well, that was enough for me. I motioned for us to move back. We could just tell Grady what we had heard and call it a Halloween.

We had just taken a couple of steps back when—

"What are you guys doing here?"

Chapter Forty-one

She wasn't talking to us.

Thank God, she wasn't talking to us.

My heart had nearly jumped out of my chest.

It was Mandy. She must have followed her brothers to the workshop.

The three of us exchanged looks. I think we all really wanted to hightail it out of there, but this could be a dangerous situation. If Mandy confronted her brothers with killing her ex-boyfriend, who knew what could happen?

I took a hunched step back toward the window. Rhonda followed. Freddie did not. We both looked back at him. I waved for him to join us, but he gave me the quick headshake no and pointed back toward the woods.

I pointed at myself and then Rhonda before putting up two fingers. I then pointed at him and put up one.

OLS was a democracy.

I then waved at him again to get back over to the window. He did, but I could tell he wasn't happy about it. Well, I wasn't happy about the fact that I had missed the first part of the conversation between Mandy and her brothers.

"No, I can't take this anymore," she said.

"Listen," Brandon said. "We shouldn't talk about this here. For all we know Freddie, Rhonda, and Erica could be right outside that window."

This time it just felt like my heart had fainted. Seriously, just keeled right over. Judging by the looks on my partner's faces, they felt the same way.

"You know, I'm the one who brought Erica into this whole mess," Mandy said with a pained laugh. "They were fine with just doing security—"

We were. We were really fine. We wanted nothing to do with this!

"But, at the time, I actually thought the Apple Witch might have killed whoever it was out in those woods."

"What?" Cam asked. "That's dumb."

"I know it's dumb. But I wasn't thinking straight, and I needed someone to talk to. I didn't know it would start all of this!"

"Why didn't you just talk to us?" Adam asked.

"I don't know! I wanted to talk to someone who wasn't family," Mandy said. "I was overtired, and not feeling well, and my imagination—"

"No, I mean it's dumb because you already know the Apple Witch didn't kill Danny because you—"

"Cam, shut up!" Adam shouted. "What is the matter with you?"

"Sorry, I—"

"No, what were you going to say?" Mandy prodded. "It almost sounded like you were going to accuse—"

"Mandy, shut up!"

"Well, yeah," Cam went on. "I mean, you know it wasn't the Apple Witch because you were the one . . . who did the thing."

Rhonda, Freddie, and I exchanged very wide eyes.

It was Mandy?

"I didn't do the thing! You did the thing!"

I gave my head a shake. So it wasn't Mandy. It was Cam.

"What do you mean I did the thing? I didn't do the thing!"

Okay, not Cam. Maybe . . .

"All of you," Mandy said. "You all did the thing to protect me, right?"

"No!" all three brothers shouted.

Boom!

A rush of chills waved down my body. Score one, Erica! The Honeycutts were not murderers! Unless of course they were lying to one another.

"We've been trying to protect you," Cam shouted, "because you did the thing!"

And just then a horrifying buzz sounded from my skirt. My hand dived into the folds . . . but there were so many folds! Rhonda and Freddie stared at me with horror as it buzzed again.

Got it!

I had it. It was fine. I hit the power button.

Maybe they hadn't heard that. Maybe—

Just then somebody slammed the window above us all the way up.

"I told you they were out there."

Chapter Forty-two

"Adam. 'Sup," Freddie said.

"Don't 'sup me, man," Adam said, "Get in here!"

All three of us straightened up. Wow, would you look at that? My legs felt very wobbly. I had expended an awful lot of adrenaline tonight.

"Maybe we should make a run for it," Freddie whispered.

"I will take you to the ground before you make it two steps toward that treeline." Adam had one of those really loud man voices. It was quite terrifying. Oh, and would you look at that? Cam and Brandon had already come around to collect us. I guess we were going inside.

Well, at least it was sounding like they hadn't murdered anyone . . . yet.

"Why on earth did you have your phone on?" Freddie hissed as we walked around the building.

"I had it on vibrate."

"Everybody knows you can still hear vibrate."

"Well, I don't remember you telling me to turn it off. And I bet if I were to call you right now, your phone would—" I cut myself off. This was seriously not an argument we needed to be having right now.

We shuffled into the workshop and stood as a group right in the middle.

Nobody said anything for a moment.

This was very awkward.

"Erica, what is going on?" Mandy finally asked.

"Well," I said, clearing my throat. "Much like you, it seems, we thought that perhaps your brothers had done . . . the thing you guys were hinting at earlier." I knew there wasn't a recording device, and I wasn't guilty, so I could have just said *murdered Danny,* but it sounded rude in my head. "So, we thought if we got them in the same room at the same time then maybe some new information would come to light."

Adam smacked Cam lightly on the back of the head.

"And it seems it has. We now all know that none of you killed Danny, so . . ." I raised a fist in the air and gave a halfhearted, "Yay!"

"How could you do that to us?" Mandy whispered.

"Well, I didn't want to," I said. "I kept telling Freddie and Rhonda that there was no way any of you could have killed Danny."

"I don't know about *no* way," Rhonda chuffed.

Freddie just muttered, "Right under the bus."

"And this is *murder,*" I said. "Murder's not right. And I was worried about Shane. What if he was next? And I was really worried about what effect the stress was having on you and the—"

Mandy's eyes flew wide.

I pinned my lips shut.

"You and what, Mandy?" Brandon asked, looking at his sister's face before dropping his gaze to her stomach. "Are you . . . *pregnant*?"

She went very still for a good second or two then nodded.

Nobody said anything, then—

"Oh my God!" Cam squealed in a high-pitched voice. "I'm so happy!" He rushed over to hug his sister. "This is so exciting!"

"Hey, take it easy there," Brandon said, pushing him a little to the side, so he could hug Mandy too. "You're going to squish my niece or nephew."

Adam was the last to walk over to Mandy. He wasn't smiling.

When his brothers saw him coming, they stopped hugging Mandy, but stayed at her side.

Mandy cleared her throat. "I know you don't want to hear this, but the father is—"

"Who cares who the father is?" Adam said, scooping his sister up in his arms. "This baby is going to be all Honeycutt."

Aww . . .

"You're not upset?" Mandy said, looking down into her brother's face.

He slowly lowered her to the ground. "No . . . I mean I was shocked when I found out about you dating, but . . . does Shane know about the baby?"

She shook her head. "Not yet."

"That's awesome!" he shouted. "Can I tell him? I'll act like I'm all mad, and I'm going to kill him, and then—"

"I think maybe I should tell him," Mandy said quickly. "Do you think . . . do you think he'll be happy?"

"Um, yeah," Adam said. "And if he's not, we'll kill him."

Suddenly everyone went still.

"Not like really kill him!" Adam shouted. "What is wrong with you people?" He shot us all a disgusted look before turning back to his sister. "Seriously though, he's been miserable since you dumped him."

"How would you know that? He's not even here—"

"He's been sending me sad texts frickin' nonstop."

"Really?"

"Really."

Rhonda and I exchanged more *aww!* faces and linked arms . . . as Freddie swatted our backs. "What are you two so happy about?"

We looked back at him.

"What do you mean?" I asked. "This is swee—"

"We didn't solve the murder. This was our shot, and now—"

Just then the door to the workshop opened.

"Oh, of course," Freddie said, throwing his hands in the air. "Perfect timing."

Grady.

Chapter Forty-three

"Hey guys," Grady said carefully. "What's going on in here?"

"Nothing," Freddie shouted. "Absolutely nothing. It was a total bust! We didn't catch the murderer if that's what you are wondering. And so help me, if you say *That's because I've already caught the killer, Freddie,* in your stupid man voice, I'm going to lose my mind!"

"I . . . have not caught the killer."

"Oh, thank God," Freddie said. "Maybe there is still time."

Grady frowned at me. "Do I have a stupid man voice?"

I shook my head.

"So, I'm thinking there is a story here," Grady said slowly. "Maybe we should all go back to the café and get comfortable."

"That's probably a good idea," I said with a nod. "This is going to take some time to explain."

Grady inhaled deeply and nodded. "Great. Can't wait to hear it."

We all moved toward the door and shuffled outside, the cheery lights of the apple orchard beckoning us in the distance. We didn't get very far before I heard Freddie say to Brandon, "Okay, be honest. You guys have been trying to get us to quit ever since we found the body, haven't you?"

Brandon sniffed and said, "Yup."

"That whole shot Erica took to the head at the paintball tournament?"

I felt Grady stiffen beside me.

"It was my shoulder actually," I said quickly. "It wasn't that bad."

"And I'm sorry about that, Erica," Brandon said. "We told you at the beginning not to take your mask off. We just wanted to shake you up a little. Not blind you."

That's true. They had said that. I mean, when he saw that I had it off he could have, you know, not taken the shot, but we could settle that over some more apple crumble.

"You sabotaged my gun too, didn't you?" Freddie went on.

"No, man," Adam said. "You just had no idea what you were doing with that thing."

"I see."

"And what about the Apple Witch?" I called out.

Everybody stopped walking to look at me. "That was you guys when we were at her house? That night in the woods?"

Suddenly all three boys looked like guilty kids again. "Yeah," Cam said. "That was us."

I knew it! Oh, if I were still their babysitter, I'd be taking away all their toys. "But who was it in the cornfield?"

"That was Shane," Adam said. "We said we just wanted to pull a prank on you guys." He looked at Mandy. "Hey, I just realized something. That's why you broke up with him—because you thought we might—"

"I thought it would be . . . safer," Mandy said quietly.

"Safer?" Adam said. "You mean from me?" He sounded pretty surprised for a guy who had held a pitchfork to another man's chest.

"I thought you guys . . . did the thing," she said in a shaky voice. "And I didn't know how you'd react when you found out about the baby."

"Nice, Mandy," Adam said. "Real nice."

"Well, come on, you thought I did the *thing*," she shot back.

"What's the *thing*?" Grady whispered to me.

I just patted his arm. I was pretty sure that the Honeycutts would be facing some sort of charges in all the covering they had done for their sister, but that could all come out in good time. And with a lawyer present.

"Just so I'm clear," Grady said, much louder this time. "Nobody has actually confessed to killing Danny, right?"

"Right," the Honeycutts answered.

"Okay then," he said, taking a breath, and we continued our march toward the café.

I trotted a few steps to catch up to Freddie. "Well, there you have it," I said. "I told you there was no Apple Witch."

He didn't answer me. But he did stop walking.

"Well, aren't you going to say something?"

He shook his head.

"You're seriously not going to let me have my moment? You, the guy who claims that saying *I told you so* is better than— Freddie?"

He didn't look right. He actually looked kind of . . . scared.

"What? What's going on?"

He shook his head. Far too quickly for my liking.

I exchanged looks with Grady. He just shrugged.

"Freddie?" I tried again, shaking his arm.

"So if Cam was the Apple Witch the first time," Freddie whispered, still not looking at me. "And Shane was the Apple Witch the second time . . ."

I shook his arm again. "What are you talking about?"

"Who is . . . that?" He raised a shaky finger and pointed over to the rows and rows of apple trees. And there . . . right in between the trees stood . . .

"The Apple Witch!"

Chapter Forty-four

"Get her!"

Wait! Who shouted that?

Oh. Okay. It was me. And I was running toward her.

"Erica!"

That was Grady shouting after me.

He was probably running too. They all probably were. But I had a head start, and their shock had made them slow.

When the Apple Witch saw me coming, she took off down a row of apple trees in a very human-looking run. "You're not getting away!" I shouted. "Not this time!"

I pumped my arms to propel myself forward, but they weren't really helping. No, my arms weren't the problem. It was all the stupid skirts I had on! My legs kept get tangled. But the Apple Witch wasn't faring much better because she had her cloak to contend with.

"Stop!" I shouted, not that that had ever worked for me when I was chasing someone, but it didn't stop me from trying. "You can't get away!" Nope. That didn't help either. "We're both going to—"

Whoa. I skidded to a stop.

Fall.

Turns out we both weren't going to fall.

Just her.

It was a hard one too. It kind of looked like she had bounced off the ground on her chest. That couldn't feel good.

I starting running again and didn't stop until I made it to the black figure writhing on the ground.

Then I sat on her.

I was worried she might try to run again, and I really couldn't do that anymore in this dress.

"Erica," a voice shouted. It was Freddie this time. "What are you doing?"

I looked around at everyone as they filled in behind me. I tried to say something, but it came out as more of a hiss.

"What did she say?" one of the brothers asked.

"I think she said *science*," Freddie said, shaking his head. "It's this whole . . . thing."

I had said *science*, just in a really wheezy voice. I was really out of breath. That didn't stop me from rubbing my hands together though. Oh, I was going to enjoy th—

Just then Freddie dropped to his knees and whipped the Apple Witch's hood back before I even realized what was happening.

"Becca," he said with a gasp. Then an *ow* because I had whacked him in the chest. He had totally stolen my Scooby-Doo moment. It only deterred him momentarily though. He then said, "So you're the one who killed Danny."

"What?" the faux Apple Witch gasped. "I didn't kill Danny. I would never kill Danny."

"Seriously?" Freddie asked.

"Seriously," she said.

"Are you sure?" Freddie asked.

"Of course I'm sure. I would never kill Danny. Danny meant more to me than anyone will ever know. He . . . he . . ."

Oh God, if she started talking about his rubber back again—

"He what?" Mandy asked, coming forward with her arms crossed over her chest.

Well, this moment was rapidly becoming pretty awkward. "Why don't we save that for another time?" I suggested.

"What is going on?" Grady asked. "Becca, why are you here? And why are you dressed like the Apple Witch?"

Her eyes darted over us. "I was looking for something."

Oh . . . crap. She was looking for the sex tapes. Of course, she was looking for the sex tapes, after I had told her I might have seen them in that beer crate.

"Hey, it's you!" Cam shouted. "You're the one on the tapes. I recognize the cloak."

I guess it was all coming out now.

Becca nodded miserably. "Danny and I were into—"

I shook my head. "You don't have to—"

"Role-play. We were into Apple Witch role-play."

"You know, Erica's right. I don't think I need to hear this," Mandy said, walking away a few steps.

"Yeah," Cam said, backhanding Brandon on the chest, "I always wondered where Grandpa got all that weird porn."

I suddenly realized I was still straddling Becca, and given everything—no, just no.

"Okay, I don't understand anything that has happened tonight," Grady said. "But forget the café, I think we'd all better head down to the station."

"Oh, but before you do, dear," a new voice said. "I

think maybe I have something that can help explain what
happened to that boy in the woods."

Freddie gasped, and we all turned to see—

"Grandma Honeycutt."

Chapter Forty-five

"Grandma," Mandy said, "what's going on?"

"Well," the Mrs. Claus lookalike said, walking toward us, "your grandfather Barney told me before he died that if a situation like this were ever to arise—"

"A situation like this?" Freddie asked. "Your husband told you to be on the lookout for a situation where all your grandchildren were running through the apple orchard with a security company, a sheriff, and a woman dressed up like a witch?"

"Yes, dear," she said. "That's right. He said if a situation like this were ever to arise, that I should give this to Sheriff Forrester." She passed Grady an envelope. "He would never tell me why."

"What is that?" Freddie asked, rushing to Grady's side. "If it's something that solves this murder, you gotta know that that doesn't count in terms of our bet."

"Bet?" Adam asked.

"Mind your business," Freddie said.

Grady opened the envelope and pulled out a sheet of paper. "It just has a string of numbers on it."

Brandon came over to look at it. "That . . . that has to

be the combination to my grandfather's old safe. It's back in the workshop."

"Well, what are we waiting for?" Freddie asked, snatching the paper from Grady's hand. "Let's go."

Chapter Forty-six

"Slow down!"

Freddie was practically sprinting back to the workshop. He was going to break an ankle if he wasn't careful.

"You know getting there first doesn't mean anything, right?" Grady shouted.

That got Freddie to slow down.

A minute later, we were all back in the workshop waiting as Grady fiddled with an old safe tucked under the counter. Well, not all of us; Becca was going through the crate of videos—even after Grady told her not to. There were bigger fish to fry. It took Grady a couple of tries, but he eventually got the old creaky door to open. He then pulled on some gloves and pulled out another letter.

We all waited silently as he cracked it open.

"Well . . . ?" Freddie asked.

Grady looked up at us. "It's a confession."

Chapter Forty-seven

"Mom, I am so sorry," I said. "I forgot to call, and then it got so late, and—"

"Where are you, darling?" the voice from my phone asked.

I leaned my head back against the wall. I was sitting on a very hard bench that didn't, of course, have a headrest. "At the sheriff's department."

"Did you find another body?"

I frowned and lifted my head back up. "No, I did not find another body."

Freddie and I had spent most of the night in this very spot. Grady had asked us to stick around, but even if he hadn't, we would have found it hard to leave. There were still so many unanswered questions. Hard to say if Grady was going to give us any answers, though. He was in his office with Grandma Honeycutt at the moment. They had been in there a long, long time now. Rhonda was around somewhere, too. She had a lot of cop friends to catch up with. And by a lot, I mean two. It was Otter Lake. Now that we were in the early hours of the morning, though,

I was thinking we might need to make a coffee run to the Dawg.

"So what's going on?"

"Well, I think we've wrapped up the murder investigation at the apple orchard. I won't go into details yet, but—"

"I knew you could do it, darling." She made it sound like I had just won the fourth-grade spelling bee. Which I hadn't. Krista Mulch had taken me out with *advertisement*. It still rankled me a little whenever I ran into her on the street. "How much longer are you going to be? Can I bring you something? A change of clothes? Something to eat?"

Just then Freddie mumbled something. He was sitting on the bench beside me with his arms crossed over his chest and his eyes closed. He was making it look like he was sleeping, but I really think he just didn't want to look at the potato trophy staring at us from the shelf on the opposite wall.

"Sorry, what was that?" I asked him.

"Tell her to bring the candy," he mumbled.

"Mom? Freddie wants you to bring the Halloween candy over. There's enough people here that it will be gone in no time."

"Oh, the candy is all gone."

"What do you mean, the candy is all gone?"

Freddie groaned his disappointment.

"How can the candy be all gone? Did you throw them in the lake?"

My mother laughed. "No, I gave it to the trick-or-treaters."

I frowned. She threw it in the lake. "Oh," I said. "Okay."

"I've found my niche market," she added.

"Huh?"

"The early-twenty-somethings."

"The early-twenty-somethings?"

"Yes, it was wonderful," she said. "They came by the boatload. And this one lovely young woman said I was her hero."

I laughed. "Really? That's awesome." I knew I liked that girl. "Did you get her name?"

"No, I forgot to ask."

Well, at least I knew where I got that from too. "Oh Mom, I've got to go. Grady is just coming out of his office."

Grady was indeed coming out of his office, leading a very tearful Grandma Honeycutt. "To think," she said, "that my Barney would be capable of something like that."

"Here," Grady said, leading her toward us, "why don't you let Freddie keep you company a moment. I need a word with Erica."

I was just about to get to my feet when Freddie grabbed my wrist. "Don't leave me," he said through his teeth.

I patted his hand. "You'll be fine."

He refused to release my wrist, so I had to pry his fingers off.

"Do you want to come into my office?" Grady asked, jerking his head in that direction.

I didn't answer. I really wasn't sure what the answer to that question was. Grady and I hadn't really had a chance to talk since everything had happened. I wasn't sure how he was going to feel about OLS's actions tonight. But, hey, at least we hadn't done anything illegal. At least I didn't think we had. I used to be a court reporter in Chicago. I didn't know all the laws in New Hampshire, but I knew there were a lot of them.

"So," Grady said, shutting the door.

"So." I rocked on my feet a little before I gestured to

the chair in front of Grady's desk. I wasn't sure if this was a sitting-down kind of conversation. He nodded, so I took a seat. "Crazy night, huh?"

Grady nodded and walked around his desk to take a seat.

"Any clue what's going to happen to the Honeycutts?"

"Hard to say," Grady said, rubbing his eyes. "I have to talk to the DA. My guess is that Cam, at least, won't be charged."

"Really?" I asked. I mean, part of me was happy, but I just didn't see how that could be the case. He had taken a dead man's phone and taken pictures with it so nobody would know he was dead. I knew there had to be a law for that.

Grady rocked back in his chair. "Well, if his story checks out, he didn't take the pictures."

"What?"

"He says he went with his grandfather and a couple of his grandfather's friends to Las Vegas for a boys' trip. He thinks his grandfather took the pictures without anyone knowing, then ditched the phone. We don't have the phone, so . . ." Grady threw his hands in the air.

"That will be difficult to prove," I said, nodding. "But come on, I'm willing to believe that Cam had nothing to do with the murder because I know him." And I had overheard a private conversation between him and his siblings. "But I can't see a DA believing—"

Grady tapped the table with his pen. "The letter. The one in the safe. It was pretty detailed."

"Oh yeah?"

Grady nodded. "Barney said that he never meant to kill Danny. He was walking through the woods one day when he came across the coals from a recent campfire. His first thought was it was just teenagers, so he decided to check out the old house to make sure they weren't hanging out in there. He thought it might be dangerous," he said, meeting my eye. He still wasn't happy about that whole thing where I had fallen through the floor. "Anyway, when he was in there, he found Danny's stash of tapes. It was pretty obvious his granddaughter wasn't the person with Danny in the videos, so, as you can imagine, he was pretty upset. He told Danny to meet him out there one night. He wrote that he wanted to put the fear of God into him and get him to leave town. Apparently though, when Danny discovered his tapes were missing things got heated. Barney told Danny that he had destroyed the tapes, even though he hadn't, and Danny flew into a rage. I guess his Apple Witch tapes were mixed up with the other ones. Anyway, according to the letter, Danny charged at Barney. Barney grabbed his coat and yanked him toward the old stove. He claims the momentum caused Danny to lose his balance and he hit his head on the edge of it. Died almost instantly."

"Oh my . . . does that match with the autopsy?"

"So far," Grady said with a nod. "There was damage to Danny's skull. And from the time line we've constructed so far, it looks like the Honeycutt brothers may have been away for a two-week camping trip at the time of the crime, so it's possible they knew nothing about it."

"But the fire? Didn't Adam start that fire at the Apple Witch's house to cover up evidence?"

"According to Adam, his grandfather started that fire. Said he covered for him because he was getting up there in age and he didn't want him to face any jail time."

"But what excuse did his grandfather give him for starting the fire in the first place?"

"He said that he had been trying to dispose of some illegal pesticides that he purchased on the Internet from China and things just got out of control. He told Adam that it would be really bad for the business if they were caught with them on the property, so he wanted to burn all the *evidence*."

"But what about the tape Freddie and I found? And why did he keep the other tapes?"

"No idea how that one got under the floor. Maybe it slipped between the boards at some point before Barney and Danny had their encounter. I mean it's possible. We both know that floor wasn't in the best of shape."

I shook a finger at him. "That we do."

"Or, hey, for all we know, maybe the Apple Witch hid it there," he said with a tired smile.

I blinked at him. "Under no circumstances will you say that to Freddie."

He gave me a small laugh. "As for why he kept the other tapes . . . who knows? I don't want to speculate."

"But are you trying to tell me that Adam just believed that whole story about the pesticides?"

"Apparently. If you believe Adam," Grady said. "What do you think?"

I brought my hand to my chest. "You're asking my opinion?"

He gripped a pen off his desk lightly on either end and nodded.

"Well, I don't think Adam killed Danny, but I know he would do anything to protect a family member, so it's possible."

Grady nodded some more and swiveled side to side in his seat. "The investigation is far from closed. We're waiting on a detailed report from the medical examiner, and we'll have to do some testing on that stove, but so far everything is adding up."

"But what about . . ." I straightened up in my seat a little bit. I felt bad for even asking this. "What about Grandma Honeycutt? How much do you think she knew?"

He shook his head and tossed the pen back on his

desk. "I grilled her for almost three hours. I think she really is just a sweet woman who was willing to keep a letter secret for her husband without ever asking him why."

"Whoa . . ."

"I know."

"That's really old-school," I said. "And just for the record, I would never be able to do something like that. It would drive me insane not knowing."

Grady chuckled. "Yeah, I kind of figured."

"Well, I never saw that coming. Any of that."

"Me neither."

We sat in silence for a moment.

"So," I said, taking a deep breath. "I guess neither one of us really won the bet."

"Nope, I think this one was a draw."

I shot him a sideways look. "So you're saying there might be a next time."

He pinched his lips together and nodded. "Maybe. Maybe. Do you think you could give me more of a heads-up on your plans though? I mean, the message you left me on my voice mail was kind of . . . bland. It didn't have a lot of urgency. I almost waited until today to call you back."

"What? Are you ser—" I cut myself off and rolled my eyes. "Freddie told you to say that, didn't he?"

Grady smiled. "You do realize our lives would be a whole lot less complicated if OLS would just stay in its lane."

"Hey, lots of private investigators look into murders. It's a legit lane for OLS to be in," I said. "But I doubt it will be that much of an issue. I mean, really, how many more murders can there be in a town the size of Otter Lake?"

"Knock on wood," Grady said. "Seriously, though,

you know how you said you can't change being who you are? That you're a private investigator and if I truly cared about you I wouldn't want you to change?"

I nodded.

"Well, I can't change who I am either. I am sheriff of this town and, more importantly, I am the guy who truly cares about you, so I'm always going to worry about what OLS is getting up to."

"Aww, I like that guy."

"So we still need to work on the whole communication thing."

"Well, how does tonight sound?" I asked with a little shrug.

"It sounds perfect," Grady said quickly. "I've got a lot of paperwork to do, but—"

"I can wait up."

"I'd like that."

We stared at each other nodding for a few moments, before I said, "Well, I'd better get back out there and rescue Freddie."

"Yeah, you should probably go," Grady said.

"Or I could stay?" I offered. "I could lock the d—"

"Get out of here, Bloom," he said with a smile. "Oh, but you can tell Freddie I'm going to have a word with Andy at the chamber of commerce."

I raised an eyebrow.

"I plan to tell him that the sheriff's department really needs more competition for the potato trophy next year. I know it's no full-page ad in the paper, but . . ."

"It'll do." I smiled and left.

Happy.

I left happy. Well, as happy as I could be under the murderous circumstances.

"Erica!"

I hadn't even shut the door yet.

"Well, I guess I had better be going," Grandma Honeycutt said, patting Freddie's hand and pushing herself to her feet. "Now you remember what I told you."

"What were you telling Freddie?" I asked, coming over to the bench.

She smiled at me. "I just wanted Freddie to know that there was nothing to be afraid of. The Apple Witch isn't real."

"Oh," I said with a chuckle. "I've been trying to tell him that for weeks."

"It's ridiculous. I've lived at that orchard for most of my life, and I've never seen a witch. It's funny how these stories can get so fanciful. Now, Dorit Honeycutt on the other hand," she said, wagging a finger and shuffling toward the door. "Her tale is one that we can all learn from."

She said it in an offhand way, but it was a funny thing to say. I just had to know . . .

"What do you mean?"

Grandma Honeycutt stopped to look at me, her hand on the door. "Sorry, what's that, dear?"

I took a step toward her. "What do you mean, we can all learn from Dorit Honeycutt's tale?"

"Did I say that?" she asked sweetly.

"Yeah, yeah you did," I said, feeling Freddie come to my side. "Were you talking about Dorit's devotion to her child?"

"Oh, of course," Grandma Honeycutt said. "That must have been what I meant. I didn't even realize I had said that." She turned to the door then stopped again. "Or maybe I meant . . ."

Freddie clutched my arm again.

"What? What might you have meant?"

"Well, let's just say us Honeycutt women have never

liked philandering men." She smiled, shot me a wink, then headed out the door.

I tried to move, but I was . . . stunned.

Freddie wasn't having that problem though. He was shaking my arm. Violently. "I tried to tell you!" he hissed. "I've been trying to tell you this entire time!"

"Did she actually just wink?" I asked. "Was that an actual wi—"

"Of course it was a wink," Freddie said, still shaking my arm. "Actually, it was more than a wink. It was practically a confession."

I couldn't say anything for a moment.

"Erica?"

I looked at Freddie. "I think . . . I'm going to have to sleep with the light on tonight."

"Oh, no way. Forget sleeping. Let's just get a bunch of snacks and watch some—"

Suddenly Rhonda was between us, arms draped over our shoulders. "Did I hear somebody say *movie*?"

"No!"

A Ghost Story

"So, ladies, what have you all learned from my little tale?"

"That if you sleep with a guy he'll forgive you just about anything?"

"Whoa! Whoa! Whoa! No, that was not the lesson. What's your last name? I'm going to have to have a word with your mother. Wow. Just wow. Would anyone else like to give it a try?"

"Never trust sweet old ladies?"

"You're getting warmer."

"Oh my God, why don't you just tell us what the lesson was, Freddie?"

"The lesson was that you don't mess around with the Apple Witch and her family. So, you know, show some respect."

"But the Apple Witch wasn't even real! You said it yourself. It was just people playing dress up."

"Just because the Apple Witch we saw wasn't real, doesn't mean that she's not real overall, Julie. And her descendants still dwell in these parts."

"*I thought the lesson was that the idea of witches was just a leftover crime of patriarchy?*"

"*Well, yes, that would be the lesson if we were, like, in school right now, Morticia. But we're not. We're at a campfire. Not eating marshmallows because . . .*"

"*What happened?*"

"*What's wrong with him?*"

"*Freddie?*"

"*Dude, did someone press your pause button?*"

"*That's not funny, man. Say something.*"

"*Why are his eyes all wide like that?*"

"*He's looking over by the trees. Do you see what—*"

"Mandy Apple! Mandy Apple! Mandy Apple!"

"*Oh my God!*"

"*It's the Apple Witch!*"

"*Run!*"

—

"*Hey, Erica.*"

"*Freddie, why were you shouting* Mandy Apple? *And why did all those Girl Scouts take off running and screaming into the woods?*"

"*I just made them think you were the Apple Witch coming to get them.*"

"*You do realize you are supposed to be chaperoning them, and not—*"

"*Oh, they'll be fine. They were all like* we want to watch movies on our phones *and* we're too cool for ghost stories, *so, you know, I just gave them a lesson in real life.*"

"*By scaring the crap out of them?*"

"*They'll thank me later. Did you bring the marshmallows?*"

"*I did.*"

"*Perfect. Let's—*"

"*Shouldn't we go after them?*"

"*What? What for?*"

"*They might get lost. Or hurt.*"

"*They're like twenty years old.*"

"*They're fifteen.*"

"*Ugh. Fine. But let's at least have a couple marsh-mallows first.*"

"*Freddie . . .*"

"*Oh my God, you suck. Fine. Girls? Come out, come out, wherever you are!*"

"*It's not working.*"

"*Well, we tried. Pass the marshmallows.*"